W9-BGM-230

the
BOOKWORM box

Helping the community, one book at a time

PRIDE & JOIE

a #MyNewLife novella series by

M.E. Carter

First Edition: November 2017
Library of Congress Cataloging-in-Publication Data
Pride & Joie – 1st ed
ISBN-13: 978-1981173082

This book is dedicated to Tie Guy and his lovely wife.

You will likely never read this book,
but that's probably in your best interest,
as you would be REALLY embarrassed if you did.

Thanks for the inspiration.
And congrats on your new baby...wherever you are.

PRIDE & JOIE

EPISODE ONE

CHAPTER ONE

Joie

S omewhere between Austin and San Antonio, out in the boondocks and away from the fast-paced, twenty-four-hour vibe that defines a big city, there's a town called Flinton.

Life moves a little slower in Flinton. People say "yes, ma'am" and "no, sir" no matter how old they are or the person being addressed is. Almost everyone attends church on a weekly basis, wearing their Sunday best, no exceptions. And big, blond hair is the norm. You know, closer to Jesus and all that. In some ways, it's a stereotypical Texas cow town.

That is, until you cross over Main Street to the south side of the area and step foot onto the university campus. Then, it turns into the typical *college* town.

Flinton State University is a huge school that boasts the college life new adults are always so excited to join. Roughly twenty-five thousand students attend classes somewhere within the boundaries of the five square miles that is the campus property. Although there's no pressure to join the fraternities and sororities, a separation between those involved in Greek life and those who aren't still exists. However, no one seems to mind, because there's a place for everyone. Clubs and organizations are available for just about any interest you can think of—dancing, reading, Frisbee golf. There's so much to choose from, it's hard to believe anyone ever goes to class. A lot of education happens outside the classroom.

Around here, cafeteria food is complained about daily. Messy buns and pajama bottoms are normal eight a.m. class attire. And you're free to be who you want to be, away from the prying eyes of parents who may question those choices.

As much diversity as there is around here, though, there's one thing that draws the entire community together.

Football.

As is true of most teams in Division I college football, if you are a part of the program, you're basically a god among men. Doesn't matter if you're a coach, a player, or a trainer. If you're on that field for any amount of time, it's clear you are a priority to the administration and other students.

I knew this before signing up for classes, but I've spent the last hour trying very hard to concentrate on the syllabus my new professor gave us and jot down notes about study groups and project requirements. Instead, my mind keeps drifting back to my son, Isaac.

He's one of the football players here at FSU, and I, his forty-two-year-old mother, am now his peer. At least in the classroom. It's not bad so far, except for the fact that I've been sitting next to some teenage skank who spent the first few minutes in this room telling her friend all about the party she went to over the weekend and some of the crazy things Isaac's teammates did.

At least, I'm choosing to believe it was his teammates. The thought of my only child doing keg stands in his boxer briefs has me wanting to run to his dorm room, grab him by the ear, and drag him home. But I won't because we have an agreement. I do my best to respect his boundaries, and he does his best to act like the young man I raised him to be.

When we first discussed my going back to school, he was hesitant about me taking classes on the same campus as him. The more we discussed it, the more we realized our paths would probably rarely cross, if at all. He's a third-year business major on the football team. I'm a first-year education major who commutes five days a week. We might run into each other in the common areas every once in a while, but for the most part, there's room for both of us to achieve our goals with minimal on-campus interaction.

At least that's what we thought would happen. But as luck would have it, sitting in the second row of my new classroom backfired on me. There was nowhere else for the party crowd who straggled in at the last minute to sit, and I've been forced to hear about the huge welcome-back shindig, which gave me way too much information about the people my son hangs out with. Just the thought that it could be him who had a random threesome makes me shudder. Some things a mother doesn't need to know.

"Are you cold?" the young blonde next to me whispers when a shiver runs through me, completely ignoring the professor's lecture. I'm trying very hard not to judge her. Usually I'm of the mindset that people are people, and we're all doing the best we can. It's hard to maintain that perspective when

3

your son's integrity may be on the line. And yes, I'm aware that I sound like an overprotective mom, but I've *been* that girl. I know how they think, and they pretty much don't until it's too late. Not to mention, being the oldest one in my class has already been an eye-opening experience. And it's the first hour of the first day.

This may end up being a long four years.

I respond with a simple shake of my head and a polite smile in the girl's direction.

"Always bring a sweatshirt with you," she whispers again. "I learned last year there's no consistency in the building temperatures. Sometimes it's really hot and other times it's freezing, so be prepared."

I mouth *thank you* at her and continue taking notes. And I do appreciate the information from her. I haven't been in college for over twenty years. This modern version is all new to me and any advice is helpful. Even if it's from a floozy.

And yes, I'm aware some grandma vernacular rears its ugly head when I'm being judgmental.

"Next time, we're going to begin our discussion on Dante's Inferno," the professor bellows, most of my classmates already packing up their belongings. I understand that class is almost over, but am I the only one waiting for him to finish? Judging by my classmates' actions it's clear—yes, yes I am.

"Make sure you have the first five chapters read before Wednesday, because we will be discussing," he continues. "You don't want to be lost or you may never catch up." The rustling of papers and laptops slamming shut gets louder. When I did my two semesters back in the day, we brought books and notebooks. Now "school supplies" mean a computer. I thought that was reserved for the well-to-do students or anyone at an Ivy League school. It's been quite the culture shock to see. Not to mention feeling completely unprepared. Take a guess who brought paper and color-coordinating pens for organizing my notes. That would be me.

"All right, all right," Professor Something-Or-Other waves his hand in dismissal. "You're free to go. But stay safe, especially all you newbies. Remember, you're fresh meat."

A few chuckles come from around the room. Probably upperclassmen who have heard this all before. Or know he's right.

"Is this your first time in college?" the girl next to me asks. For wearing jammie pants, no makeup, and partying until the sun comes up, she appears remarkably refreshed. It's so unfair that I had to be up at five-thirty to have time to cover the dark circles under my eyes before driving here, and she probably rolled out of bed ten minutes before class started, not a circle to be seen. Damn these children and their young, flawless skin. I should have enjoyed it more when I had it.

"I took a few classes many years ago," I respond, shoving my antiquated note-taking methods in my new satchel. It's dark leather and big enough to hold all my supplies, plus everything I may need in the event of an emergency. I love it. "Unfortunately, most of my credits didn't transfer."

She makes a face. "That sucks. My mom had the same problem when she went back to school a couple years ago. Like, how unfair is it that she had to retake them all? I swear, all the administration at this school does is nickel-and-dime us."

I actually got more credits than I expected, considering my classes are so old. But I don't say that. She's young and idealistic. I'm sure it would fall on deaf ears anyway. College kids are notorious for hating anyone who works for their college. "I'm just glad I got credit for my freshman English class. It's too bad I have to retake algebra, though."

She grimaces again. "Ew. I hate math classes. Just one more to go and I'll be finished with numbers for good, I hope. Anyway, I'm Mia. If you need anything or whatever, I'll be here three days a week. And I know how hard it is to go back to school at your age, so I'm happy to help."

I feel my eyebrows shoot up in surprise at her dig, but quickly bring them back down. I'm pretty sure she wasn't trying to be rude, and since I've spent the morning judging her party-girl ways, my guilt tells me I need to give her some grace. She is, what, nineteen? Twenty? I don't think most of us have a good lock on our filters until we're in our thirties. And even then, it's iffy.

"Thanks, Mia." I smile back at her and situate my bag over my shoulder. "I'm Joie. And same goes to you, even though I'm not sure what kind of help I can give you since I'm new."

She shrugs. "I'm sure something will come up. Maybe a recipe or something." With a small wave, she turns and beelines her way out the door with the rest of the crowd.

I take a few seconds to pull my printed schedule and map out of my bag. I could use the university app and my GPS to help guide me to my next location, but I'm too overwhelmed to try to make it all work. Old school is my comfort zone when I'm nervous. I love technology as much as the next guy, but give a girl a minute to catch up to the millennials.

No, that's not right. These kids are too young to be millennials.

Oh boy. I'm beginning to feel ancient.

As the last one out of the room, I don't have to fight the crowd as much to get through the doors. Most students are coming inside for their next class, not going outside, giving me a moment to pause and observe the scene around me, taking in my feelings about this new situation. Frankly, I'm giddy.

Twenty-two years ago, I was in my second semester of college when I found myself pregnant. One too many parties and one too many bad decisions meant inevitably forgetting birth control and my oops baby decided it was time to come into the world. Hence, the reason I can peg a party girl from a mile away.

Don't misunderstand; Isaac was the best thing to ever happen to me. For the first time, there was someone else who was more important than I was. Well, in my eyes anyway. And there was nothing I wouldn't do, nothing I wouldn't sacrifice to give him the life he deserved.

Which means my plans to get a degree, even though I was undecided on my major at that point, were put on hold as I became a wife and a mother. The wife part only lasted a couple of years, but the mother part stuck. It wasn't easy. My entry-level job as the receptionist at a local construction company didn't pay much, but the lovely elderly woman who acted as the office manager trained me well, so advancement was imminent when she retired.

We still lived paycheck to paycheck, but my job provided the ability to pay all our bills and buy a small house in a decent neighborhood. Plus, because I worked with your typical good-ol'-boys, when Isaac started playing football, they pooled their money to make sure he had whatever equipment he needed. And most of the guys showed up for a least a couple games

7

each season. Considering his dad was never around, I know my son appreciated their support as much as I did.

Leaving the company after that many years was hard, but just like always, the guys were thrilled I was finally in a place where I could live out my dream. I've only been away from my job for a week, and I've already been texted six times, called twice, and had one person beg me to come back. His offer included a year's supply of strawberry margaritas. My favorite. I guess the new office manager is a bit of a stick-in-the-mud.

As good as that offer felt, I'm right where I need to be. My desire to be a teacher began the moment I stepped into Isaac's first grade classroom as the volunteer homeroom parent. It was just a matter of waiting until he graduated and went off on his own to be able to follow through with my dream. And his new scholarship is a god-send. It enabled me to only get a small student loan and live off my savings for a few years.

Yep, it took twenty years longer than most, but I'm really lucky to be here, and I know it.

Stepping off the last step, I stare at the map, making sure I'm heading toward the science building for my nine o'clock biology class. I can't help but smile. I'm here. I'm finally here. Following my dreams with nothing in my way.

"Oof!"

Except the big body I just ran into. It was definitely standing in my way.

"Oh shit. Are you all right?" His deep voice and slight drawl make it take a second longer than it should to pull me out of the fluster I feel at seeing my giant satchel lying flat on the sidewalk, half of my belongings scattered on the ground.

"I'm okay," I reassure him, bending over to put all my belongings back in my bag. "I wasn't watching where I was going."

He bends down to help, and it suddenly hits me that he seems familiar. But of course he does. He's one of Isaac's coaches. Coach Jack Pride. I've never seen him up close before, just from a distance at home games. And even then, because this is Isaac's first year as a scholarship athlete, they were the best tickets my tight budget could afford, which wasn't close.

I'm surprised to notice how attractive he is. He's built like an athlete—big and broad shoulders, with muscular biceps peeking out of his short-sleeved white polo. He's not as trim and fit as his players, but I'm pretty sure he doesn't put in the same number of hours in the gym they do. But he definitely takes care of his "dad bod." His salt-and-pepper hair is cut short, though it's still long enough that the slight breeze runs through it. Coach Pride can't be much older than I am, but the words "silver fox" keep running through my mind.

"I'm embarrassed to admit, I was messing with my phone when I ran into you." He gives me a lopsided grin, and I bite my lip. He's cute. Really cute.

We get all my stuff back in my bag and stand up, accidentally touching when he hands it over to me. Feeling the warmth of his fingers is nice, as much as I'm hesitant to admit it.

You know it's been a long time since you've been touched by a man when the graze of fingertips makes you feel slightly woozy.

"Do you know where you're going? I'd be more than happy to help you find your way to your...um..."

"Next class." I smile at his feeble attempt to not make assumptions. I'm sure I stick out like a sore thumb next to all these kids.

Did I just call them kids? I'm gonna need to tone that down if I plan to make any friends around here.

"Ah. I thought you had that student vibe to you." He smiles with very straight, very white teeth, offset by the tan he maintains from hours of practices in the sun.

"Is it that obvious it's my first day?" I flirt back, shocking even myself.

"Only by the overstuffed bag," he jokes.

We stare at each other for a few second before I start screaming internally. *Focus, Joie. You're here to get a degree, not troll for men.*

"Well, um…thanks for helping me pick up my stuff. I'm gonna head over to the science building now." I gesture toward the direction I think I'm supposed to go. "It's that way, right?"

He seems to snap out of his own internal dialogue. "Oh! Yeah. It's just past the student center. The orange brick building on your left. The only orange building this school has. Can't miss it."

I give him a thank you and a small wave, turning to walk away. Taking a deep breath, I try to shake off the moment. As attractive as he is and as lonely as I can sometimes be, I have goals and a reason for being here. Finding a man is not one of them.

But now that I've seen Coach Jack Pride up close and personal, football games are going to be much more fun.

CHAPTER TWO

Jack

I t is hot as fuck out here.

But when is it not? August in most parts of Texas reminds me of the different levels of hell in Dante's Inferno, which I only remember because all of our players are required to take Lit I. Some areas are hot and humid, and it feels like you're cooking in slow boiling soup. Some places are hot and dry, and it seems as if your skin is burning off whenever you're in the sun. In Flinton, we have a breeze. Yes, we're in a relatively flat area, but we're surrounded by rolling hills so the wind loves blowing through.

Unfortunately, in late summer that breeze is so hot, it's like the devil himself is breathing over your shoulder.

Did I mention it's hot as fuck out here?

"Come on, ladies!" my boss and the man in charge of this field, Hank Stellan, taunts. "We're playing football, not prac-

ticing for a dance recital. Get your heads out of your asses."
He bangs his clipboard for effect.

I barely notice, my mind too busy searching for inconsistencies on the field and patterns we can tweak.

Hank and I have worked together with this team for over a decade, and we have our coaching practically down to a science. He watches the overall picture and screams obscenities for most of the practices. I stand with my arms crossed, chomping on my gum, scrutinizing the tiny details that can make the difference between a good player and a great player. After practice is over, Hank and I meet and discuss what we each saw.

It's a good system; led us to four national titles in the last ten years. It's not a sweep of all the trophies but still something to be proud of.

Scratching the back of my neck, I curse myself for not wearing sunscreen again. I can already feel the sunburn coming, and we're not halfway through this practice. This isn't my first rodeo. I should know better. But I keep forgetting to pick up some 50+ SPF at the store. Sheila used to make sure I always had it in stock, so it's taking some time to get into a new routine.

I chuckle to myself. *It's been three years, Jack. You should be in a routine by now.*

But I'm not. You can call me helpless or a good-ol'-boy or lazy, but I'm not really any of those things. Sheila was just really, really good at running our home. I never had to make a grocery list or put my laundry away. She did all that. I took care of the bills. She took care of the rest. It was simple and perfect for us, and I guess I still have a hard time remembering I'm the only one in charge of all that now.

What can I say? I'm a middle-aged man who settled into my ways a long time ago. This old dog likes those tricks.

My mind begins to wander as we wait for everyone to get into position on the field. I find myself thinking about the dark-haired beauty I ran into earlier today. Who does she take care of? A husband? A boyfriend? Just herself? What brought her to Flinton State and how long is she going to be here?

"Dammit!" Hank yells next to me, banging on that damn clipboard again. I chide myself for losing my focus on my job. I'm here to win football games, not troll for women. "What the hell was that? You aren't holding a greased pig. It's shouldn't be that hard not to fumble."

The players get in position again, and I cock my head as I watch our tight end's stance. He seems hyped and jittery. That's nothing new. Lots of our players get hopped up on endorphins when they play. But his take-off on the hike is half a second too late.

"Take-off drills," I comment to Hank.

"He's pushing late?"

"About half a second." Which means he's late getting across the field. Which means he's having to reach that much farther to make the catch. Which means he's screwed when a member of the opposing team is gunning for him.

"All right that's enough, ya bunch of pansies!" Hank bellows and stomps onto the field. "Let's set up for take-off drills."

Someone hands me a water bottle, although I'm not sure who. I typically don't pay much attention to anyone on the field other than the players. It's not because I don't appreciate them. I just get hyper-focused by my job.

As the assistant coach for the Flinton State Vikings, I've seen a lot of players either make it or break it on this field. My goal is to help them make it. Not only so we can win, which means job security for me, but so they can go on to have successful careers. We've had several kids receive very lucrative offers in the pros. Hell, two years ago, we gave the NFL the number two draft pick in the country. That means paying attention to anyone other than the guys who are actually passing the pigskin around isn't my priority.

But I certainly appreciate whoever remembered to put ice in this water. Squeezing a good-sized gulp in my mouth, I cringe as the icy water gets that much colder when it mixes with my minty gum. It's almost uncomfortable, despite how refreshing it is for such a hot day. I think it was 107 degrees last time I checked. But losing the gum isn't an option. Five years ago, when Sheila got cancer for the third time, I finally quit smoking. In its place, I chew gum. Lots of it. And I suppose it keeps my breath minty fresh, so I shouldn't complain.

"Fucking typical Texas heat," I grumble to myself, making a petite female trainer stop and eyeball me. "Ma'am." I nod in her direction. She shakes her head and walks away, handing out more water.

One of the guys catches my eye and I find myself watching him run drills. He's not the biggest player on our team, but he's definitely bulked up since he made it as a walk-on two years ago. And he hasn't lost his grace as he's grown. That's a huge problem for most college players.

Let's face it. Boys aren't done growing until they're practically out of college, so these guys are constantly having to relearn their bodies and how to manipulate them for maximum effectiveness. For instance, pull-ups aren't the same after suddenly growing four inches. The floor isn't as far away, but your arms seem longer. And that's not the only time rapid growth makes things hard. Every time you think you know how to do something, your body changes, and you have to re-learn it all over.

Crossing my arms and keeping my eyes on our guy, I watch as he explodes from the ground, attacking the tackle dummy with such force, it throws the training coach off balance. But I can see where he can do better.

"Stevens," I call and wave him over. He rips his helmet off and jogs my direction.

"Sir?"

"How are those tackles feeling?" I keep my eyes off him and on the field. No use in making anyone on the team get too comfortable. I'm their boss, not their friend. Their feelings are of no consequence unless it carries onto the field. Don't get me wrong, I care about each one of them on a personal level. But during workout practice is not the time or place.

"They're feeling pretty good," he replies. "I'm concentrating on powering through my legs like you said, and I think it's working."

I nod once. "Make sure you don't forget you have an upper body."

"Yes, sir."

"Use your legs to explode, just like you're doing, but once you get to your opponent, don't forget to push off with your arms. Draw on your back muscles to make that same kind of explosion with your upper body and knock his ass to the ground."

"Yes, sir."

Always so polite. His mama raised him right.

"And Stevens"—I turn and stare him down—"if Coach Matthews isn't flat on his ass after knocking into that dummy, you're doing it wrong."

The kid spouts a lopsided grin. I can see motivation in his eyes. As a coaching staff, we don't put up with shit. Our players will show us the respect we deserve. There are no exceptions.

However, putting one of us down because we're tackling too hard doesn't count. That's just good football.

"Yes, sir," he says one last time and runs back to his position when I wave him off in dismissal.

Hank sidles up next to me, instinctively knowing something's about to go down on the field. He just doesn't know it's Matthews yet.

"Still think he was a good addition to the starting lineup?"

I nod once. Even though Stevens wasn't talented enough to get here on scholarship originally, he's worked his ass off, always with a good attitude, and it's paid off. He plays football for the love of it, not as a way to make money and get girls. At least, that's not the vibe he gives off. When the university randomly opened up a little more scholarship money, we gave it to him. It took a bit of convincing, but I still think he was the right choice.

"Yep. He's about to flatten, Matthews."

We both watch as Stevens gets into position again. Just a few short seconds later, he explodes off the field, his thick legs using all their strength to launch him across the short distance. As he connects with the tackle dummy, it's obvious his entire lower body is doing the bulk of the work. But then, just a micro-second into the exercise, his upper body gets in on it. The force of it throws Matthews, who is standing behind the dummy to hold it stable, completely off balance, and he barely has time to register that he's going down before he ends up flat on his back.

Hank and I snicker.

"That right there is why I stand behind the decision to put him on the books," I point out, still chuckling. Matthews frowns over at us and flips us the bird, making us laugh a little harder.

Watching one of our own get mowed down is fun sometimes, but playtime is over. We have a job to do.

Hank begins yelling and banging on that damn clipboard again. And I get back into my cross-armed, gum-chewing stance, eyes studying the field, spotting other small problems that can be fine-tuned.

This is college football. Here in Texas, this is life. And I'm damn proud to be a part of it.

CHAPTER THREE

Joie

"Where are the dice?" My best friend, Amanda, stares blankly in the game cabinet, trying to find all the supplies for Bunco night while I work on setting up a third card table. We love game night. Once a month I host it at my place, and all our gaming friends come over for the fun.

Or course, "gaming" means a whole different thing to us than it does to our children. Face-to-face interaction for one. A variety of snacks for another. And of course, the alcohol. Because what game night would be complete without mimosas and margaritas? They're made with fruit juice, which means the calories don't count. Plus, after my first full week of classes, I need to relax and reset my brain.

"Check the drawer." I gesture my head that direction. "I didn't want them to get pushed to the back and the container to accidentally pop open."

She shifts her attention and within seconds raises them in the air. "Found them. What else do you want me to get out?"

"I was thinking about Farkle and maybe Scattergories," I grunt as I fight with the table leg.

Amanda stands there observing me, an amused smile on her face. "You okay there, Joie? Looks like that table leg is stronger than you are."

I grunt again, pulling until it pops into place, and let my breath go. "I got one with the strongest legs I could find. We're not having a repeat of last month's table debacle."

Amanda starts chuckling. "Every time I think about it, I still laugh."

"That's because you weren't stuck on bottom."

Gamers, live action or video, can get pretty competitive. Just because this group is a little older doesn't mean we've become passive. Things can get heated really quick. The last time we played Bunco, Amanda and I both went for the dice at the same time. The table couldn't hold our weight and collapsed underneath us while our friends watched in horror.

I blame the fact that it was an old table, because I refuse to believe we're too heavy.

Amanda comes over and peers at the leg supports I'm still putting in place. "That seems really solid. But if it ends up not being able to support the weight of two grown women, we may have to consider celery and peanut butter as our regular snacks at these shindigs."

"Well then, it better not break, because I'm not giving up those cake balls Drea brings," I jest.

"Quick! Add more supports," Amanda jokes, making me laugh.

Amanda and I have known each other since our boys were in middle school football. She and her husband, Jeff, have become good friends of mine. We all used to sit together at games and would trade off transporting the boys to and from practices. They're really more like family to us than friends.

"How are your classes going anyway?" she asks, as she unfolds the plastic chairs and puts them around the tables.

"Good! I'm not enjoying taking college algebra again." She grimaces, which is exactly how I feel. "But I am taking an educational psychology class, which I really like, and it kind of keeps my eye on the prize."

"That's great. I really admire you for going back to school. I have zero desire to ever step foot in a classroom again."

"It's kind of a culture shock, that's for sure. I never thought of college kids as being young, but I'm so old now, they all look like babies."

Amanda grabs the rest of the games and puts one on each table. We set it up like stations. Pick your game of choice and go for it. We'll have a couple of intermissions, allowing people to move around and enjoy it all.

"Well yeah," she says, opening a couple decks of cards and shuffling, "they're literally half your age."

I shake my head. "That just blows my mind. How did we get this old?"

"That's life, I guess." She shrugs. "Better not blink or we'll be sixty."

"No kidding."

We meander our way into the kitchen and start pulling out our special game-night glasses. I got them for Christmas a few years ago from Isaac. Each glass has the logo of a different board game on it. I love them. But I only pull them out once a month.

"Speaking of, have you run into Isaac on campus yet?"

"No!" I vehemently shake my head. "And I don't want to. I don't want to be known as the football player's mom any more than he wants to be known as the football player whose mommy followed him to school."

Amanda chuckles again. "I didn't say you had to interact. I just wanna hear how big both your eyes get when you run into each other and how awkward it is as you run away from each other. Cause you know that's what'll happen."

"I've been practicing my unaffected facial expression for that moment. See?" I shoot her my best nonchalant look.

A laugh bursts out of her. "I can't tell if you're about to have a psychotic breakdown or are constipated."

"Hey!" I half-heartedly complain because I'm sure she's right. I've never been accused of being a good actress. Typically, what you see is what you get with my emotions.

A knock at the door and a "Hello!" yelled from the front bring us out of the kitchen and back to game-central.

"What do you have here?" I take a giant box out of our friend Brenda's hands and carry it to the sofa.

"Phew. Thanks." She hands Amanda a plastic bag, probably of food, that she's also carrying. I'm hoping it's her famous green sauce dip for tortilla chips. "I was cleaning out my closet today and found all these purses. Most of them I haven't used more than a couple times. I figured some of you might want one. Otherwise, they're going to Goodwill." She plops down on the couch and begins thumbing through the goodies. "There's some good stuff in here."

One of the bags catches my eye, and it's like a homing device to me. It's black and shiny and *huge*. Pulling it out of the box, I open it wide and feel giddy at all the room inside. Reaching my hand in, I find my entire arm will fit inside. That means plenty of supplies will also fit. I stick my head all the way in, and when Amanda starts snickering, I realize I may be taking this a little too far.

"What are you doing there, Joie?"

"Making sure it's perfect." I pat down the outside, pushing all the air out and admire that there are no nicks or scratches on it. It's in amazing condition. "Yep. This one is mine."

"Don't pick the first one," Brenda argues. "Maybe there's a better one."

"Nope. There's nothing better." Seriously. This purse is exactly what I need. You can't find them this size and of this quality anymore. Trust me. I've tried.

"What are you going to use it for?" Amanda seems confused by my all-consuming love of this bag.

"My new job!" I announce, eliciting another confused look. Poor Amanda. Sometimes she can't keep up with my energy. Of the two of us, she is definitely the more subdued. Always has been.

She shakes her head just slightly. "I'm sorry, your *what*? I thought you quit working."

Hiding my new treasure in the game cabinet so no one will try to steal it, I respond, "I'm picking up a little part-time job to help pay a few of my bills. Maybe have a little spending money."

Kasey continues digging through the purses while we chat. "At the construction company? What do you think of this one?" She holds up her find for me to assess.

"White is hard to clean and once the bottom gets dirty, it'll ruin the leather."

"Good point." She puts it back in the box and keeps searching for a treasure. "Where is this new career of yours?"

"At Carnival Station."

Amanda and Brenda both stop, mid-movement, and size me up, like they're waiting for me to say I'm kidding. "The bouncy house kids place?" Brenda finally asks.

"Yes. But I won't actually be working for Carnival Station. I'm going to be the entertainment."

"I'm confused," Amanda says, looking even more baffled. "What kind of Carnival Station are we talking about here? Is it a strip club after hours or something? Because I just can't picture you taking your clothes off for money."

"Oh stop." I grab a deck of cards and begin shuffling mindlessly. "It's not a strip club. Once a week, I'll go to the restaurant part to make balloon animals for the kids and read stories. Paint faces. Things like that."

"That sounds kind of fun." Brenda tosses a purse back in the box, and Amanda immediately picks it up. She really does have a lot of bags to choose from. "Does it pay well?"

"Nothing significant. But even a couple hundred dollars not taken out of my savings each month helps."

"You did a really good job saving enough money to go to school without working. Not a lot of people would plan like you did." Amanda holds up another find. It's a Coach purse, a very light lavender color, straps long enough to put over your shoulder, but not too long. It's beautiful.

I nod my head in approval, and she sits down, clearly pleased.

"I only started saving ten or twelve years ago. And thank goodness Isaac earned that scholarship. There's no way I could've gone back this year if I was trying to pay for both of us."

"He's worked hard. He deserves it," Amanda says with a shrug as she walks toward the front door, probably to hide her new treasure in the trunk of her car. "Now if he could pass some of that motivation off to my kid, that would be great."

Poor Amanda. Her son, Nicholas, hasn't fared very well in college. He decided not to play ball, instead focusing on his studies. So far, he's been on academic probation twice and had one pregnancy test taken by his girlfriend. That's the only time we cheered for him failing a test.

Amanda opens the door and startles. "Oh! You scared me!" she says to one of our friends who was getting ready to knock.

Several women laugh as they make their way into my house, Drea handing me a container full of cake balls. Drea is my favorite.

Within minutes, a couple dozen women gather around the various tables, plates full of snacks and drinks in their hand. Some card game is making people laugh across the room. And someone brought dominos for a rousing game of Chicken Foot in my kitchen.

But Bunco...Bunco is where it's at tonight. Three tables are set up on our side of the room and the dice start to roll.

Within minutes, the fast-paced game of chance is going at full speed. We roll for 1's. Then 2's. By the time we move up to 3's, we're moving fast and no one is talking.

I watch as Amanda shakes the cubes up and drops them on the table. They bounce once, twice, three times and slide to a stop.

"Bunco!" Amanda yells, and the scramble is on, each person around our table grabbing for the dice. Brenda launches herself across the table, reaching as far as she can, with me right behind her. The upper half of my body lands next to her and a loud *crack* echoes around the room.

Suddenly, the room is in slow motion as the table wobbles underneath us...

And collapses.

Drat! I hate celery and peanut butter.

CHAPTER FOUR

Jack

Y ou wouldn't think games could take a lot of out me, since I'm not the one running up and down the field. But you'd be surprised how exhausting standing in the heat for several hours at a time can be. Add onto it the anticipation of game-day mornings, followed by the adrenaline rush during the game, and yeah...Once the stadium empties out and the cameras stop rolling, I'm like a dead man walking. I just want to drive home and grab a cold beer, a pizza, and some SportsCenter. No going anywhere. No doing anything. No talking to anyone.

The one exception is my baby sister, Greer. She's had it rough lately with her asshole of an ex-husband going to prison for some sort of tax fraud. It's put her in a huge bind financially, because she no longer gets child support. Not to mention all the liquid assets she had obtained in the divorce were confiscated because the feds said they weren't his to divvy out in the first place. Thank goodness my parents had left us both a decent-sized inheritance he couldn't touch. It's the only reason my sister is staying afloat.

But possibly the hardest part of the whole situation is how it's affected her kids, my niece and nephew. Julie and Oliver are fourteen and sixteen years old. While Julie is the picture of a normal teenager, Oliver is not.

Born with a double cord wrapped around his neck, forcing an emergency C-section, doctors suspect Oliver has significant brain damage. More damage than they originally realized. Up until he was about six, he seemed perfectly normal. But once he started school and the other kids matured, he just ...didn't. He began having a hard time with his impulse control and the left side of his body seemed unusually weak. That's what tipped off the doctors to potential right brain neurological damage. Add on that he has a high-functioning autism diagnosis.

Needless to say, when Greer and the asshole divorced, it was hardest on Oli. The change of structure and dynamic took some getting used to, as did transitioning back and forth on his dad's weekends. They finally seemed to have Oli in a good place when the feds stepped in and threw it all into an uproar again. The loss of his dad, however crappy of a dad he was anyway, has thrown Oli into a really bad place. Even if Greer won't admit it.

"We're fine, Jack. I promise."

"Based on how wobbly your voice sounds, I seriously doubt that," I quip back. "Wanna tell me how it's really going?"

She sighs, and I can tell she's on the verge of tears. "Oli got suspended again."

"Shit," I mutter.

"I can't keep doing this, ya know? Thank goodness I work for myself and can set my own hours, but I have to be able to concentrate in order to edit proficiently. I can't do that when he's around. He needs too much supervision." She sighs again. "I don't know how to help him, and I feel like I'm drowning sometimes."

"Why don't you move here?" I suggest for the umpteenth time. I'd love to have her down here, but she's resistant. "We could use the money from the sale of Mom and Dad's house and get you something here that'll work."

"And uproot Oliver again? I'm not sure he'd survive any more transition."

I shrug, even though she can't see me. "Maybe. But at least I could help get him off your hands sometimes. A little Uncle Jack time might do him some good. We could go fishing, or I could take him to tour the stadium. I know a guy who might be able to get us in," I joke.

She giggles, which relieves some of my worry. When all she needs is to vent, she still has her sense of humor. When she's really hit her limit and needs help, that humor is gone.

"I don't think he cares about seeing a football stadium right now."

"What? What are you teaching him?" I rant playfully. "No nephew of mine is going to miss out on the love of the game. It's a Texas tradition."

"Sorry. He's obsessed with Pokémon right now."

"The little yellow thinga-ma-bobber?"

"That's the one."

"Huh." I think for a second while I turn on my blinker and turn onto my street. "I mean, I guess I can play that Pokémon

Go crap or whatever. I don't understand it at all, but I'm sure he could show me."

"Shut up." She laughs. "Just keep your ears to the ground for any amazing residential or educational programs that might meet his needs. Something's gotta give one of these days."

Pulling into my complex, I navigate my way through the parking lot to my spot. "If I come up with anything, I'll let you know. And you tell Oli he better not be disrespecting my sister, or I'll show up to have a man-to-man talk with him."

"Would you quit with that? Last time you had a man-to-man talk, you took him for ice cream and brought him home sugared up."

"But he was respectful when he came home, right?"

She huffs. "Uh huh. Until the sugar crash when he started crying."

Yeah, that part I didn't anticipate. I've never had kids. How would I know?

"Anyway," she continues, "I'm gonna go work for a couple hours while I wait for Julie to get home from the movies and Oli is sleeping. The game went okay today?"

"As okay as can be." I pull the car into my spot and cut the engine. "Just exhausting as always."

"Don't push yourself too hard. You're an old man now. I don't want you to break a hip or something."

My sister the comedian.

Running my finger through my hair, I argue, "I am not that old."

"Uh huh. That salt-and-pepper mop on your head is a choice?"

My hand stills. Damn. She got me on that one.

"Okay, okay, whipper-snapper. I gotta go." I clamber out of the car, struggling to carry my phone, keys, and the pizza I stopped to get. "Beer and pizza are calling my name."

"All right. I love you, big brother. Thanks for letting me vent."

"Love you, too. Anytime."

We disconnect and I perform a balancing act as I climb the stairs to my unit. Once inside, I immediately drop everything on the coffee table and head toward the kitchen for a beer.

On the way, I pass another empty pizza box, four empty beer bottles, a bag of McDonald's trash, and a six pack of toilet paper sitting on the counter. It's opened and only has two rolls left in it.

Damn. When did I become such a slob?

My eyes gravitate to the picture of Sheila and me on the fridge, and I know exactly when things became disorganized around here.

In the photo, we're standing in front of the Karekare Falls on the North Island of New Zealand. It's the last trip we took before she died...her bucket-list vacation. We had a full month in Australia and New Zealand. Everything she wanted to see, we saw. Everything she wanted to do, we tried. I didn't have a bucket list, but if I had, that trip definitely would have fulfilled it.

Three days after we came home, her best girlfriends threw her a surprise party. All our friends and family came. People from the law firm she used to work for. People from college. Cousins she hadn't seen in years. It was an amazing night.

A month later, they all came back to help me bury her. That was a rough time in my life, but when the cancer came back for a third time, I knew she didn't have any fight left in her. And it was okay. She went on her dream vacation, she partied with her friends, and she passed on at home in her bed. I'll never regret any of it.

But of the two of us, she was the housekeeper. Even three years later, I still have to remember where I store the vacuum when I actually use it. I guess with it just being me, I don't think about it. As long as there aren't bugs running around, picking up isn't my priority.

"I really need to spring for a maid," I say out loud, as I pop the top off my beer and take a swig, meandering back to my favorite chair and plopping down in it. Turning on SportsCenter, I grab my dinner and sit back to relax.

A razor commercial comes on. You know the kind I'm talking about...the guy shaves with the magical razor blades and suddenly a hot woman shows up out of nowhere, attracted to his clean-shaven baby face.

It's a stupid commercial, but suddenly the woman I ran into the other day crosses my mind. She was cute. Really cute. Tan skin and a bright smile. Her dark eyes crinkled a bit at the corners when she flashed her grin at me. She was obviously older than most of the other students, which was nice to see. Reminds me that it's never too late to start over.

I peek over at a framed photo of my wedding day all those years ago. We were young and idealistic. Ready to face our future head-on, no holds barred. Life had different plans for us, though. But we made do and loved each other through it all.

Before she died, Sheila made me promise I wouldn't pine over her loss forever. That I'd find love, someone to start a new life with. Up until this week, I've never considered it because no one has caught my eye, but for some reason, the woman I bumped into the other day has.

It's been three years. I'm not really grieving the loss of Sheila anymore, even though I miss her every day. Maybe she's right. Maybe I do need to find companionship.

I think on it a moment longer before making up my mind with a single nod of determination.

It appears Jack Pride is going out into the dating world again.

CHAPTER FIVE

Joie

I hate science with a passion. Which Isaac thinks is weird because I like doing things like putting Mentos in Coca-Cola bottles to see the explosion and making homemade slime. But I guess those don't really count as college-level experiments as much as they're considered kindergarten games.

In order to play those games with five-year-olds in an educational setting, however, I have to pass the college-level part. That includes my very first biology exam, which I don't feel prepared for. Hence, why I'm studying Mendel's Laws and genetics vocabulary while my lit professor is talking about Dante's Inferno.

Wait. That's not right. We finished that last week. He's talking about *Everyman*, a 15th century play that examines the Christian faith and what man must do to obtain eternal life.

It's not a bad play. I didn't fall asleep while reading it over the weekend. But it wasn't riveting either, which actually works to my advantage because I don't want to pay attention to the discussion anyway. I have the principle of segregation to brush up on.

Which I don't understand. At all.

I am in so much trouble.

"I don't remember a guy named Mendel in the play." Mia keeps her eyes on the professor as she whispers to me. She's practically bundled up like an Eskimo today—thick jacket, scarf, beanie with a pompom on top, pulled low over her ears. It's always cold in here, but she's taking it a little too far.

"It's Mendel's Laws," I whisper back. She blinks at me, my words obviously not computing. "The analysis of genetics?" Still nothing. "Didn't you take Biology I?"

She peeks over at my notes. "Oh!" *And there's the lightbulb.* "I knew the name was familiar. I hated that class."

"Is there a problem, ladies?"

Mia snaps to attention, her spine pencil-straight at the boom of our professor's voice startling her.

I shake my head and smile. "No sir. Just making sure we caught it all. I got Fellowship and Goods. I missed Knowledge."

He squints his eyes and pauses, trying to determine if I'm lying. We both know that I am, but even I'm impressed with how fast I'm able to pull those key points out of thin air. Unless he wants to come up here and see what I'm writing to prove I'm not really paying attention, we both know it's not worth calling my bluff. Quickly, he comes to that same conclusion and continues on with the lecture.

As he paces to the other side of the room, Mia breathes out slowly. "Thanks. I can't get kicked out of class again. I almost lost three credit hours last semester for that."

Fantastic. I'm sitting next to the one person at this whole university who gets dropped from classes because she can't stop talking.

I don't respond, hoping she catches the hint that I don't want to chit-chat right now. I want to pretend to listen to the lecture while I study and stay in the professor's good graces. Unfortunately, I have no such luck when she leans back to stretch.

I hear her soft gasp and know something exciting just happened in her world, and I'm about to learn all about it, whether I want to or not.

"You know Isaac Stevens?"

Glancing up from my notes, I take in the excitement on her face.

"Only someone really important to a player, like, *really* important, like a girlfriend gets to wear a player's team sweatshirt," she practically hisses, grabbing my arm. I pull away slowly and take in my outfit.

It never occurred to me when I grabbed Isaac's old hoodie from freshman year, the one he grew out of, that anyone would think anything about it. It's nothing special. Just the ratty one I wear around the house when I feel chilled. I thought I was showing school spirit like a normal student who buys clothes from one of the university stores. Guess not.

"How did you know that? It's just a hoodie," I whisper.

"It has his name and number embroidered right on the front." She points at the emblem, getting awfully close to my boob. *Slow down there, tiger.* "Only the uniforms worn by the players have that."

Huh. I never put that together. Before I can get another word out, she squeals quietly and grabs my arm again. Does this girl have no boundaries?

Actually, I know the answer to that. I've been sitting next to her for over a week now. She's not hard to peg.

"Are you dating him?" she pries excitedly. I open my mouth, but she keeps going before I can answer. "I didn't know he was into older women. I bet there's so much you can teach him, if you know what I mean." She wiggles her eyebrows, making me grimace at her implications. "I hear football players have a *lot* of stamina."

"Okay, stop," I interrupt, putting my hand on top of hers. "Yes, I know him. No, I'm not dating him. I'll tell you more later, but stop talking before you get us kicked out."

She sits up and mimics zipping her lips, just as the man in charge turns again and begins walking to our side of the room again. I go back to pretending to listen while I study, and Mia goes back to doing whatever she does when she's not using up all the oxygen in the room.

Her silence is practically deafening. Unfortunately, it does nothing to help me feel like I'm accomplishing any sort of learning. Science just isn't my thing.

The sounds of bags being packed breaks my concentration, and I realize my time is up. I have about fifteen minutes until my first college biology exam and nervous doesn't even begin to describe how I feel. Mia, however, despite the fact that she can probably spot a football player's embroidery from a hundred yards away, isn't astute enough to notice my attempt at a mad dash. Go figure.

"So, if you're not dating him, how do you know Isaac Stevens?" I should have known she wouldn't let it go.

I smile brightly at her, even though I don't really want to go there, knowing once the rumor mill starts, I'll be getting a call from my son. He's not ashamed of me, quite the opposite. He just doesn't want to be razzed by his teammates. I get it.

No, I don't. I've never been a twenty-year-old boy. But I understand his reasoning for not making a production out of it. Mia here, she will definitely be making a production out of it. I just smile politely, like my lovely mother taught me, and answer her.

"He's my son."

Mia squeals and throws her hands over her mouth, bouncing on her toes. "Ohmygod, are you kidding me?" She grabs my arm again, her mouth dropping open like an amazing thought just crossed her mind. "I've been hanging out with Isaac Stevens's *mother*?"

I quickly shrug her off again, reaching for my things. I have fifteen minutes to cram while walking. I don't have time for this conversation. Actually, I wouldn't want to have this conversation even if I didn't have a test to get to.

"I wouldn't say we've been hanging out, Mia. We're in a class together." I maintain my smile for politeness as I try to refocus her.

"But we talk all the time," she continues, a starry-eyed look taking over her eyes. "Isaac is the cutest. Ohmygod, could you introduce me to him?"

Oh good. The first person to figure out my connection with the Vikings football team, and it's the groupie who's practically determined to get me expelled from my lit class, right along with her.

"Maybe sometime," I concede, trying to brush her off as I throw my satchel over my shoulder and pick up my notebook.

Her eyes light up like I've agreed to set her up on a date with my son. Which I didn't. And won't. "But listen, Mia, I have to run. I have an exam in"—checking my Fitbit, I realize I'm running out of time—"thirteen minutes. I have to go."

"Okay," she calls behind me as I race up the stairs. She was so sidetracked by the idea of my son, she hasn't packed up her things yet. This is bad. Very bad. "We'll talk more about it in a couple days."

No, we won't, I think to myself. Who Isaac dates is up to him, but if I ever set him up, it's not going to be someone who uses up that many words every day. I know Mia is lovely in her own ways, but she needs a few more years to mature. Like maybe a decade or so.

Walking out the door, it takes my eyes a second to adjust to the sunlight. I only have, oh no, twelve minutes. I need to book it.

Staring at my notebook, I begin reading through my genetics vocabulary again as I walk, making sure there are no key pieces of information I'm forgetting. I have no idea if vocabulary will even be on the test, but if I don't understand the words, I'm screwed either way.

Suddenly, I walk right into a wall.

"Oof!"

It all happens like it's in slow motion. My notebook goes sailing through the air. My bag bursts open and things pop out. My arms fly up as I tumble backward. But before I can hit the ground, strong hands grip my arms.

"Shit! Are you all right?" his deep voice inquires.

Jack Pride. For the second time in as many weeks, I've literally run into him on this sidewalk in front of this building.

I have never been more embarrassed in my life.

He sets me upright and leans down to grab my things.

"I am so sorry," I declare, feeling the heat rush through my face. I hope he can't see the blush. "That's twice I wasn't watching where I was going."

He chuckles and stands, handing me my notebook and the pens that apparently hit the ground when we collided. It could be worse. Those pens could be tampons.

"Don't be so quick to blame yourself. I was sending a text instead of paying attention."

"Oh." There's something I was supposed to be doing, but suddenly I'm sidetracked by the movement of Jack's biceps while he runs his hands through his hair.

His salt-and-pepper hair, that was hidden under a ball cap until he took it off.

To run his fingers through it.

Oh my. I can't even have coherent thoughts around this man. What is happening to me?

"I hope I didn't hurt you," he says with a smile.

My brain finally seems to kick back in. "Oh! Oh, no. I'm fine. Just embarrassed. This is why I don't walk and chew bubble gum."

He smiles, so I think he caught my lame attempt at a joke.

"What has you distracted anyway?" He gestures to the notebook in my hands.

"Biology. I have my first test, and I'm a little nervous about it."

"Science isn't your thing?"

"Not at all," I admit. "But it's a necessary evil. I'm trying to do my best."

He leans in to me and lowers his voice. "I'll let you in on a little secret."

His scent has me feeling all googly. That's not even a word, but it's how he makes me feel. He smells like cologne and mint and a little bit of sweat. But not in a bad way. More of a musky way. I find myself angling toward him to hear this revelation. "What?"

"Typically, the students that make the best grades are the ones who took a few years off before they came here. It's like they want it more." He smiles at me and I go all googly again. "I'm betting you're going to ace this test."

Well isn't that one of the nicest things anyone has said to me on this campus?

I lean back and smile at him. "Thank you. I needed that boost of confidence. I've been way more nervous than I should be over some dumb vocabulary."

"I get it," he remarks with a shrug. "When you want something that badly, your nerves can take over. Just take a deep breath before you start and stay focused. You'll do fine."

It's cute how he goes into coaching mode as he encourages me. It's exactly what I needed. Especially since I have...

I get a glimpse of my Fitbit again.

"Oh shoot! I have to be there in nine minutes!"

I bend over to grab the last remaining item off the sidewalk that he initially missed. Oh good. It *is* a tampon. I knew that sucker wouldn't stay concealed in my time of embarrassment.

"Hey, I know you have to run," he asserts, politely ignoring the feminine product in my hand, "and this might sound crazy, since I don't even know your name. But we seem to keep running into each other so, what the hell, would you like to have coffee with me?"

That stops me dead in my tracks. "Me?"

40

He takes stock of our surroundings. "Well, yeah. I don't see anyone else around I'm interested in conversing with."

There aren't many people around at all. Classes are about to start, and I'm going to be very, very late if I don't hurry up. Apparently, Jack misunderstands the concern on my face when his eyes get wide and he pales a bit, which is hard to do with his tan.

"Oh fuck. I'm sorry," he quickly says. "I didn't think about the fact that you could be married. I'm so sorry."

I feel my own eyes widen, but I don't have time to put much thought into anything except reassuring him and getting to class. "No! No, I'm not married." I hold up my left hand to show him my bare fingers, like it's proof or something. It seems to work because he visibly relaxes. "Um, sure. I could go for some coffee."

The smile that crosses his face makes me go all googly once again. "Great! I assume you have a car?" I nod. "There's a fantastic coffee shop about three miles from campus. Down on Northend Road. Aptly called Northend Coffee."

"Yeah, I've seen it driving in."

"It's far enough from campus that usually only locals hang out there. Meet me there? Say around one?"

I bite back another smile. When I drove in today, I noticed the coffee shop. I was planning to stop there on my way home to study for a while, but this sounds much better.

"I'll be there. But I really do have to go. I don't want to be rude but I have..." Glancing at my Fitbit again, I grimace. I'm going to have to run now, and I hate exercise of any kind.

"I know. Go," he says kindly, and I turn away, beginning my jog. "Good luck! Remember to focus!"

I wave over my shoulder and hold onto my satchel as it bounces. I'm feeling strangely confident in my scientific knowledge now, *and* I have a date with Coach Jack Pride.

Poor Mia would never stop talking if she caught wind of this.

CHAPTER SIX

Jack

The jingle of the bell above the door is surprisingly loud compared to the quietness of the room. Or maybe it's just because I'm over six feet tall, and it's right above my head as I walk into Northend Coffee.

Either way, a quick glance around the room shows no one notices my arrival, which is exactly the way I like it.

There are a few people sitting at various tables around the room. Most are involved in conversations, although a few are reading a book or working on a computer. And then my eyes register the one I'm here to meet. The unnamed student who I literally keep running into. She's sitting at a small round table against a wall and she's...what is she doing?

Is she making balloon animals?

I smile as I watch her, waiting behind a few people to get my java. She's concentrating really hard on twisting the balloon this way and that, taking a few seconds here and there to tap her phone before resuming her twisting. I assume she's watching some sort of instructional video.

As the latex begins to take shape and look like some sort of animal, the delight on her face becomes apparent. She's almost finished. She's almost made a dog or cat or something...

Then she loses her grip, and the thing deflates in her face with a Pfffffffffffff. I can't help but chuckle lightly at the way her eyes scrunch tight and her mouth grimaces when the air blows all over her.

But I also can't help admiring how she doesn't get discouraged. She just taps her phone a few more times and reaches into her giant bag to grab a new balloon.

Good god, how many bags does this woman own? They keep getting bigger.

"Here, Coach." Joe, the barista behind the counter, offers me a large cup of coffee. It takes me a second to register what he's talking about. I didn't realize it was my turn to order. "I saw you come in and figured you wanted your usual."

Accepting the cup from him, I nod and hand him my credit card. "Yeah. Yeah, thanks. That's perfect."

He rings me up quickly, making small talk about the weather. That's one of the things I like about this place. They treat me like a regular person, no one special. I love my job and all, but sometimes I like to not have to talk shop every second of every day. It's why I avoid most of the establishments closer to campus.

I take a sip of my straight black dark roast and turn to walk in her direction. She's still working hard on those balloon animals, and I'm really curious to find out why.

"Hi." I don't mean to, but my interruption makes her lose her concentration and causes another balloon to deflate right in her face. I can't help but laugh while I apologize. "I'm sorry. I didn't mean to startle you."

"You didn't," she claims with a smile. "I'm just not very good at this anymore."

Taking the seat across from her, she starts putting her project away.

"Don't stop on my account," I try to reassure her. "You look like you're on a mission."

"Oh no," she protests, still packing her things up, "I need the reprieve anyway. There's only so many times I can blow one of those buggers up before I start getting lightheaded. I need to build up my lung capacity again."

I pause, cup halfway to my mouth. "Again? As in, you used to do this?"

She nods, obviously pleased at surprising me. "Years ago, I used to work as Mrs. Clown at kids' birthday parties."

Well, I certainly wasn't expecting that.

"That sounds…" I try to come up with an accurate description that doesn't sound offensive. She continues to smile.

"It sounds weird, I know," she declares, letting me off the hook, "but it was fun. I got to hang out with kids and put smiles on their faces. There are worse things to do for money."

Sadly, she's got that right.

"I have many more questions about your career choice," I playfully chide. "But I need to backtrack for a second because I've never properly introduced myself." I reach my hand out across the table in offering. "I'm Jack Pride."

She smiles and takes my hand in hers to shake it. It's small and warm and soft compared to mine. "Joie Stevens."

"Joy? That name seems to suit you."

She quirks her head just slightly as our hands release, and she picks up the coffee in front of her. "How so?"

"Well, the sole purpose of that Mrs. Clown job was to make kids smile, right? Can't get much more joyful than that."

"Ah," she remarks in understanding. "I guess it does fit. Too bad it's not spelled that way."

"No? I didn't realize there were different way to spell it."

"It's j-o-i-e. Apparently, it's French."

"Oh la la," I joke, and then cringe internally. It's been a while since I've flirted with a woman. I'm off my game.

Joie doesn't seem to think I'm cheesy though. She just laughs. "I know. It's pretty and all, but it can get annoying having to help people spell it. Or pronounce it."

"Well then tell me Joie, with the French spelling..." Fucking hell. Can I get anymore stupid sounding? "Why are you sitting here working on making balloon animals again? Decided to get back into the biz?"

She shrugs. "Actually, yes. Now that I'm going back to school full-time, I decided it would be smart to work a couple days a week to help keep my student loans down. First year teachers don't make a whole lot of money, and I'd rather not owe Uncle Sam for the rest of my life if I can help it."

"Ah. An education major."

"Yep. Hopefully early childhood. As you can see by my willingness to make party favors and wear clown shoes in an effort to make children happy."

"For what it's worth," I remark, "I think it's admirable that you're willing to put yourself out there like that."

"Thank you. And wish me luck. I haven't been in this line of work since my son was a baby. I'm a little nervous."

I take another sip of my joe, enjoying the easy banter we have going. "How old is your son now?"

She pauses for a moment, like she's trying to decide how to answer. But the moment passes quickly, so I don't think much of it. "Almost twenty-one. I can't believe it. Where did the time go, ya know?"

It's hard to believe this woman is old enough to have a twenty-one-year-old child. She must have been a baby herself when she had him. As my thoughts distract me, I stop paying attention to where I'm putting my cup and it loses its balance, falling to the side.

"Oh shit," I exclaim, grabbing a handful of napkins out of the dispenser, trying to mop up the liquid before it ends up in a bigger mess. "Quick, move your stuff."

Joie says nothing, but digs in her giant bag for a second before pulling out a round cloth something and quickly wiping up the mess. Snatching my cup up, she quickly wipes another round thing around my cup, cleaning it off. In just seconds, the table is back to normal and the only evidence that anything happened is a handful of dirty napkins and those two round disks.

Watching her, I know I have an astonished expression. She, on the other hand, looks like nothing even happened.

"How the hell did you do that?" God love her, she genuinely appears baffled by my question. "Are you a magician, too? How did you clean it up that fast? What are those things?"

"Oh." She begins to laugh as understanding sets in. "I am almost embarrassed to admit that those are nursing pads."

My eyebrows furrow. "They're what?"

She just giggles. "Nursing pads. You know…nursing moms put them in their…" She gestures toward her chest, which is the wrong thing to do because of course my eyes drift downward. "They put them in their bra for when their milk leaks."

I grimace and make her laugh again.

"Wait, wait." I hold my hands up and shake my head in confusion. "I thought your son was twenty-one."

"He is. Almost."

"Do you have another kid or something?"

"No," she says, still smiling and perfectly relaxed at the conversation having turned to breasts. "My niece is only two. A couple years ago I was in the car with my brother when one of our drinks spilled. I grabbed the first thing I could find on the floor of his car and it was a nursing pad. Turns out, it was the most absorbent thing I'd ever used to clean up a spill. And it fit right at the bottom of the cup holder. So I went out and bought some. I always have a few on hand for times like this."

I blink once. Twice. "That is both the weirdest and most genius thing I've ever heard."

"I know!" she exclaims. "It's very unconventional, but if it works, it works."

We both take a sip of our coffee, a little bit lost in our thoughts. There is definitely more to this woman than meets the eye. She gives a very calming, easy-going vibe. She's comfortable to be around. And she's very comfortable in her own skin. I could get used to this.

"So, Jack Pride," she flirts, "how is it that a good-looking guy like yourself ended up asking a gal like me to coffee?"

I quirk an eyebrow at her bold statement. There's no pussyfooting around with this one. I like it.

"Honestly, I haven't dated at all since my wife died." Her smile drops, but I'm quick to reassure her. "No, no. Please don't feel sorry for me. It was three years ago, and while I miss her, I'm not sad about it all the time. It sucks, but watching cancer ravage her body was worse, so don't make that face."

Joie immediately loses the pity expression. "Sorry. You're right. There must be a weird comfort in knowing she's not suffering anymore."

I sigh. "There is, believe it or not. It was her third diagnosis and the least promising. Instead of prolonging what she felt was the inevitable, we did everything she had ever wanted to do. We made some amazing memories those last couple of months."

"What kinds of things did you do?"

"Well…" I rub my lip with my finger tip as I think back to those last months. "First thing we did was create her bucket list. We added the little things like renting a Porsche for the day and splurging on a really expensive handbag she'd only use a few times. Things like that."

"Hey…she had the right idea," Joie says with a smile. "Never underestimate the necessity of a really good handbag."

I glance down at the monstrosity hanging off the back of her chair. "I can see that. I suppose that wasn't a bucket list item after all, as much as me getting my shit together and finally buying her one."

Joie nods like that was the right answer as I continue, "Once we had the list written, I pulled the biggest, most expensive one she had written down, and we went and did it."

"What was it?" Joie sits still, like she's waiting with anticipation on what my answer is going to be.

"We went on a whirlwind tour of Australia and New Zealand."

She lets out a gasp. "Oh, how amazing!"

"It really was." I smile proudly. "I have never seen landscape like that before, and I'm sure I'll never see it again."

"Did you see any kangaroos?"

I chuckle. "Sure did. We stayed far, far away from those bastards. They're mean."

Joie lets out a laugh, and I can't help but laugh along with her. I appreciate that she's not focusing on Sheila's death, but on her life.

"I'm glad you got to do that with her. She's a lucky woman to have a husband who would drop everything to head Down Under."

I shrug. "It's what she'd always wanted to do, and I wasn't gonna let her leave this earth without seeing her biggest dreams."

Joie smiles again, resting her arms against the table as she listens to me, completely engaged in our conversation. A warm feeling runs through my chest, and I realize this is what dating in my forties should feel like. None of those bull-shit games I see my players playing. None of that drama. Just two people enjoying each other's company. Maybe this will be fun after all.

"Anyway, I'm sure I could have started dating sooner, but working at a university makes it hard to find people in the right age category, if you will."

She nods in understanding. "If it makes you feel better, even if you don't work with a bunch of new adults, it's slim pickings out there."

"Yeah?"

"Yeah. I was the office manager at a construction company for close to fifteen years. I was surrounded by men. Still, nothing."

I chuckle as she smiles. "That's just sad."

She shrugs back at me. "It's the way of the dating world, I suppose. You're lucky to be on a date after only a couple years. I've been single for, what, eighteen years and can count the number of dates I've had on one hand."

I blink rapidly as I digest her statement. "Eighteen years? Good lord woman, how did no one snatch you up yet?"

"That's very flattering of you to say," she responds. "Maybe I'm picky. When you're left alone to fend for yourself at the age of twenty-two with a two-year-old, you tend to change your standards."

"Holy shit, that's young," I remark, mostly to myself, even though I said it out loud. "And your parents didn't help you?"

She sighs and sits back, getting more comfortable. "They tried. But I was a headstrong young woman. I'd been giving them trouble for years…sneaking out, partying behind their back, eloping when they warned me of the idea. I think I was determined to prove I could do it. Like letting them help would somehow be recognizing they were right about my behaviors."

That admission makes me smile. "When did you finally get over it and let them help?"

"I'm not sure I have. But I have apologized many times for the way I treated them. Especially once Isaac became a mouthy teenager."

I bark a laugh. "Yeah, I've heard teenagers have a way of making your parents seem much smarter than you give them credit for."

"So, so true." She grins. "You haven't experienced the teenage years yourself?"

"Nope. When Sheila was diagnosed with cancer the first time, the radiation pretty much eliminated that possibility. But my sister has two teenagers right now and, oh boy, have I heard some stories."

We continue sitting in the coffee shop, each ordering a second cup that I pay for this time, and talk until our cups are empty and it's time for me to head back to the stadium.

As we stand and Joie begins gathering her things, I realize I like this woman. I *really* like her. She's nice. She's beautiful. She's charming. And she's short.

I usually go for tall ladies, but Joie is so full of personality, she seems to tower over me in some weird way.

"Listen, I know you're busy with your studies and your new job"—she flashes me a smile at the mention of those damn balloon animals—"but I'd love to take you to dinner. If you're interested?"

"Sure." There's no hesitation in her answer. "I live about forty-five minutes away. On the outskirts of San Antonio. Is that a problem?"

"That's actually perfect. There's an amazing pizza joint out there we can go to. No suits. No dresses. Just casual and fun."

"Sounds good."

We exchange phone numbers, and I walk Joie to her car, carrying her giant-ass bag that weighs damn near a hundred pounds.

"How do you lug this around?" I grunt when we get to her small four-door, and I toss it on the back seat.

"What can I say? I'm stronger than I look."

52

Somehow, I don't doubt that.

"I'll call you in the next couple of days and maybe we can get together this weekend?" I offer, confident she won't change her mind.

"Sounds good. I'm sure I'll run into you on campus, probably literally, sometime soon," she jokes as she climbs into her car, ending our coffee date with the same humor we've had the whole time. Then, with a smile and a wave, she cranks the engine and is gone.

I watch as her car drives away, shoving my hands in my pockets.

Dating in my forties might not be that bad.

CHAPTER SEVEN

Joie

It's been years since I've been on a date. Okay, it probably hasn't been that long, but it feels that way because somehow, someway, over the years, "Isaac's mom" has been my main personality and "Joie" became secondary. In all facets of my life, including dating.

It happens. When you become a mother, life wraps around raising that little person, and it's easy for your own likes and dislikes to get lost in the process. An opportunity to hang out with Jack as a woman enjoying time with a man was a real treat for me. And as much as I didn't want to get my hopes up about his intentions with me, it's too late.

Fortunately for me and my hopes, Jack didn't wait those two days to call. No, by the next afternoon, we were texting back and forth.

It started with a *How did your biology test go, anyway?* which turned into *How long do coaches have to be at the sta-*

dium on a regular day? and pretty much every mundane, irrelevant, yet enlightening question in between.

I'm no stranger to texting. Amanda and I are the worst
about sending each other inappropriate memes or jokes at the
least opportune times. But something about texting with Jack
is different. It's flirting, but it's not over the top. It makes me
feel good. Makes me feel special. It's just fun.

I giggle as I read the most recent message from Jack. I
shouldn't laugh at his frustration of grown boys refusing to
throw their lucky socks in the laundry, making the locker room
smell like it's full of dead fish, but I do. Any mother who has
raised a teenage boy knows this pain, so I can sympathize.
Plus, somehow, I've turned into a giggly girl around him.

I have to remind myself to put my phone away. It's time
for study group, and I need to find the room and focus.

Following the signage on the wall, I locate room 3B in the
northeast corner of the library and open the door.

Wow. *Once again, I'm the oldest person in the room,* I
think to myself. I know everyone in here has to be in my class,
otherwise they'd be in a different study group, but I only recognize one person. Nick is a bit older than the others by a few
years. He enlisted in the Army straight out of high school and
spent eight years in the service. When he got out recently, he
decided he wanted to be a teacher. A high school teacher, to be
exact. In his words, "Teenage boys need more strong-male role
models," and so here he is.

Of course, he didn't tell me any of this information. I
overheard him telling the cute blonde he sits next to in our educational psychology class. They sit in the row in front of me,
so it was hard not to eavesdrop. Plus, there aren't many men in
the class, and I was interested. I could be ashamed of myself

for listening in on someone else's conversation, but hey, at least it wasn't reality TV.

As I take a seat across from Nick, I notice everyone else staring at their phones. I suppose the discussion hasn't started yet. Either that, or they're really good at bouncing back and forth between social media and the topic at hand. Or they're very bad at studying.

Either way, I refuse to pull my own phone out of my satchel again. I don't need the extra distraction Jack's texts bring.

Well, I don't *need* it. Want? That's another story.

"Excuse me," I ask the person sitting next to me. She's a tall woman, probably about twenty. She has long dark hair and large dark eyes. She seems friendly enough. "What time does the group start?"

Before she can answer, Nick jumps into the conversation. "Professor Ellis said it's an informal study group. I guess that means anyone can start us off, right?" He swivels his head back and forth as he waits for someone at the table to respond and gets mostly shrugs instead. A few heads nod. There's one laugh.

That was from someone not paying attention at all, but still playing on her phone.

Nick shrugs. "Okay. Well then, I guess we should get going. The syllabus says our first test is going to include Piaget's cognitive development stages. Should we start there?"

Papers rustle and laptops are flipped open. Someone asks, "Is this test going to be essay or multiple choice? Does anyone know?"

No one does, so we all agree the best course of action is to assume it's an essay test and get all the details memorized.

We begin going over the topics, Nick giving us the most direction by throwing out questions, and it seems to help. Until he starts to get stuck.

"I think the hardest thing for me to remember is the sensorimotor stage," Nick says. "I don't know why I can't remember object permanence. It seems so simple."

"Maybe it would help to come up with some real-life examples," I suggest. "For instance, when my son was about a year old, he thought it was hilarious anytime I would put a dishrag over his head, pull it off, and yell, 'There he is!' It was like a modified version of peek-a-boo."

"Oh, that's a good example," someone says, the click of typing keys speeding up.

"It doesn't just work for object permanence," I continue. "He was also learning how to manipulate the hand towel. And he was in control of it. When he put it on his head, it stayed. When he pulled it, it moved. It falls under recognition of the ability to control an object as well."

I get a few more nods of understanding and watch as people continue jotting down my examples. Other people have ideas, too, mostly from their years of babysitting or having younger siblings.

An hour later, we all feel pretty confident that we have the developmental stages down and could get through almost any question Professor Ellis throws at us. To be perfectly honest, I didn't find this part of the lecture that difficult to grasp. But I guess I do have an advantage, being that I've watched all the stages as they unfold in real time and with a real child. They just get to read about it in a boring book.

Collectively, we decide to take a break before moving on to the multiple intelligences. This is where I start to get confused, so I'm glad we're doing it next.

As my study-mates stretch and grab for their phones again, I reach into my bag and pull out some treats. I really want to be seen as a regular student, but let's face it. My natural inclination is to make sure these kids are fed. It's a curse.

"I know we're not supposed to have food in the library, but I snuck these in anyway." I grin and drop the paper plate full of double chocolate brownies in the middle of the table. They're moist and chewy, and I know they taste amazing because I had three of them before they finished cooling this morning.

Yes, I made brownies at six o'clock in the morning. When the neighbor's dog wakes you up and you can't go back to sleep, you might as well be productive, right?

It doesn't take long for everyone to grab a brownie, or three, and the moans of enjoyment surround me.

"Wow. Thank you so much," the tall girl next to me says, kindly. Stephanie is her name. I make a mental note to remember that.

We all start milling about, and one of the guys approaches me, I assume to thank me as well. He's a huge guy. At least six four and well over two-hundred-fifty pounds. I assume he plays football, but I'm not going to ask. I want to be respectful of my agreement with Isaac. For him, but also for me. I've been *Isaac Stevens's mom* for so long, it's kind of nice to just be *Joie* sometimes.

"You're Isaac's mom, right?"

Welp, so much for being my own person for a while.

It's not his fault he figured me out, and he doesn't mean it as an insult. I smile at him and put out my hand. "You caught me. I'm Joie."

His giant paw grabs my tiny hand, and he gives me a solid shake. "Brian. It's nice to meet you, Ms. Stevens."

"Oh, please, Brian. Call me Joie. I'm here as a student, not a mom."

"Okay, Joie."

"How did you figure me out, anyway?"

After Mia's meltdown over Isaac's old hoodie the other day, I stopped wearing it around campus. I didn't want to accidentally out myself and potentially have another embarrassing conversation where the underlying theme is incest. Naturally, that means I'm curious how this guy knows me.

"Well, it took me a second because you're really young to be his mom."

Ah, flattery. It's like being carded at the grocery store for booze. We all know the cashier is full of crap, but it makes us feel good anyway. "I'm not that young. I'm forty-two."

He shrugs. "That's not old. Forty is the new thirty, and all that."

I've not heard that one before, but I'll take it. It makes me feel younger than I am, which I have no problem taking advantage of.

"I guess you and Isaac have the same smile." He squints at me strangely before saying, "It's kind of creepy how much you look alike actually." I'm not sure if I want to drop my head on this desk over his audacity, or laugh at the statement. Either way, he's not done. "But I still didn't put it together until I ate one of your brownies."

What one has to do with the other, I'm not sure, but my confusion must be apparent.

"Isaac brought some to practice once last year." He rubs his neck and glances at the few remaining treats on the table, longing on his face. "The only person who makes brownies like that is my mom, which is why I remember. Kind of made me a little less homesick when I had them."

Now I remember. I had made several dozen for a bake sale the Presbyterian Church was having, but I overbaked. They're Isaac's favorite so I didn't think twice when he took the overage with him. I had no idea he shared them with his team. He was just a walk-on player at that point. But clearly, he knew his teammates well enough to know a little treat from home could make a big impact.

I pat Brian on the arm. "Well, I'm glad they gave you a little taste of home. Where are you from?"

"Wisconsin."

"Wow!" I exclaim. "You're a long way from home."

"Yes, ma'am," he says politely.

"You like it so far?"

"I've had some time to get used to it," he responds with a sheepish grin. "I'm a sophomore, but I red-shirted last year. I like it better now that I'm getting some playing time in on the field."

Just a sophomore. This guy is huge, and yet, he's still so, so young to be this far away from home.

"Do your parents get to come down for any games?"

His cheeks pink a bit, and I can tell I've embarrassed him. "Oh no, ma'am. We can't afford to be flying back and forth except to get me home for summer and back. But it's all right. They watch all my games on television. And this year, they're having big potluck barbecues. All the neighbors and my old church friends go over and watch the game with them."

I can tell by his wistful expression that he misses Wisconsin. I supposed being homesick isn't uncommon for the college crowd. Especially if you can't get home for the holidays. And then it hits me...

"Wait...what do you do over the holidays?"

"What do you mean?"

"I mean, where do you go if you can't afford to fly home?"

He shrugs. "I stay here."

I blink a couple of times before I realize my jaw is hanging open. It never occurred to me some of Isaac's teammates, these *kids*, would be spending the holidays alone. Granted, if the Vikings get picked up for a bowl game, it's likely they'll play on Christmas. But there is so much time surrounding those few games.

Pulling myself together, I smile at him and pat his arm again. "Maybe I'll have Isaac bring you guys some more brownies over the holidays."

His eyes brighten. "That would be great, Ms. Stev...uh... Joie." Suddenly his attention is diverted by someone grabbing the second to last brownie, leaving one lone treat. I smirk, knowing he is about to tackle anyone who gets between him and the prize he is gazing at. "Anyway, thanks again for bringing these," he says without meeting my eyes, his glued to the chocolate as he rambles over to the table. As soon as he grabs it and takes a bite, his eyes roll in the back of his head and a deep moan comes from his throat.

I chuckle under my breath, taking his reaction as the best compliment I could ever get from a giant college football player.

Turning back to my studies and taking a seat, I make a mental note to find out more about what accommodations the athletes who are stuck here over the winter break receive.

And I revel in the fact that forty is the new thirty.

I wonder if Jack realizes he's going to dinner with such a young woman. I'll have to text him later and find out.

CHAPTER EIGHT

Jack

"That's what I'm talking about!" Hank exclaims, banging his hand on his desk.

We're watching clips of last week's game. More specifically, clips of each player. Hank's eyes are riveted to the screen as we watch Stevens explode off the line, knocking the other team's defender right on his ass.

"Woo-ie. He's gotten good over the last year." Hank sits back, a shit-eating grin on his face. "He's what, a junior?"

I nod. "Red-shirted the first year, so as long as he's still on a five-year graduation plan, we've got him for another two years after this."

He swivels his pencil between his fingers, a tell-tale sign that he's thinking. "I wonder how he'd do on the offensive line."

"You thinking left guard?"

"Maybe." The pencil keeps moving. "Lyles is having a tough time keeping people off our QB."

"I noticed that," I agree. "I was gonna watch him a little more closely at practice this week. But I have a bad feeling it's not his skill that's causing his problems."

"Christ," Hank grumbles and tosses his pencil on the desk. "I fucking hate when they lose their focus."

Having their egos stroked for so long because of their skill level, combined with getting out from under the watchful eye of Mommy and Daddy, can be a disaster waiting to happen for some of these young men. More than a handful of times, we've watched kids who worked their asses off throughout high school get to college and fall on their face. The girls, the parties, the freedom...football stops being a priority and that's when the problems begin.

"We all fell into that party trap in college. It comes with the territory. You know that."

He points at me like I'm the offender here. "Not as a scholarship recipient. I don't give a shit if his daddy is a pastor and he's never gotten any pussy until now. A few parties is one thing. But when you can't do the job you're paid for, it's over the line."

"Agreed." I sit back and cross my arms over my chest. "Let's call him in. Show him the clips. Remind him of what he's got to lose and put the fear of God in him."

"Whatever we have to do." Hank scrubs his hand down his face in frustration. "I hate adding extra work to our day because some snot-nosed kid has to be called out for being a fuck-up." He points at me again. "And he damn well better not get shit-faced at the scholarship gala.

I don't want our donors anywhere near that kind of shit."

I chuckle. "I'll take care of it. I know how the gala stress-es you out."

"You have no idea," he claims, pinching the bridge of his nose. "Renee spent five hundred dollars on a new dress for this hullabaloo." I let out a low whistle. That's a lot of dough. "Every fucking year she drops a shit-ton of money on this thing."

Once a year, as a thank you to our sponsors, the boosters have a huge fundraiser gala. It's all cocktail dresses and ball gowns, suits and even some black tie. We make the players, not just football players, but all the school athletes, wear a monkey suit, too. There are caterers and live music. It gives the sponsors the opportunity to meet the kids who are receiv-ing the money from the boosters. It also gives them incentive to open their wallet again and give more. They love it.

The team? Not so much.

Hank? Not at all.

"You're the head coach. You don't have a choice but to be there."

"Yeah." He sighs then considers me. "Are you bringing someone this year? Tell me you'll have a date I can pawn Renee off on, so I don't have to hear her commentary about all the other dresses this year."

I chuckle. "Nope. No date this year."

He groans and rests his feet on his desk.

"Although, now that you mention it, I do have a date this weekend."

His eyebrows lift slightly in surprise. Hank was here when Sheila was diagnosed with breast cancer the second time. And he was here when she was diagnosed the last time. When the doctors told us it was terminal, he was one of the first people I called. When I told him about taking Sheila on her dream trip, he didn't skip a beat and helped me figure out how it could be done without losing my job. Turns out, it wasn't that hard. I used all of my vacation and sick leave then went unpaid for the rest of it. But having him fast track the paperwork helped so much.

Yeah, Hank's seen me at my worst. And while he knows I'm not living in emotional despair, he knows I miss her. It's no surprise his curiosity is piqued.

"Anyone I might know?"

"Unless she's a trainer and I don't know about it, nope."

His eyebrows furrow. "Why would she be a trainer? Are you...is she a student?"

I open my mouth to answer him, but I realize that this might be against my employment contract, and it never occurred to me until now. Sure, she's older, and I don't teach any classes, but this might be a direct violation of university policy.

His eyes widen and his jaw drops. "Jesus, Pride. Cradle rob, much?"

I glare at him. "You know me better than that." He stares at me in disbelief, so I knock his feet off his desk, jarring him from his relaxed position. "It's true. She's in her forties and going back to school now that her son is out of the house."

"Where'd you meet her?"

"That's where it might get sticky." I run my hand over my five o'clock shadow while I think. "I ran into her outside the Cooper building. Literally ran into her. About knocked her over." I chuckle, thinking about her bag practically exploding and the look on her face when she realized there were feminine products on the ground. I played it off well, but it was still cute seeing her blush.

"Why were you at the Cooper building?" he asks. "That's a hike from here."

"I had to go talk to Merrick's adviser."

"Shit." Hank rubs his eyes. "Again?"

Benjamin Merrick is a fantastic defensive tackle. Observant. Quick on his feet, especially for his size. Efficient at his job.

He's also dumb as a box of rocks.

That boy has done tutoring, extra credit, study groups. Anything and everything we've required of him, he has done without complaint, but he can barely stay in eligibility. We finally worked with his advisor to change his major from kinesiology to communications. There was less math and science, and even then, it was only basic freshman-level stuff.

Unfortunately, less math and science meant more essays and literature. Which also goes over his head.

"It was actually a surprisingly good meeting." Good is a relative term, but I'm trying to stay positive about the guy.

"Yeah?"

"Yep," I say with a nod. "Not only is he maintaining his eligibility status, he's on track to graduate at the five-year mark. Just like we were hoping."

Hank squeezes his fist together and pumps it in victory. We've pulled out a lot of stops to help this kid be successful. Not just in football, but so he's prepared for life.

"I've gotten a few whispers about him being drafted, too," Hank confesses.

"Good. If he goes in, we need to make sure to help him get a good financial planner. I can't imagine what kind of job he could hold down once his career is over, except maybe coaching. But you know how few jobs there are." Hank nods. "If he can get a decent deal and a good planner who can help him out, it'll help tremendously for after he retires."

The thing about Merrick is he's not stupid in general, just with his studies. But unfortunately, that means an agent or financial planner that doesn't have the best intentions, could easily swindle him out of a lot of money. Hank and I have made it our mission to help ensure that doesn't happen. Our players are like our kids, and we don't want to see them fail.

"I'll let you know if those draft whispers turn into shouts so you can call his mama and tell her what we're gonna do. She knows her boy's been hit one too many times in the head."

"I won't start the conversation like that." I chuckle and lean back in my chair, stretching my legs out. "But she's a nice woman. I'll give her a heads-up."

"Speaking of nice women…"

I groan and run my hands through my hair. "I don't know what to do. I know it's frowned upon to have a relationship with a student. But I always assumed that was more about a coach dating a player or a professor dating his student. Not a coach dating a forty-something, non-traditional, education major that takes classes on the exact opposite side of campus, and they never cross paths."

"Unless you're tracking down an advisor."

I narrow my eyes at him. "And how many times am I going to have to put this much work into a player's studies again? Not many."

"I don't know what the official policy is because I've had this ball and chain for such a long time." He flashes his wedding ring at me.

I snort a laugh. "Don't let Renee hear you say that."

He waves his hand around. "Do you see Renee in this room? I'm not that stupid." Linking his fingers together and putting his hands back behind his head, he continues, "But I kind of think you're right about it being a common-sense thing. She's your age, you'll never be in charge of her, so the worst that can happen is she can manipulate you for a few tickets. But that would be your own damn fault if you fell for it."

"You mean like Matthews did?"

Hank doubles over laughing, while I sit with a shit-eating grin on my face. "The stage-five clinger! I forgot about that!"

Several years ago, Matthews met some woman at a local bar one night. Brandy, Bambi, Candy...who knows what her name was? For their first date, he brought her to the gala. Apparently, she got a taste of the good life and wanted more of it. Why she thought Matthews could provide it, no one knows. But she did. And he couldn't shake her. After taking her out on two dates, she was talking about moving in and marriage and babies...the whole nine yards. She would show up in the office with a picnic dinner because she "loved" him.

We thought it was hilarious because he legitimately didn't know how to get her to understand he wasn't that into her. He finally had to lay it out and make her cry. And by cry, I mean race up to the office so she could scream and wail and call him all kinds of names you wouldn't hear coming out of my mouth, and I cuss more than a sailor, all in front of an audience—us.

Since then, the dumb ass has fallen into that trap two more times. Never as severe as the stage-five clinger. But not without us slapping him upside the head a couple times for being an idiot.

Hank is still chuckling and wiping tears from his eyes. "You gonna bring your co-ed to this year's gala?"

"We haven't even been on a date yet. I'm not introducing her to any part of this team until I know they're razing me for a good reason. We're not the only ones who were there for the clinger."

We both start laughing again. "Well good," he says. "I'm glad to see you getting in the saddle again. I hope you waited this long for a good one."

Me too.

CHAPTER NINE

Joie

When I open my front door, standing on my stoop is a very dapper Jack Pride. He looks delicious. Which is something I'd never think, let alone say, if that means anything as to how handsome he is tonight.

He's wearing jeans and a polo, but something about the way he carries himself makes it obvious he's a coach. Like he commands respect, even if he's not on the field. I like it.

He lets out a low whistle as he takes me in. "You look amazing."

I feel the blush heat up my cheeks. "Thank you." I didn't pick out anything special. Just a nice pair of skinny jeans with a white, flowy top that makes me feel like the baby gut I've had for twenty years is concealed. "Do you want to come in? Or…I mean, do we have a reservation?"

He laughs, a slow chuckle rumbling out from him. "No, we don't have a reservation. But I don't need to come inside. I'm a growing boy, so I'm ready to eat."

Oh yeah. I like this guy. I like his sense of humor and his wit. I like the way he watches me like I'm beautiful. I like that he says it out loud. And I kind of like that he doesn't want to come in.

I know, I know. It's been a *long* time since I've been with a man. But I've always subscribed to the belief that I'm worth waiting for. If you don't want to build a solid relationship with me first, I'm not important enough to you. And that means you don't deserve these goods. The fact that Jack doesn't try to come in means a lot. Like he might be on the same page as me. Which would be one more thing to like about him.

"Okay." I turn, flashing him a smile over my shoulder. "Let me grab my purse."

It's hanging on the hook right next to the door, so it takes me no time at all to snag it, pull my keys out, and lock up behind me. I'm strangely nervous and hyper-aware that Jack is walking really close to me, so I don't notice his ride until we're right up on it.

I stop and my eyes go wide. "That is a giant truck."

Jack chuckles and pulls the passenger door open for me. "I live in Flinton, Texas. Are you really that surprised?"

I shrug in agreement because he has a point. Five-passenger, extended cab, extended bed, extended everything isn't really uncommon around here. I just can't figure out why they're necessary unless the owner works in construction or on a ranch.

After climbing into the cab, and I do mean *climbing*, I take a few seconds to regard my surroundings. The front is clean. The back? Not so much. There are dozens of empty water bottles littering the floorboard. A few fast food bags, too. It's like he transported half the team home in this thing. Which may not be completely off-base. He is the assistant coach. I'm sure that kind of stuff happens all the time.

Before I can think any more about it, Jack jumps into the driver's side and cranks the ignition. He glances over at me with a smile. "Got your seatbelt on?"

I nod and off we go.

"Where are you taking me, anyway?"

He glances at me and smiles before focusing on the road. "I figured I'd run with the pizza idea. There's a little place about fifteen minutes from here. DiPashi's Cuicino. I hope you like authentic Italian."

"I do. But how in the world did you find a place like that around here? You live in Flinton. That's forty-five minutes away from here."

"Sheila, my late wife"—I nod in recognition of her name—"used to hate going out to dinner anywhere near Flinton." He chuckles, a soft look on his face and I know he's remembering her fondly. "She hated the notoriety of my job. *Hated* it. So it became our thing to find hole-in-the-wall restaurants."

"And what did she think of DiPashi's Cuicino?"

"Didn't like it."

His unexpected answer makes me laugh out loud. "But you're taking me there to eat?"

A wide grin lights up his face. It should be weird talking about the woman he was married to for so many years, especially since he clearly still thinks the world of her, but it's not. It's almost comforting to know there must be something special about me for him to think I might be the same caliber as she was.

"She didn't hate it because the food is bad," he clarifies. "She hated it because she's not a fan of authentic Italian. It's owned and operated by this couple who moved here from Sicily. Sheila was fine with Americanized Italian, but she wasn't a fan of all the basil and olive oil."

"Well, no disrespect to Sheila, but she's wrong," I joke.

"You like that kind of food?"

"I like any kind of food, but authentic is right up my alley. Italian made by someone from Sicily? Yep. Greek made by someone from the island of Lefkas. Let's do it. Mexican made by someone from Guadalajara? Bring it. I'm a foodie with that stuff."

"Well, good. It'll be nice to eat with someone who appreciates good cuisine." Suddenly he grimaces and shakes his head. "Ah shit, I'm sorry. I guess it's not really good dating etiquette to talk about your wife with the woman you're taking to dinner."

I smile, partially as reassurance. Partially because I like his slight Texas drawl. It's kind of sexy. "I don't mind. It's nice knowing those kinds of relationships still exist. There are so many horror stories out there, I like hearing about the good ones."

He glances my way a few times, still trying to keep his eyes on the road. "I take it you had one of the horror stories?"

Crinkling my nose, I think about my answer. It's been so long that I really am over it. But that doesn't mean the memories are happy.

"I was a bit of a wild child for a few years," I begin.

"Really? You seem pretty stable to me."

"Having a baby when you're practically a baby yourself forces you to grow up pretty fast."

"I take it Isaac's dad didn't stick around?"

"Nope," I say, popping the p for effect. "Years ago, I was really angry that Isaac's dad left. How could he leave me on my own with a two-year-old? We *both* had this baby, ya know? We were *both* responsible." I sigh as I put my thoughts in order. "But now that Isaac is the same age I was when he was born, my perspective has changed a bit. I understand how it happens."

"You don't mind so much that he left anymore."

"Oh no," I correct him. "It was still the wrong thing to do. If Isaac ended up in the same position, you better believe I would beat his little butt if he responded the same way." Jack chuckles, which makes me laugh. "It's true! I'm not one of those moms who think my child can do no wrong. I know he can. And I'll be damned if he grows up to treat his own child the way he was treated."

I glance over at Jack, who is staring at me. Thankfully we're at a stoplight.

"What?" I ask, beginning to feel self-conscious about his eyes on me.

Jack turns to face ahead as the light turns green and presses his foot to the gas. "You don't know how rare that is these days."

"What? Holding my kid responsible for his actions?" He nods. "Really? I thought that was just decent parenting."

"I've been coaching for a long time, and I'll tell ya, there's been a shift in recent years." Jack shakes his head like he's trying to rid himself of some bad memories. "The guys still respond to us because we run a tight ship, but the trust we used to have isn't there as easily anymore. It's like the minute we turn our backs, they forget everything this team is supposed to stand for."

"I wish you were exaggerating, but I sit next to a chatty Cathy in my lit class. I hear way too much."

"I wish I could say what you've heard is wrong. But I doubt it strays far from the truth."

I keep watch out the passenger window as we drive. I probably should tell Jack he knows Isaac, but we've been on one date. Even if we decide to see each other again, it doesn't mean it'll happen. If it does, though, I'll fess up. It shouldn't make a difference since he's dating me, not my child. But at some point, I guess it's only right that they both are aware of the connection.

A familiar building goes by and I recognize exactly where we are. "Oh look! That's the Carnival Station I'm working at now."

Jack leans forward to see where I'm pointing. "At that clown job?"

A giggle escapes me. "It's not a clown job. I don't wear a red nose. I just make balloon animals and do some face painting."

He quirks an eyebrow at me in disbelief, so I cave.

"Okay, fine. I put on the clown shoes and wig for a few annual events."

We both laugh as we continue our conversation. We talk about my parents who still live in the area, and his parents, who are both unfortunately deceased. We talk about my brother Greg and his ridiculous idea of buying a house sight unseen, specifically so he could live next door to his girlfriend.

Jack is fun and funny. And before I know it, we're seated inside the restaurant, perusing the menu. We haven't been here five minutes and I already love it. It's a tiny place, maybe a dozen or two tables situated around the single room, white tablecloths and folded fabric napkins on top of all the tables. The silverware is polished and shiny and mirrors on all the walls give the room the illusion that it's bigger than it is. Quiet music is piping through the speakers. And the faint smell of basil and cheese wafts through the air, making my mouth water.

"I can't believe this place is here," I remark as I continue to take in my surroundings. "It's so quaint. I love it."

Jack eyes don't flicker up from his menu. "You're gonna love the food even more. What are you in the mood for?"

I smirk. He wasn't kidding when he said he was hungry. "It all looks really good. Do you have a favorite?"

He folds his menu and places it down in front of him. "I know it doesn't sound like anything special, but the pizza is unreal. How does that sound?"

"Sounds like an easy decision." I slap my own menu on the table with a grin in his direction. "I'm sold. You decide the toppings because I'm game for anything."

As if she's been listening for her cue, our waitress immediately approaches. Since I haven't been here before, I let Jack do all the talking. I'm not terribly picky, and I was being truthful when I said anything was fine. I like trying new foods and new flavor combinations. When she's done taking our order and making sure our drinks don't need to be refilled, she leaves us to our conversation.

CHAPTER TEN

Jack

Joie leans in, elbows on the table, and gets comfortable. "You said you have a sister?"

I swallows the drink I was taking before answering. "Yeah. Greer. She lives in Kansas with my niece and nephew."

"Where your parents were?"

"Yeah. Now that my parents are gone, I keep trying to get her to move down here, but so far, I've been unsuccessful." A wave of sadness passes over me, but I'm not sure if it's over the loss of my parents, or over missing the last part of my family.

"Is she worried about changing custody arrangements or something?"

I snort a humorless laugh. "Uh, no. Her ex-husband, the asshole, is sitting in prison for tax fraud, so all those arrangements are pretty much null and void."

Her eyebrows shoot up in surprise. I know she's trying really hard not to be shocked, but it's hard when a bomb like that has been dropped on you. I felt the same way when Greer first told me.

"I probably shouldn't have just blurted that out," I chuckle. "I guess I get a little overprotective of her and the kids."

"It's understandable," Joie says, pulling herself back together. "Deadbeat dads are bad enough. But being in prison means there's no way he can help provide for them."

"Not that he was big on that before he went in, the fucker," I grumble under my breath as I take another sip of water.

She's smiling at me. I'm not sure why my indignation causes her to have that reaction, but I'm not going to dwell on it.

"If your parents are gone and the ex is in prison, what's her hesitation in moving?" she inquires. "Her job?"

"Nah. She works from home, editing books or something."

"Oh, that's cool."

"Yeah." I can feel my face light up when I talk about my baby sister. I'm so proud of her, I can't help it. "When she first divorced the asshole...um...sorry," I apologize, realizing my language may be offensive to her. I don't think it is, but I try to be a gentleman and that means being respectful. "I mean, when she first divorced her ex, she wasn't sure what to do. But she was into reading and knew there had to be a way to make a living in that arena. She took a bunch of classes or something and earned all these certifications. Now she has her own editing business. Has two or three people working under her and all these authors come to her for help." I lean back and cross my arms over my chest as I speak. "She's made a very good living for herself and the kids. And she can be there whenever Oli needs her."

"Oli?" Joie questions.

"My nephew. He had some brain damage at birth and was diagnosed on the autism spectrum, so he's a real handful." I know some people think it's odd that I don't speak about my nephew like there's anything wrong with him. Just very matter-of-factly. But to me, it's not this huge thing. His disability is a part of who he is, and I refuse to treat Oli like he's fragile or like being autistic is a bad thing. Sure, it creates some additional challenges, but it's just who he is.

"Anyway, there are times, usually when he's having growth spurts, that he can get really out of control at school. Greer has to be able to drop everything when that happens, so being her own boss has really helped out. Well, unless it's summertime."

"Wait…what happens over summertime?"

I shrug. "Oli can't be left unsupervised or he gets into stuff. He has a really hard time with impulse control, so you have to watch him like a hawk."

"What about, like, a day care or something?" I can tell by the expression on her face that she knows it's a terrible idea, even as the words are coming out of her mouth. But it's hard for most people to understand the gravity of having a special-needs child.

"He's sixteen, so he's too old for day care," I explain. "And even if he wasn't, the first time he flipped, they'd kick his ass out. Day cares don't take too kindly to chairs being thrown around the room. There's nothing she can do except ride it out and pray he finally starts to mature some."

"And there's nothing like a group home or something." Joie's face immediately reddens as she throws her hands over her mouth, eyes wide. "I can't believe I said that," she grumbles. "I'm so sorry. I didn't mean to sound like she should get rid of him or something."

"You didn't," I reassure her, although I'm not convinced she's actually reassured. "It's a discussion Greer and I have had many times. We've actually explored that option because he's almost bigger than she is. At a certain point, she can't protect herself or Julie, my niece, if he goes into a rage. She's trying to do what's best for him, but she has another child to think of, too."

The thoughtful look on her face shows she didn't even think of that. But why would she? It's hard to understand how much parents have to deal with when they have a mentally-disabled child. Oli is my nephew, and I still have a hard time wrapping my brain around it sometimes.

"Unfortunately, Oli doesn't qualify anywhere," I continue. "Either the facility doesn't accept kids on the autism spectrum or they don't accept kids with aggressive outbursts. Or they don't accept her shitty insurance. Or they do but the payout on her end is still five thousand dollars a month *if* insurance approves it. She's in a no-win situation. That's the big reason I'm trying to get her down here. She needs my help."

"And she doesn't want to uproot her special-needs child who might have a hard time with the transition."

I nod once. "That's exactly it. Oli has had so much change lately, Greer's afraid a big one like moving to a new house, a new town, a new school, would throw him over the edge."

"That's understandable. Kids on the spectrum are so routine-oriented, I can see why she'd be concerned."

I run my hand through my thick hair as I relax more into our conversation. I like feeling comfortable enough to talk to her about my family…even the hard parts. "I keep listening for any resources down here that might be able to benefit him. Maybe a different school program or something. I don't know. I'm sure the right fit is out there. I just haven't found it yet."

"Is he good with animals?"

"Loves them. He's like an animal whisperer. Never met an animal he didn't like and never met one that didn't like him."

"I actually heard about a program the other day."

My eyebrows shoot up. "What kind of program?"

"I don't know which one, but one of the high schools around here apparently busses some of their special needs kids out to a local ranch to work like a co-op type thing."

I lean forward, intrigued. She has my full attention. "To work with the horses and stuff?"

She shrugs. "I'm sure that's part of it. It came up in my educational psychology class the other day. I guess the guy who runs the place helps teach the kids different skills and sometimes even hires them for day-to-day tasks, if they have the capabilities."

I rub my chin thoughtfully. "This is something I need to research. That sounds like it could be right up Oli's alley."

She nods in agreement. "Especially if he's high functioning. He could learn a lot of different skills that could help him down road with work."

I look at her, really look at her, and smile. "Thank you for that information. I'm gonna make a few calls and see what I can find out. Anything I can do to help my sister and my nephew, I'll do it."

Before she can respond, our waitress returns, carrying a giant pizza. The pan alone is half the size of our table. My mouth waters as I take in the black olives, mushrooms, pepperoni, and the most cheese I have ever seen on a thin crust pie in my life. Once the plates are in front of us, I give her the go-ahead.

"Let's dig in," I say with a smile. So we do.

It's so greasy and gooey, we have to wedge a knife underneath each slice so the cheese doesn't just slide right off before it reaches our plates. The first couple bites have to be eaten with a fork for that reason, but there are no complaints from me. In fact, I think Joie moans in enjoyment a little too loudly when she takes her first bite. My brain forgets about the pizza that's halfway to my mouth when she does it, and sure enough, I end up with a pie crust in my hand, the cheese fallen back onto my plate. Joie, of course, laughs about it. Probably because she's not the one trying to put her pizza back together.

Between the two of us, we eat the entire pizza. Not even a string of cheese is left on the platter. Then we sit back with a pair of Italian cappuccinos and just talk. About school. About jobs. About life.

After several hours, we realize the restaurant has been cleared out and it's time to leave. I take Joie's hand as we talk to my truck, letting go only to climb in on the other side, then grabbing it again as we head back toward her place. The contact makes me feel tingly. I guess you forget how much you miss the intimacy of physical contact until you get it back.

When we arrive at Joie's house, I help her out of the truck, and take her hand once again.

"Would it be presumptuous of me to tell you to clear your schedule for the next couple weeks?" I ask as we meander to her door.

"A little," she jokes. "But I'd probably do it for you anyway. Is that your way of saying you want to take me out again?"

I can't help but chuckle at how direct she is. "I would very much like to take you out again. We have an out-of-town game this coming weekend, but would you be interested in doing something the following Friday?"

"Friday, Friday." She furrows her brow and thinks for a moment. "Wait, don't you go to that gala thing next Friday?"

I feel myself stiffen. How in the hell does she know that? Suddenly, I'm wondering if running into her, twice, wasn't so innocent after all. The mess Matthews got himself into runs through my brain and I have to ask her. "How do you know about the gala?"

She shrugs. "Doesn't everyone? Mia, that girl in my class, makes sure of it."

She's right and I feel myself relax. I can tell she's trying to read my expressions, but there's nothing to read. Sometimes I forget how far removed I am from campus talk, because I'm isolated in my little world. Not all women are out to bag a football player or a football coach. And Joie has never struck me as anything but honest, so I push those thoughts right out of my mind.

"That means Friday night is out," I finally say, rubbing my hands up and down her arms when she shivers. The night has turned chilly, which is odd for September. "Saturday's are hard because we have games, and I never know when I'll be back, but I can do a late dinner if you're game. Or even Sunday evening."

She nods and places her hands on my waist, as my hands are still on her arms. "Sunday would be perfect. I'd like that."

"Sunday evening it is."

Suddenly, as plans have been made and the evening comes to a close, the air begins crackling around us.

"Joie," I say quietly, my eyes staring at her lips. "I'd really like to kiss you. Is that okay with you?"

She nods and I lean in. Just as I'm about to make contact, she giggles.

I pull away. "Why are you laughing?"

She covers her mouth with her hand. "I'm sorry. I'm nervous."

"About what? A kiss?"

"Yes," she says, still shaking. Only now I don't know if it's laughter or nerves. "I don't mind you kissing me. In fact, I want you to. But the anticipation gets me anxious so you're not gonna be able to go slow. You're just going to have to go…"

She squeaks when I take her by surprise, slamming my lips to hers. She's not laughing anymore. Oh no. She's kissing me back. Her lips are soft and plump. And she tastes slightly of cappuccino. It only lasts a few seconds—no reason to have a make-out session on her porch—but it's pretty damn perfect.

When I pull away, her eyes are still closed and her lips still puckered. It takes a few seconds for her lids to flutter open, and when they do, all she says is "Wow." I smirk and give her another peck.

"I take it that means it was okay?"

She clears her throat and licks her lips. "See how much better it is when all the nervous anticipation doesn't get in the way?"

A laugh bursts out of me. "Much better." I run my hands down her arms, a small grin on my face. "I need to go."

"Yeah."

"I'll call you tomorrow?"

"Yeah."

One last kiss and I let her go, even though after tonight, it's the last thing I want to do.

CHAPTER
ELEVEN

Joie

F riday afternoon and the week is finally over. It was a busy one, with a major essay due in my lit class, another test in biology, a group project in educational psychology, and working two days. I wasn't sure how I'd do as a returning student. It's been so long since I've studied or taken notes, I was afraid it would take a while to get in the groove. So far though, I'm doing well. And I'm proud of how good my grades are. I'm pulling a straight four-point-oh.

Jack and I haven't seen each other since our date almost two weeks ago. But we've texted and called regularly since then. It's nice being courted. Especially since he has this quiet calm about him. It almost offsets my constant movement. Which is weird since we don't see each other a lot. But even over the phone, we just seem to balance either other out.

He has this gentle drawl when he speaks. It gives me the impression he doesn't talk a whole lot, but when he does, it's important. I like that. So much of life is filled with unnecessary words and games. I have no desire to deal with that stuff anymore. In my early twenties? Sure. I was the queen of drama. Now? I have too much life to live.

And by life, I mean a *Twilight* movie marathon with Amanda tonight. Even a modern woman like me needs to relax with some rocky road ice cream and a sparkly vampire sometimes.

My phone rings as I walk across campus to my car.

"Hey, honey," I greet Isaac, as I shift my backpack to a more comfortable position. "What are you up to?"

"Hey Mom. I'm finishing up at the gym before the gala tonight."

"Oh, that's right. I forgot that was tonight. Did you rent a tux?"

"Uh, no," he snarks in that tone only a young adult can use, making it clear you asked a ridiculous question. "I'm sure some bazillionaire will wear a tux, but we're just required to wear a suit, so I'm wearing that navy one we got last year."

"Oh good. I'm glad it finally came in handy." I chuckle. "I was starting to wonder if I made that investment for nothing."

A warm breeze blows through, making my hair ruffle. Geez, I need to get it cut or something. This messy bun isn't working for me anymore.

"No, I've worn it before. But listen, Ma," he says on a rush, "what are you doing tonight?"

"Tonight?" This is an odd question. He never asks about my plans. While we're close, I'm still his mother, which makes me way less interesting than anyone else in his life.

"I'm sitting my tush on the couch and snuggling up with Edward Cullen."

"Eww," he responds. "I have no idea who that is, but if he treats you wrong, I'll kick his ass."

I bark out a laugh, amused and yet appreciating the sentiment. "It's a movie, Isaac. Edward Cullen? *Twilight*?"

"Umm...no. Didn't interest me in high school. Doesn't interest me now. But does that mean you're free tonight?"

I furrow my brow, now that he has my mom hackles raised. "What do you mean by free? What's going on?"

"My date for the gala cancelled at the last minute, and I was hoping you'd want to go with me."

I stop dead in my tracks. This gala is a big deal. A really big deal. It's not an event where you just grab a dress out of your closet and go. Most of the women are getting their hair done and mani-pedis. And I'm walking across campus in yoga pants and a sports bra, wondering when I can get to the salon so I can get my unruly hair under control. "The donors love it when the parents come, and I think you'd get a kick out of the whole thing. It'll be fun."

His unexpected statement pushes aside my anxiety momentarily.

"Wait just a minute," I chide playfully. "Are you saying you're ready to introduce your teammates to your mother...the nontraditional older student who studies among them?"

He laughs. "Yeah, I heard you're in Brian's study group. He seems to like you, so I figured...whatever, I'll ask my mom. They'll all be cool with it."

A grin lights up my face. "I'm not sure if Brian likes me or my brownies, but I suppose if it doesn't go well tonight, I could try to win the rest of your teammates over with some baking."

"Does this mean you'll go?"

I sigh and pick up my pace, knowing I'm running out of time. "Yeah. I'll go."

"Cool," he says nonchalantly, having no idea I'm panicking on the inside as my mental checklist of what needs to be done continues to get longer. "I'll pick you up at seven since it starts at eight. Is that okay?"

"Perfect. I'll be ready." At least I hope I will be.

"Awesome. Thanks, Mom. I'll see you in a bit."

We disconnect and I immediately dial Amanda's number.

"Whatup?" she asks when she answers on the first ring.

"Amanda!" I practically yell. "I'm freaking out."

"Why? What's wrong?"

"Isaac just called. Amanda, his date cancelled on him, and I have to go to the gala with him. Tonight."

"Uh...the gala that starts in less than five hours?" she asks calmly. But I know she's not actually calm. She's switching into planning mode.

"Yes. That gala."

"The one you have no dress, no shoes, and no plans for?"

"Amanda, I need your help, not a list of all the reasons why I'm stressing," I assert, getting to my car and pulling out my car keys.

"Sorry. Okay. I have a couple dresses I wore to Jeff's office parties in the back of my closet. I'll grab them and head over to your place." And planning-mode Amanda, who I love, comes out in full-force. "They might be a little big, but at least one of them fit me thirty pounds ago, so we might be able to work with it."

"You know where my house key is?" I throw my backpack on the passenger seat and slam the car door behind me.

"Inside that weird fake rock thing you seem to think is inconspicuous but we all know is a burglar's dream come true?"

"Har, har," I respond. "Yes, there. And pull out my sewing machine while you're at it!"

"Where is that?"

A quick check for traffic behind me, and I back out of the parking space, trying not to peel out of the lot. "In the spare room closet. Up on the shelf."

"Oh lord," Amanda complains. "If I drop that thing on my head and hemorrhage in my brain, tell Jeff I love him. And to learn how to pick up his dirty socks from the floor if he wants his next wife to stay with him."

"Okay, Debbie Downer," I say with a laugh. "I'll let him know."

"How long until you get here?"

"I just got on the road. It'll be forty-five minutes at least."

"Oh shit." Amanda starts laughing, like she does when she's feeling stressed. "You better book it. You have a forty-five-minute drive here and another forty-five minutes back. That only give us...oh hell...three hours to get you gala ready."

"I know!" I take a deep breath as I roll to a red light. If I'm going to be ready on time, I need better luck and for all these lights to stay green. "I'm gonna let you go so I can concentrate."

"I'll be there with dresses and shoes laid out to try on and the sewing machine, well, on the table since I have no idea how to set it up."

"Sounds good." I can breathe a little better, knowing Amanda is already hustling. We don't have time to waste, and we're going to cut it close, but we can pull this off. "I'll see you as soon as I can."

As I hang up the phone, my mental list keeps running through my head.

Dress, shoes, shower, Amanda can do my hair while I do my makeup, clutch, no need for a pedicure; I'll wear heels.

The biggest problem is the dress. Fingers crossed we can make something work, even if we have to sew together a quick rig to get through the night.

My phone beeps with an incoming text. A quick glance shows Jack's name on the screen. I really need to text him back and let him know about my change in plans tonight, but it'll have to wait until I'm not driving, and I have time. Because time is something I'm short on right now.

CHAPTER TWELVE

Jack

I yank at the tie around my neck, wishing it would loosen up, but knowing my efforts are futile. I can't take it off until this shindig is over, and that's at least two hours from now. My only saving grace is the bottle of Shiner my fingers are wrapped around.

A hand claps me on the shoulder. "Looks like the donors are enjoying themselves," Hank states, holding a beer as well. "As much as I hate getting all gussied up and shit, at least it wasn't for nothing."

I survey the room and sure enough, everyone is laughing and smiling. Apparently, they consider a swanky gig like this a good time. I don't get it, but I don't have to. As long as the people with the deep pockets are happy, that's all that matters.

"A couple people have already said they plan to double their donation," I remark.

"Good," Hank says with a nod and a swig of his beer. "We need some new gear. I'd rather not rely on our chunk of ticket sales for that, since we're hoping to update our uniforms next year. You know how stingy the university can be."

"Especially since the box office is probably raising their cut next year."

His eyes widen. "Where'd you hear that?"

"Radio. I heard something the other day about our third-party vendor raising costs across the board. Not just with us. Concert venues, amusement parks, all of it."

Hank groans and rubs his face. "Shit. You know that means we're gonna get screwed."

I nod. "Either us or the ticket holders. They've gotta make up the loss somewhere. It's a good thing we shook so many hands tonight. We may have to rely on them until it all stabilizes again."

We both take a drink and watch the activities around us. Our scholarship recipients are doing a great job of hobnobbing. They're all talking to patrons instead of hanging out together. No one has had too much to drink. They all seem comfortable making small talk. They are our elite, and tonight they're once again proving why. I'm proud of them.

"Where'd Renee go?" I search the room trying to catch sight of the blue dress and giant hair she's sporting tonight.

Hank seems unconcerned with her whereabouts. "Last I saw her, she was chatting up a group of eye candy." The term sounds derogatory, but that's how we refer to the new girl-friends that inevitably show up every year.

In the world of football money, there are two kinds of scholarship donor: the old money alumni who love the school, love the team, love the game; and the new money alumni who love being able to brag to their friends about how much money they've donated. They are easy to tell apart. The old money alumni have been around longer than we have. They never miss the event, bringing their wives who have also been around longer than we have, shaking hands with the coaches and talking shop. The new money alumni bring whatever woman they're dating or are married to at the time and ignore her, so they can compare dick and wallet sizes with other new money alumni the whole time.

Hank and I have seen some of these donors bring a different girlfriend all ten years we've been doing this. The men get older, but the eye candy stays the same age. Still, donors are donors, so while Hank and I are available to anyone who wants to shake our hand, Renee seeks out the women who may feel out of place and help them feel more comfortable. Women who have a good time make their men happy. And happy men make bigger donations.

Welcome to the wonderful hierarchy of Texas money.

"She did a great job tonight," I say to Hank. "I'm glad she was able to hook us up with that party planner. It's about damn time someone remembered to bring drinks for real men."

I hold up my Shiner, and he clinks his bottle to mine, a gesture of solidarity. When I go to take a swig, I realize I'm empty.

Clapping him on the shoulder, I say, "I need to refresh. I'm gonna head to the bar. You good?"

He shakes his beer. "I'll go with you. I'm about out." We make our way through the sea of people to the nearest drink station, smiling and nodding at people along the way. "Don't look now..." Hank pretends to whisper, but does a terrible job of it, "but I think Matthews didn't learn his lesson the first time."

He gestures with his head and I glance to the left. Sure enough, Matthews has just arrived, a blonde bombshell attached to his arm. He has a huge smile on his face, obviously proud to be escorting her around. She has…well, she has stars in her eyes. They all have the same look when they come to the wrong conclusion…big, wide smiles as their big, wide eyes take in all the lights and glitter around the room. Hell, I can practically see her brain thinking this is the kind of lifestyle Matthews will be able to provide her. And she has it wrong. So damn wrong.

Sure, Hank makes a lot of money. But he's the head coach. All the responsibility falls on him. Me? I don't come close to what Hank makes, and I'm his right-hand man. So, I know for a fact what she *thinks* Matthews can provide and the *reality* of what he can provide are not the same.

"That man will never learn." Hank shakes his head before tapping the bar twice, holding his bottle up so the bartender knows what we're drinking. "How quickly do you think until he has to make her cry?"

"Oh no. That's not a stage-five clinger," I disagree. "As soon as she goes back to his place and realizes he lives in a one-bedroom apartment, she'll be off to find the sugar daddy she really wants."

He snorts a laugh. "I suppose it could be worse. She could be showing up with picnic lunches and pledging her undying love."

"Poor guy. I guess we'll need to be a little nicer to him on Sunday after she's gone and he's trying to figure out where he went wrong."

Hank snickers and pats me on the back. "I'm heading over to try and drag my wife away from her new circle of friends. You gonna be okay?"

I flash him a thumbs up while I swallow my beer. "I need to make another circle around the room. I'll catch you later."

He walks away, and I turn to leave my mostly full bottle on the bar. I have more hands to shake and I'd rather not be toasted while I do it. Just as I turn to walk away, I run into a body behind me.

"Oof," we both say and instinctively I grab at the woman's arms to keep her from falling. Then I realize who it is. "Joie?" She gives me a sheepish smile.

At first, I'm happy to see her. But then her beauty takes my breath away. I've only seen her on campus or in jeans. I've always thought she was beautiful. But this...this is completely different. She's stunning in a simple red dress, cut just low enough for my imagination to run wild. Her thick hair is dark and wavy, part of it pulled back in some fancy, glittery clip.

But then I realize she's here. At the gala. Uninvited. How the hell did she get in without an invitation? These things are monitored by security, and she's not on our donor list.

Surely there's a simple explanation though, right? I don't see stars in her eyes. I never did. She only saw me as Jack. Right?

Out of the corner of my eye, I see Matthews and his date walk by, and all the woman trouble he's run into comes to the forefront of my mind. He didn't see it either. He's a seasoned dater, has dealt with a clinger more than once, and he still doesn't see it. I haven't dated in twenty years. Which means I wouldn't see it either.

I need to nip this in the bud quickly. The ability to provide these kids with updated gear could very well ride on this night, and no donor is going to dig deep if she goes ape-shit on me like that stage-five clinger did on Matthews.

Which is too bad because I really thought she was an amazing person. I guess I've been out of the game for so long, I'm not as good of a judge of character as I thought I was.

"What the hell are you doing here?" I growl in her ear, trying not to make a scene.

The smile immediately drops from her face. "I'm sorry. I meant to tell you..."

"You weren't invited, so why are you here?" I know I sound harsh, but I need to make it clear that this is not okay. "We went on *one* date, Joie."

"Excuse me?" She pulls away from me, acting startled and maybe a bit hurt. "What are you implying, Jack?"

"I didn't invite you, Joie. This is a big boundary problem."

The anger flashes in her eyes, and for a split second I wonder if I'm in the wrong, but I push the thought away. "You think I showed up here for you? Like you take me for pizza one time and suddenly I can't be away from you? Can't be without you because you're such an amazing catch?"

"Well, didn't you?" I challenge. I don't have time for these games. I need to get her out of here quickly before this escalates any more.

"No," she says incredulously. "My being here has nothing to do with you. But it's good to know you think so highly of yourself before I committed to that second date."

I scoff. "Then what the hell are you doing here, Joie? This is a closed event."

An arm wraps around her shoulders and I look up to see Stevens, drink in hand, huge smile on his face. "There you are, Mom. I've been trying to find you. I see you met my coach."

Mom? Stevens is her son? My heart drops as I put it all together. Joie Stevens. Her son's name is Isaac. Isaac Stevens. I have no idea how I missed this connection before or why she didn't tell me. But right now, it doesn't matter. All I know is I just made some huge assumptions without asking her first, and if the fury in her eyes is any indication, I royally fucked this one up.

"I did," Joie says, plastering a fake smile on her face. I know it's fake because it's not reaching her eyes. Those are still shooting daggers. Until she peers up at her son. Then her pride is evident. "Isaac speaks very highly of you, Coach Pride. He's always talking about how much you're helping him with his game. How much you've taught him about never jumping the gun until you have all the information in place so you don't mess up a play. How you encourage the boys to be strong men. To be respectful, both on and off the field."

I wince. Not only did I insult her, but she's driving home what a dick I was and how she expected better of me. Frankly, I expect better of myself. Damn that Matthews for putting me on edge. Okay, that's not fair. Matthews didn't do anything except be an idiot. This one is all on me.

I clear my throat. "Well, he has great potential. You've done an amazing job raising him. Most of our players aren't as respectful."

"Most people in general are stuck in their own self-absorbed bubble," she says, directing her glare back at me.

Ouch. I deserve that. "Yeah, um…about that…" I begin, rubbing my chin as I try to figure out how to apologize without tipping Stevens off.

Instead, she cuts me off. "Anyway, I'm really glad Isaac has such a good coach. And thanks for the scholarship. Now, if you'll excuse us, I know there are quite a few people Isaac would like me to meet."

Stevens seems confused but doesn't argue. "Um, yeah. Nice to see you, Coach."

I nod in acknowledgement and try to catch Joie's eye, hoping she'll see my apology, but she completely ignores me as they walk away.

"Who was that?" I don't even have to check to know Hank is standing next to me again.

"I thought you went to search for your wife."

He taps the bar and gestures to the bartender for service. "I found her. She sent me back for more booze. Apparently the older she gets, the more she needs to drink her way through the conversations with eye candy." I snort a laugh, my eyes still on Joie, who is charming some of the donors. Damn, she's beautiful. I wish I'd told her that before I fucked everything up. "Two Shiners and a Lemon Drop," he tells the bartender before turning back to me. "Like I said, who is she?"

"Hmm?" I pretend not to know who he's talking about.

He gestures Joie's direction. "Red dress. Hanging with Stevens. He never struck me as the kind to go for a cougar, so I'm guessing she's not his girlfriend. You were talking to her a few seconds ago and now you look like she kicked your puppy. What gives?"

I sigh and decide it's better to just fess up. "That's Joie." His expression doesn't change at all. "The nontraditional student I went out with a couple times."

His head whips over in their direction, and he whistles. "She's good looking, man. But that still doesn't answer the question of what the hell she's doing with Stevens."

He hands me another beer, and I take a swig before answering. I wasn't going to drink anymore, but after the shitshow that just went down, I need the alcohol. "Apparently, he's her son."

"And he didn't beat your ass or make a scene? Smart kid."

"I'm guessing she hasn't told him. And I'm guessing she never will now that I accused her of being a stage-five clinger."

He stares at me blankly for a several seconds before a belly laugh bursts out of him.

"Oh, come on," I argue, punching him on the arm. "It's not funny."

"I disagree." The asshole wipes a tear away from the corner of his eye. "I think it's really funny. Is that why she keeps looking everywhere but here?"

"I'm guessing so."

He's still chuckling as he claps me on the back. "Good luck fixing that one." He walks away, two drinks in hand still muttering, "Stage-five clinger" under his breath.

"Asshole," I mutter. Although I'm not sure if I'm talking about him or me.

CHAPTER THIRTEEN

Joie

"I want an elephant!" The towheaded five-year-old doesn't ask. She demands.

Unfortunately, I don't know how to do elephants yet. I always screw up the trunk. "Uh...how about a dog?"

She stomps her feet and squeezes her little fists. "I don't like dogs. I like elephants!"

I blink a few times, trying really hard to keep the smile plastered to my face. I've only been here for thirty minutes. I have two and a half hours to go. If this is the way all the kids are going to act today, I may not last my whole shift.

"Okay." I muster up as much fake brightness as I can. "I'll do my best." And by *do my best*, I mean I make a dog, then shove a deflated balloon through its face for the trunk. Shock of all shocks, the world's most delightful child is thrilled with the creation and skips away to show her mother who is sitting in the corner chatting up a friend.

I sigh before beaming down at the next child, putting on my fake smile again. He's small, maybe three, and has his thumb in his mouth.

"Would you like a puppy?" His eyes widen and he nods, never taking his eyes off what I'm doing. Normally I would be chatting him up, trying to draw him out of his shell. But I'm not into this today, which stinks because it's usually the highlight of my week. I love entertaining the children and bringing some joy to their day. Especially on special occasions like this one where I get to dress up in a red, curly wig and giant floppy shoes.

Typically, I wear my normal clothes, paint a cute rainbow on my face, and I'm good to go. But it's the five-year anniversary of this particular location, so as a celebration, management asked if I'd come in the complete clown get up. Of course, I don't mind. But even with the hustle and bustle of all the people wandering in and out, attracted by the music and free ice cream, my heart can't get on board with the job today.

It's been close to a week since I last talked to Jack. He's texted me several times since Friday night, apologizing for jumping to conclusions. But I haven't responded.

The thing is, I understand why he was surprised to see me at the gala. I never told him Isaac was in his football program. I planned to tell him. It was never a secret. But with Isaac springing the event on me at the last minute and barely having time to get ready, I ran out of time. I take responsibility that he was blindsided. But that's not the part that makes me hesitate to respond to him.

I've thought a lot about it over the week and what raises all the red flags for me is the nasty way he insulted me. Instead of hearing me out, he automatically assumed the worst of me. When I tried to explain what was going on, he cut me off and jumped to conclusions.

I get that this is a misunderstanding. A very dumb misunderstanding. But I swore when Isaac's father left, I would never settle for less in a relationship than what I deserve. What I deserve is how Jack has been to me before that night: kind, attentive, flirty, caring. But what I don't deserve is how he was at the gala: unkind, rude, judgmental, harsh.

In all truth, I could probably give him one more chance because of my part in it. But he needs to work for it. He needs to prove to me this isn't his normal pattern of behavior. He needs to go out of his comfort zone to make this right. And yes, that is a lot to ask after only one date. Well, two if you count the coffee. But I won't settle for less. Fair or not, I need a man. A *strong* man who can keep up with a strong woman like me. I need a Viking.

Not as in the mascot of the team. I have no obsessive interest in athletes. What I mean is, I need a man who is strong enough to not be intimidated by my strengths, but is equally unintimidated by my needs. I need someone who admires the things about me that a lesser man would be intimidated by. My independence. My ability to provide for myself. The fact that I don't *need* him, I *want* him. A man who recognizes that he needs to go above and beyond when he's wrong, because a couple of apology texts is bare minimum, and I deserve more than bare minimum.

And that makes me sad because I really hoped Jack was a Viking. At this point though, he's just a man.

I hand the tot his balloon animal and a huge smile lights up his face.

"Tank ew," he practically whispers before running off yelling, "Mama! Mama! A puppy!"

His excitement is infectious, and I flash my first real grin of the day. Zeroing in on the next child in line, I go through my normal spiel, "Hi! I'm Joie the Clown! Would you like a balloon animal? Or maybe a sword?" Before the little girl can answer, movement catches the corner of my eye, and I look up.

"Jack," I breathe, blinking a few times to make sure this is real.

"I think she wants a hat," he says, confusing me.

"What?" I feel like I'm in a dream and none of this is making sense. Not him being here. Not what he's saying. Not his gesturing to the kiddo standing next to me. He seems nervous, which I've never seen before, and he has dark circles under his eyes. Another thing I've never seen before. It's all very confusing.

"Your customer. I think she wants a hat."

"Oh. Oh!" I exclaim as my brain starts working again and I address the small child. "I'm sorry. Yes of course, you want a hat!"

My fingers fumble as I twist and turn the balloon, forcing it to finally take shape. Jack just stands there the whole time, watching me. It makes me nervous. Or maybe I'm giddy. I'm not sure, but what I do know is my hands are shaking. He's here. He's *here*. He's gone out of his way to track me down. But why? What does he want? Waiting for my answers is excruciating.

Finally, I get the project together and place it on the little girl's head. Turning to the next kid in line, I announce, "We have lots of time to do more balloon animals. I'm going to take a tiny little break, and I'll be right back, okay?" A collective groan follows. "I know, I know," I agree. I understand their frustration. Waiting patiently is hard on them. "But this is a good time to go finish eating your lunch or to go potty, so you don't miss out on the face paint when I come back!"

It's like a lightbulb of multi-tasking has gone off in all their little brains, and they all take off towards various parts of the room, each asking their mother for something different.

Taking a breath, I stand up and walk toward Jack.

"Nice outfit," he teases.

I smile and check out the bright yellow jumpsuit I have on. "It's a special occasion today. Figured I'd go all out."

"I see that." He sizes up the restaurant, taking it all in. "The parking lot was packed. This is quite the event."

"Five years of being open is no small feat these days." He nods but doesn't say anything, so I finally do. "Why are you here, Jack?"

He runs his hand through his salt-and-pepper hair and takes a breath, like he's calming his own nerves. "I came to apologize in person. Not because you haven't responded to my texts, but because it's the right thing to do." I feel my eyebrows rise as my interest is piqued, but he's not done. "I said some harsh things to you that night, and I was wrong. I never should have spoken to you like that. Never should have jumped to conclusions. I questioned my own judgement of character, and I should have trusted my gut to know when someone is interested in me for me, and when they have ulterior motives."

"Why didn't you?" I challenge.

He chuckles lightly. "Matthews, one of our practice coaches. Did you meet him that night? He was with the blonde?" I stare at him blankly. "She wore a bright yellow dress that had the giant slit up the side. I thought it was going to malfunction all night."

"Oh, that one." I nod. "She got super plastered and tried to start a fight with the bartender."

"Yeah, that's her. Anyway, he doesn't have the best luck with women. The gala was mild compared to what happened a couple years ago."

"What happened a couple years ago?" What I really want to know is what the heck this has to do with Jack begin a terrible jerk to me. But I assume he'll get there eventually. Plus, there's no way this Matthews guy has dated someone worse than the woman he was with the other night. Color me intrigued.

"He got involved with this woman. He thought she was really nice and it turns out, she was psychotic. Really psychotic. After two dates, she started showing up at the stadium and at his apartment, questioning why she hadn't heard from him. Even brought her mother one time so she could introduce her to 'the one.' It got really ugly when he broke up with her. At first, I thought he might have to take out a restraining order."

This sounds like a reality TV show, or the beginning of a *Law and Order* episode. Part of me wants to know more. But I can't let him get away with treating me disrespectfully. "What does that have to do with me?" I cross my arms over my chest, making it clear I don't appreciate being compared to these unstable women.

"Nothing, really." He shrugs and shoves his hands in his pockets. "Hank and I were talking about it right before I bumped into you. It was fresh on my mind. And having seen the guest list, I knew your name wasn't on it, so I just...I just ..."

"Assumed I was stalking you?"

He has the wherewithal to look sheepish. "Kind of. For a second."

"It was longer than a second, Jack."

"It was," he jumps in, admitting his mistake. "I was disappointed because I really like you. And then I jumped to some wrong conclusions."

I quirk an eyebrow at him.

"And I was a total and complete dick in front of a whole lot of people, and probably embarrassed you in the process."

"You got that right," I mutter, glaring at the floor as his explanation sinks in.

"For that, I'm so sorry. But Joie"—I peek up at his face, observing the soft expression—"why didn't you ever tell me your Isaac is the same person as Stevens? My player?"

Now it's my turn to sigh because this is the part where my fault comes in. "You know how you like to get out of Flinton to go out to eat because it keeps you a little more anonymous and you can just be Jack instead of Coach Pride?" He nods. "I've been Isaac Stevens's football mom for a lot of years. I was enjoying just being Joie."

I glance up at him and watch a small smile of understanding cross his face. "You were enjoying being a woman out with a man. No pretenses of who people think you are because of what you do."

I nod again. "I really was going to tell you. I wasn't trying to keep it from you. I was just waiting for our next date to do it, after I knew you had a genuine interest in *me,* and it wouldn't scare you off. And then Isaac sprang the event on me with only a couple hours to get ready"—he grimaces with understanding—"and I didn't have time to text you. I really did try to tell you when we ran into each other."

He grabs my hand and holds it between us, trying to be discreet in front of the kids. "I know. I've thought about the exchange so many times over the last few days. And I really am sorry. Can you forgive me? I really like you, and I'd like to keep getting to know you. Not Isaac's football mom. *You. Joie.*"

I smile at him and nod. "Yeah, I can forgive you." Pointing a finger at his chest, I continue, "But listen here, Bucko. If you ever talk to me like that again, there won't be any more chances, got it?"

He smiles. "Yes, ma'am."

"Okay," I say, relaxing. "Now I know you want to kiss me and make it better, but I'm at work and have a job to do, so it'll have to wait. Plus, my clown nose gets in the way."

I squeeze the red ball, and he chuckles. "Can I stay and watch you work? Maybe take you to a real dinner after you're done?"

"Um…that's two hours from now. But if you really want to…"

"I do," he interrupts.

I head back to my chair and sit down, children immediately clamoring around me, making requests, which I'm more than happy to comply with. When I glance up, I see a little boy pulling at Jack's hand. He looks down and smiles at the child.

"Can you paint my face?" the child asks.

Jack's expression changes. His eyes flash up to mine, a cry for help written all over his face. I ignore it and wait to see how he responds.

"Uh…the only thing I know how to draw is a football."

"Yes!" the boy yells. "I love football!"

Jack sits down, grabs my face paint, and goes to work. For the next two hours, Joie the Clown and Jack the Coach paint faces, make balloon animals, and read stories. The kids all seem delighted to have another adult to torment, which makes me laugh several times.

And when I see the demanding child who refused anything less than an elephant putting colorful barrettes in Jack's hair without him so much as flinching, my heart softens. He may just be my Viking after all.

CHAPTER
FOURTEEN

Joie

For a September evening, it's a little chilly. The air has cooled and a breeze is blowing through, so it's the perfect night to wear a Flinton State hoodie. It's also perfect for Saturday night football.

For the first time ever, I have decent seats at a home game. I'm not really sure if it's because of Isaac or because of Jack, but either way, I'm not complaining. Fifth row at the forty-five-yard line for free beats the heck out of nose-bleed seats I pay for any day.

As the team makes their way down the field, following the line of scrimmage, my eyes can't help but gravitate toward the assistant coach. He's wearing a white polo and black pants, with some headphones over his ears. He stands with his feet apart, arms crossed over his broad chest, always chewing that gum. Is it weird that I find him sexy like this?

My eyes stop their perusal and lock on the small bruise on his temple, causing me to giggle under my breath remembering how he got it.

After Jack showed up at my job and I opted to give him another chance, he made good on his promise to take me out. Not only did we go to dinner that night, last weekend he really surprised me by signing us up for juggling classes. He said kids love it when clowns juggle, and it would be one more skill I can pull out of my pocket to keep them entertained.

I disagreed with his thought process, based on the fact that I don't plan to juggle anything in a small restaurant with children crowded around me. That's just asking for someone to get hurt. Nor do I ever plan on show-boating when I become a teacher. But still, it sounded like fun so I agreed to go.

We spent four hours learning the basics of juggling. First with two balls. Then with three. Then they had us juggle different items like plastic cups and stuffed animals. We both did pretty good. The problem came in when Jack decided to try his hand at bowling pins.

He wasn't ready. I knew it. The instructor knew it. Everyone in the class knew it. But Jack was determined to get it right. All was well for about ten seconds, and then he lost his concentration. Before his brain could catch up with his hands, and he could stop the tossing, the pins crashed into each other, ricocheting around and smacking Jack right in the face with the hard edges.

When I finally stopped laughing, I realized one of the pins had knocked him so hard, he had the beginning of a nasty bruise on the side of his face. Naturally, I started laughing again, while pulling a portable cold pack out of my purse. He then started laughing over the randomness of my having a portable cold pack with me.

He and my brother Greg are going to bond over my giant purse of surprises someday. I just know it.

Despite his injuries, we had a wonderful time that night. Shortly after he knocked himself silly, the class ended, and we went out to dinner again. This time at an authentic Thai place. We ate real Krathong Tong followed by Lad Na, which had this *amazing* gravy. If I didn't already enjoy Jack for his witty conversation, I'd probably still date him just for the fantastic restaurants he finds.

Just like before, Jack walked me to my door that night, but didn't try to come in. Instead, he gave me a sweet, lengthy kiss, his tongue barely sweeping against mine when our lips connected. In some ways, I was hoping he would have kissed me harder, but I also appreciated he didn't want to put on a show for my neighbors. That's not my style.

Of course, the texts and phone calls haven't stopped. And as worried as I was in the beginning that he would distract me from my goals, he doesn't. He asks about my classes all the time. He asks about my projects and tests. Whenever I get nervous, he shifts into coach mode and encourages me. It's really sweet. And really cute. And I now understand why Isaac likes him as a coach so much.

My last assignment for the week was turned in this morning, so my mind has been on this football game all day. I've been looking forward to it. Seeing both my men on the field, without the aid of binoculars, has made me practically giddy.

"Can you believe how close we are?" Mia screeches in my ear.

Well, I *was* giddy. Then I arrived, and I realized I was sitting next to Chatty Cathy. I have no idea how she scored her seat, but I suppose since she hangs out with the team, someone had an extra.

I nod politely in agreement with her. It's not that she's here. In all truthfulness, she's a sweet girl. She's just a lot for someone my age to take in sometimes.

"Oh, there's Isaac!" She begins tugging on my arm. "Are you going to call him? Maybe he'll see us!"

I shake my head in amusement. I'll give her one thing—at least she's honest. Even if it is to a fault.

But while she's batting her eyelashes at Isaac, I'm watching Jack. Compared to the other coach, who is pacing and screaming and banging on a clipboard, Jack is that steady calm I love. He doesn't say much, but when he speaks, his players stop and listen. It's fascinating watching how respected he clearly is. He really is a Viking. Not just to me, but to others as well. That is so endearing to me.

Suddenly, as if he feels my eyes on him, he turns, and we make eye contact. It's only for a second, but I see his lips quirk up briefly as he winks at me. I give a quick wave back, not holding back my smile.

He turns his attention back to the game, but the player standing next to him looks at me quizzically.

Isaac.

Who apparently thought my wave was for him, if his slow wave back at me is any indication. He looks confused, and I don't blame him. I've never once waved at him from the stands. But right now, I'll let him come to whatever conclusion he wants. Mia starts shrieking "He sees us! He sees us!" and I burst out laughing at the ridiculousness of the whole thing. How many incorrect assumptions can be made at once?

It appears my other Viking, and this time I *am* referring to the mascot and players, may need to come have a sit-down conversation with me soon.

PRIDE
&
JOIE

EPISODE TWO

CHAPTER ONE

Joie

I take it back. I take it all back. College is harder than I thought it was going to be.

Yes, I have a 4.0 GPA. Yes, most of my professors know me by name. But I am surviving on caffeine to get everything done.

Midterms were harder than I expected them to be, and if I want to keep my grade point average where it's at, I can't afford to slack off. That means long hours in the library. Studying on weekends. And lots of review groups.

Like the one I'm in right now.

Educational psychology may be my favorite class, but it's also the most intense. It's not that the content is even hard. I raised a child; I've seen most of this before. I just have names for it all now. But it's so time consuming.

Initially, we were required to read *Pollyanna* by Eleanor H. Porter, pick a particular character, and come up with a basic psychological summary that fits their behaviors in the book. That was all fine and good. It was a children's book, so the reading was easy. And there weren't deep psychological issues. It was more about pinpointing basic behaviors. But then a similar real-life assignment was sprung on us.

Twice a week, for an hour per day, with a minimum of four weeks, we sit in a local elementary school classroom, where we have to pick a child to observe and write a case study on them, just like we did with the book. We're not allowed to put names or identifying features, for privacy reasons obviously, and we can't interact with the child. Just observe behaviors.

While I find it fascinating, and I really love getting into the school, the only days I have time for this extra work are on Tuesdays and Thursdays. The days I work. It's only three hours out of my day, including drive time, but those six hours a week used to be spent getting things like laundry and grocery shopping done. Now that's all put off until weekends, cutting into my study time, which means I have to study later during the week...

It's a vicious cycle. Hence, the venti upside-down caramel macchiato I'm nursing at eight o'clock at night. I'm going to be sitting in this conference room chair for several hours, and then I have to drive all the way home. I need the caffeine desperately.

Tonight, we're going to go over our case studies as a group and pinpoint any holes or missing bits of information. Basically, a tweaking session before the first draft is turned in. But in true college-kid fashion, not everyone is here yet, so we're waiting for the stragglers.

My phone dings with a text just as I take a drink of my java. The name flashes on the screen briefly and lips immediately quirk up. It's Jack.

Jack: *Late night on campus?*

Me: *How did you know?*

Jack: *I just saw your car in the parking lot. Do you need anything? Coffee? Snacks? A kiss?*

I bite back another smile and try not to giggle like a school girl. Even though I technically am one.

Me: *PDA probably isn't allowed in the library. Especially with one of your players in my study group.*

Jack: *Let me change the question...dinner Friday night? Without a library full of eyes?*

A laugh bursts out of me, and I quickly cover my mouth when I realize how loud it is. I glance around and only a couple people are looking at me, but most don't even turn their heads away from their phones. Smiling again, now that I know I didn't draw too much attention to myself, I respond. Because that's what Jack does to me...makes me smile.

Me: *You're on.*

I put my phone down and Brian Anderson, Isaac's teammate and fellow brownie lover, catches my attention. He's sitting next to me, eyeing me skeptically.

"What?" I glance around quickly to see if he's really looking at me or just in my general direction.

Tilting his head toward me, he lowers his voice almost to a whisper. "Who's the dude?"

I will my face not to flush. As Jack's player, the last person I want to fess up to is Brian. Isaac probably needs to know about this first. "What dude?"

"The dude you're texting?" He gestures toward my phone.

"How do you know I'm texting a dude?"

"The look on your face."

I lean in more, whispering, "What does my face look like?"

He straightens in his chair and holds his finger up so I'll wait for a minute. Then he turns to Stephanie, who is sitting next to him. She's a tall, pretty girl. About twenty. I've seen her look at Brian with stars in her eyes before. Apparently, he's noticed.

Moving in close to her, he flashes her a flirty grin. "Hey."

She looks momentarily bewildered but responds with a quiet "Hey."

"You look really pretty today."

I roll my eyes at how thick he's laying on the charm. Beyond a few questions and answers in this group, I don't think Brian has ever spoken to her before.

"Thanks." Stephanie bites back a giggle, a blush creeping up her cheeks.

Brian turns back to me and points over his shoulder at her. "That look."

My jaw drops and I smack him playfully on the arm. "I do not! And that was so rude!" I situate my body so I can see around him to address Stephanie directly. "Ignore him and his fake charms. He's trying to prove a point."

She shrugs. "He called me pretty, so whatever."

I just shake my head. I don't understand this age group. They're funny and energetic and idealistic…and I'll never understand the relationship dynamics they have. Welcome to the generation raised on electronics, I suppose. Always with their faces in a screen. Never having to learn people skills.

Or I'm just old and out of touch.

"So anyway…" he continues. Crap. I was hoping Brian would be distracted. No such luck. "Who's the dude?"

I blow my bangs out of my face as I prepare to do something I normally have a strict moral code against. I lie. "There's no dude. And even if there was, it wouldn't be your business anyway."

"Uh huh." He turns his body toward me and puts his hand on my chair, a smirk on his face. "I don't believe you, but I'll let it go for now. As long as you tell me one thing." I quirk my eyebrow at him, giving him my best mom glare. It doesn't work. "Does he treat you right?"

My heart softens at his true concern, and I smile at him. He may be ornery, but he's a good kid. I saw it in him the day he introduced himself to me and thanked me for the brownies I brought. And he continues to impress me with small things like making sure the man I refuse to admit I'm dating is good to me.

"I'm guessing Stevens doesn't know yet, does he?" I crinkle my nose and shake my head, finally admitting what he already knew. "I won't tell him, because that's not my place. But make sure whoever the dude is, he knows you have the entire Viking defense backing you up if he so much as looks at you sideways."

I pat him on his forearm. "Thank you, Brian. But I promise, that won't be necessary."

He nods at me once then turns back to Stephanie. "You really do look pretty today. That wasn't just a line."

She blushes again, and I shake my head at his audacity. What a little player. I hope Stephanie keeps her eyes wide open with him. He's sweet to me, but probably because there's a certain amount of respect that goes with being his mom's age. And because I bring snacks.

Suddenly, the door flies open and a disheveled-looking Nick comes racing in, hurriedly throwing his backpack on the table. "Sorry I'm late, guys. I got caught up in band practice."

"You play in a band?" Brian asks. He looks impressed by this latest news.

Nick keeps yanking his notebooks and laptop out of his bag. "Yeah. I play trombone in the Viking Marching Band."

Suddenly, Brian doesn't look as impressed. Somehow his reaction doesn't surprise me.

"Anyway, did I miss anything?" Nick sort of fell into the role of leader of the study group. Every time we meet, he's prepared with a plan on how to get things done and helps the group stay on track. I don't usually mind. It just means the rest of us don't have to take on that responsibility and keeps us from just wasting our time being here.

While waiting for him to settle in, I grab my phone off the table and shoot off another quick text to Jack.

Me: *We've been caught. Brian Anderson says to tell you that if you hurt me, you'll have him and the rest of the team to answer to.*

I look around the room as I wait for his answer. Everyone is finally getting ready for what is sure to be a long night.

Jack: *You tell that little shithead he better watch himself, or he'll be doing extra frog squats until his legs give out.*

Before I can respond, another text comes through.

Jack: *And then tell him I appreciate him looking after you. But he's got nothing to worry about. That is, if we really have been outed.*

Busted.

Me: *I'll pass along the info from my anonymous "dude" if it comes up again. Gotta run. We're starting.*

I throw my phone in my black satchel and take another sip of my coffee, ready to begin a long night of discussing the development of behavior patterns.

CHAPTER TWO

Jack

I knock on the front door and glance around the neighborhood while I wait. I've been here before. Several times. But the more I'm here, the more I like the area of town Joie lives in.

It's a quaint little community with smaller homes. Well, smaller for Texas anyway. When they say everything's bigger in Texas, they weren't kidding around about square footage.

But I really like it here. She lives on a cul-de-sac, although not in the actual circle. But from this vantage point, I can see a few small kids riding their bikes in the street while their mothers sit on lawn chairs and chat. That's who seems to live here most. Families with small children who are in their starter home. Retirees who don't want the upkeep of a larger house also take residence here. The mixture of the two stages of life make for a nice, homey feel.

The door swings open and Joie greets me with a smile. She's holding a hand towel and has an apron on. Her hair is held back by a bandana, WWII pinup style. She's so cute, even when she's not trying to be.

"Did I catch you at a bad time?" I ask as I step over the threshold.

She leans in for me to kiss her quickly. "I'm just cooking dinner."

Closing the door behind me, I follow her into the small kitchen. "Cooking dinner? I thought we were going to order in?"

"We were. But then I realized I have all the ingredients for enchiladas, so I figured we could save the money and eat this before the it all goes bad."

That's Joie for ya. She's smart. She's kind. She makes a mean balloon animal. But she's also practical. I admire how much tenacity she has, but how she balances it with a forgiving heart. She really is the whole package, and as I watch her cook dinner for the two of us, I can't help but remember how lucky I am that she gave me a second chance after mistaking her for some psycho, looking to date a coach.

The thought alone makes me wince. In all honesty, I wouldn't have blamed her if she told me to hit the road after that clusterfuck. I jumped to some pretty harsh conclusions with no evidence to back it up. But instead of writing me off as just another meathead, she handled herself with grace and maturity...and made me find her to grovel. The fact she knows her worth and wasn't about to put up with my shit made me like her even more.

And now she's making me a home-cooked meal. Could I get any luckier?

"Seems like you're going to an awful lot of effort just to feed me."

She doesn't look up as she continues stuffing some sort of chicken mixture into a tortilla, rolls it, and places it in the baking dish. "You would think. But seriously, this is the world's easiest enchilada recipe. Mix shredded chicken with cheese and salsa. Slap it in a tortilla. Voila! Homemade enchiladas."

"It's not something authentic your mother taught you how to make?"

That causes her to glance at me with a smirk. "I guess I never told you I was adopted. My parents are as white as white bread can be. I'm lucky my mother knows how to cook macaroni and cheese from a box."

"Oh, I didn't know. I'm sorry. I didn't mean to bring it up." I rub my hand down my face, hoping my face doesn't reflect the embarrassment I feel. She shoots me a quizzical look.

"Why are you sorry? It's not a big deal. It's just the way my family came together."

I scratch the back of my neck, trying to be careful as I proceed. "So it's not like, a secret or anything?"

Finished with the tortillas, she dumps what looks like a whole jar of green salsa on top of the enchiladas and begins sprinkling cheese on top. Okay, that's not a sprinkle. That's a deluge. Just the way I like it.

"What is this, the 1940's?" she asks, and I chuckle at the reference, considering the bandana she's wearing would have anyone confused about the decade we're in. "Adoption isn't a shameful thing. I mean, mine wasn't exactly ideal. Anyone being adopted out of child protective services has been through the ringer. But it doesn't minimize who my family is to me."

"Do you ever...um...I mean..." I feel my face flush. There's so much I want to ask, but I don't want to open any old wounds accidentally. Why was the state involved in her childhood? Was she hurt? Does she remember it? None of it is my business, but I can't help my curiosity.

"You can ask me anything, Jack." She opens the oven and carefully slides the baking dish in. "I'm pretty much an open book. Not much offends me."

"I know. I just feel like a dick asking these questions."

"You mean like how I feel when I ask about your wife's death?"

I stop and look at her. "Huh. I guess it's kind of the same thing, isn't it?"

She tosses the hand mitts on the counter and leans back against it, shrugging. "If by that, you mean it's a just a thing that happened, not a thing that controls your life, then yes."

I nod once in understanding. "Okay. Well then, I'm just wondering if you ever thought about looking for your birth parents."

She turns toward the fridge and opens in, reaching to the back and pulling out a bottle of wine. I can't help but wish the wine was in the very back so she could stay bent over a little longer. That's a nice view.

"When I was a teenager, I thought about it. I thought about it a lot," she says as she grabs and corkscrew from the drawer and tries to screw in it in the top of the bottle. She's so short, though, I can already tell it's going to tilt and slide off the counter if she presses down too hard. "In hindsight," she grunts as she continues to fight with the bottle, "I think I used my adoption as an excuse to be a jerk to my parents, to act out on all my hormones. But then when I had Isaac, it sort of hit me." She's continuing to struggle with opening the wine so I finally take it out of her hands to help her out. "Thanks." She shakes her hands out like she hurt her wrist in the process. "Anyway, it hit me that I don't really want to know them. Child protective services doesn't pull kids into the system unless something is seriously wrong. They don't have the manpower. They don't have the beds. They don't have the time to harass innocent families."

"You don't think so?"

She thinks for a second. "Let me clarify that. I'm sure somewhere out there, in all of the thousands of caseworkers, there's one who has a vendetta against someone else and would use their position to go on a power trip. Stranger things have happened." I nod in agreement. "But that's the exception to the rule. I've read my paperwork. My birth parents were horrible people. When the caseworker picked me up, I was filthy and malnourished. They found a dead roach in my diaper. How gross is that?" I grimace because, yes, that's really gross. "So short answer, I got lucky. I got really, really lucky to have the parents I have. They took in a frightened, underdeveloped toddler, stuck with me through my rebellious teenage years, and supported me as a very young, very stupid single mom. I know how blessed I am." A grin crosses her face. "Even if my mother is a horrible cook."

A laugh bursts out of me and I put the wine down on the counter, taking two steps toward her to cup her face in my hands. "And I am so, so blessed they did because I couldn't imagine not being here with you right now."

Leaning down, I cover her lips with mine, kissing her softly. Her hands reach around my neck and her fingers wrap around the hair at my nape. I love kissing her. It's slow and gentle. A few sweeps of the tongue. It's unhurried. It's passionate. It's restrained because…well, because we haven't gone there yet, and we don't want to get all riled up.

That's another thing I like about Joie. She's in no rush for this relationship to get to the next level. She's content with us taking our time, getting to know each other. Getting to trust each other. Making sure we really are a good fit, personality-wise, not just because we're attracted to each other. It's meant a lot of cold showers for me, but I prefer that to the messiness of getting too attached too quickly. This way is so much better.

Plus, there's something to be said for anticipation.

All too soon, the kiss winds down. I open my eyes in time to see Joie lick her lips and clear her throat. "Um…wow. Um …" I can't help how my ego inflates knowing I've kissed her silly. "Stop looking at me like that. I know I'm a little incoherent right now."

I chuckle and pull her into a hug. "Sorry. It's a giant stroke to my ego when I kiss you senseless."

"Please," she jokes back. "I'm not senseless. My brain was just resting for a minute."

"Okay, well now that it's working again, what do you need me to do?" I rub my hands up and down her back and kiss her head. She's so short, but I like it.

Pushing me away, she turns to the cabinet to grab a couple plates and hand them to me. "You can set the table. Napkins are on the counter over there and silverware is in that drawer. I'm gonna start cleaning the kitchen while we wait for dinner to finish up."

"Yes, ma'am. You wanna sit outside?"

"Yeah, that would be great." She beams. "I love this time of year, when it's cool enough to take advantage of my patio furniture."

A small eating area is just off the kitchen, a few steps away. Right through the room is a side door that goes to a patio overlooking the yard. The wrought-iron table is covered with a blue tablecloth, and the chairs have matching blue cushions. It doesn't take but a few minutes to set everything two people need, so I have time to head back in and really look around the house.

A large living area connects to the eating area. For such a small home, the space is massive. She has two good-sized couches, an overstuffed chair, and a giant television situated around the fireplace. And yet, it doesn't feel cramped at all. Over the mantel is a large framed photo of Joie and her family. She and Isaac are the darkest ones in the picture. A tall, blond man with a beard holds a little girl with brown ringlets. I'm assuming it's her brother and niece she is so fond of. Her parents look older, but she's right when she says they are whiter than white bread, which makes me chuckle to myself. They're all sporting wide grins. Just one big happy family.

Moving over to a bookshelf, I take in pictures of Stevens as a baby and a very young Joie smiling with pride as she holds him up to the camera. There are a few of his elementary school pictures. One in his high school football uniform, in the obligatory one-knee on the ground pose. And finally, an action shot during a game in his Vikings uniform, probably a color copy of a newspaper photo. It's clear how much Joie loves her son and how involved she is in his life.

The one thing that concerns me is how clean her home is. There's no clutter. There's no crap sitting around. Everything is put away. Placing my hands on my hips, I make a mental note never to take her to my apartment. I don't think she'd enjoy what a slob I am. I may need to finally splurge for that maid I keep talking about. If my apartment could look anywhere close to like this, it would be worth it.

The sound of a timer going off has me heading back to the kitchen. "Was that dinner I heard?" I joke when I hear the slam of the oven door.

"It was." I find Joie scooping out a very cheesy enchilada and placing it on a plate.

"Holy shit, that looks good," I exclaim, putting my arms around her waist and leaning over her shoulder to get a good look. "How much cheese did you use?"

"Uh...two pounds, maybe?"

"For just the two of us?"

She shrugs. "You can never have too much cheese. It's so bad for you, but I don't care. You only live once, and I plan to live it up! Cheese is my version of partying."

Once everything is dished out, I grab the plates and she grabs the wine. "Why did I already set plates out if you're going to dish everything out inside?"

As she slides the door open, a sheepish grin crosses her face. "Because I forgot. I do that every time, so I always end up using double plates."

That little tidbit of information actually endears me to her. In the time I've known her, she seems to do excel in most everything she does. I like knowing she has little quirks, too.

"More wine?" she asks as she pours.

I gesture toward my glass. "Since you're already topping me off, sure."

She flashes me a flirty smirk, and we dig into our very, very cheesy and delicious dinner.

CHAPTER THREE

"**W**ell? What did you think?" I ask as we work together to wash what few dishes are still dirty.

After eating, Jack and I sat outside, finishing the bottle of wine and enjoying the cooler temperatures. I love this time of year. It's warm enough to wear short sleeves, but cool enough that you can wear jeans without having a heat stroke. Don't get me wrong, it's not chilly. But when it's been in the upper nineties for months, eighty feels like a cold front. This mild weather is why people move to Texas and suffer through the summer. Every other season is amazing. If only summer wasn't about six months' long.

"I think I've been selling myself short." Jack wipes the hand towel over a plate I just gave him. With only two of us, there's no reason to use the dishwasher. "If I had known it was so easy to make a decent meal, I wouldn't have been surviving off fast food all these years."

"You're telling me you've never googled anything about easy-to-make recipes?" I chide playfully, handing him some clean silverware to dry.

He thinks for a minute. "No. Can't say that I ever have. I guess I just assumed it would be too much work for me to figure out."

I giggle. "Oh, Jack. I know you're set in your ways and all. But the internet really is your friend.

He scoffs. "I know that." I raise one eyebrow at him. "Okay, fine. I only use it when I'm at work. Who needs the distraction when I get home?"

"You mean the distraction from ESPN?"

"Exactly," he says with a grin. "I knew you would understand."

We continue with our lighthearted banter as we finish the dishes. Once my hands are dried off, I lean against the counter to brace myself. "What time do you have to leave tonight?"

He crinkles his brow. "What do you mean?"

"Don't you have an early morning or something?"

He shakes his head and licks his bottom lip. I notice, because I've noticed every time he's licked his bottom lip tonight.

While we were eating.

After drinking his wine.

Just now.

I'm kind of jealous of his bottom lip.

His eyes seem to darken, and I know his thoughts are venturing the same direction as mine, and I wonder if he's as nervous as I am. "Are you wanting me to leave?"

Suddenly, the air seems to get thick in the room. It's sexual tension. I haven't felt it in years, but I'd recognize it anywhere. It's not something you forget because it's been so long. In fact, I'd say the feeling is magnified *because* it's been so long.

I clear my throat and try to remember how to breathe when I whisper out a "No. I don't want you to leave."

He stalks two steps my direction. "You want me to stay?"

I nod and lick my own lip in anticipation.

"How long do you want me to stay?"

This is where it gets sticky for me. I'm battling myself. I want Jack to stay all night. I *really* want Jack to stay all night. But I need to know where we stand first. I need to address that before anything else. "That depends," I finally admit.

"On what?" He runs his hands over my hair, pulling the bandana off my head and dropping it on the counter. I completely forgot I was wearing it and for a split second, I hope I don't have hat head. Especially in this moment.

"It's been a long time since I've been with a man, Jack."

He wraps a lock of my dark hair around my finger. "How long is a long time?" he says quietly as his eyes roam over my face, taking in each of my features.

"Um…I think Isaac was in middle school the last time I had sex."

Jack freezes and looks me straight in the eye, the moment gone. "Middle school?"

I nod.

"He's a junior in college now."

I nod again.

"So, you haven't been with a man in almost a decade?"

I quirk an eyebrow and purse my lips. "You say that like it's a bad thing."

"No, no," he defends quickly. "It's not a bad thing. It's just...Wow, Joie. That's a long time. Did you not date or something?"

I shrug. "I dated, but I don't get how people can just drop their pants for anyone. This third date rule people do now? That's such crap. I'm not embarrassed or a prude or anything. I'm just not interested in giving the milk away. This cow is worth more than that."

His head bobbles slightly as he considers my thoughts. "I can see that. So then why are we having this conversation now? We haven't been dating that long."

I take a deep breath, sucking in nerve along with air. "I guess I like you more than I've liked anyone before, maybe ever." His eyes soften, and a shy smile crosses his face. "So I'd like to take you to bed with me. But before I do, I wanna know where your head is at. When it comes to us."

He scratches his jaw while he thinks. "I tend to be old school, ya know? Not as proper as my parents were, or anything. But like you, I don't see how people can get physical with someone they don't know and never see them again. There's so much more to sex than only getting off." He begins twirling that lock of my hair again. "It's intimacy. It's sharing mutual pleasure. It's connecting on a spiritual level."

Oh boy. I'm getting hot just hearing him describe the emotional part of intimacy. I'm a goner if he starts talking dirty. Which makes me wonder, does he talk dirty? I kind of hope he does.

"And I like milk. But I don't want free milk. I want the cow, too. For as long as she'll let me have her."

My brain screeches to a halt. "Wait...did you just...did you call me a cow?"

"You started it. But yeah, that sounded way better in my head than it did coming out of my mouth."

I lean my forehead on his chest as the giggles overtake me. He wraps his arms around me and we laugh. It's wonderful, and intimate, and perfect. Finally, he pulls away and kisses me on the lips. It's slow and sensual. And over all too soon when he continues our conversation.

"In all seriousness, though," he says, as I continue kissing him. Only this time, my lips are moving down his neck as he rubs his hands up and down my back. "I'm okay with not pushing that part of our relationship until you feel comfortable. I'm not in this to bag you and get out."

"I don't think that." I continue my trek behind his ear and his breath begins to hitch as he tries to keep talking.

"Well, good. But let's be honest...we're in our forties. We're tired. There won't be an all-night sex marathon, and the anticipation isn't going to kill either one of us. Plus, there are preparations to consider."

"Preparations? What kind of preparation?"

"You know. Birth control and stuff."

This time I pull away and look him in the eye. "Jack, my tubes are tied."

He pauses. "Really?"

I shrug. "Yeah. I had it done several years ago. I was having some serious bleeding issues so my doctor took out half of my uterus, and I had my tubes tied at the same time."

"Wait. Bleeding issues? Like heavy periods or something?"

I wrap my arms around his neck as we talk. "Way worse than that. I ended up in the hospital a couple times because my iron count was so low. I was literally bleeding out. Even had a couple transfusions."

His jaw drops open. "Joie! That's terrible!"

"That's why they finally did it. Haven't had any problems since." I kiss him gently on the lips. "It also means, there is no chance I'll accidentally get pregnant."

He freezes for a moment and then moves at lightning speed, bending down and scooping me up by the thighs.

"Jack!" I squeal. "You're going to throw your back out!"

He wraps my legs around him and carries me down the hall. "Jesus, woman! How old do you think I am? I'm not decrepit!"

I laugh as he struts straight through my bedroom door and squeal again as he tosses me on the bed. Before I can make another sound, he's on me, kissing his way down my neck, gently moving my shirt to the side so he can kiss my shoulder. I haven't felt lips on my skin in so long, it makes me tingle all over.

"This is going to sound really bad," I sigh, "but you better take your shoes off before you get dirt on my bedspread."

The rumble of his laugh reverberates through my whole body. "You're worried about dirt on your bed at a time like this?"

"You don't want that dirt anywhere near our bodies once we're naked."

"The woman has a good point." He practically launches himself off me and all the sudden is stripping out of all of his clothes, not just his shoes. Those go first, followed by his socks, but then his shirt comes off and...

Holy moly.

He's fit. Not quite a six pack, but darn close. A smattering of dark hair sprinkled on his chest. His biceps—oh my. They flex and stretch as he removes all of his clothes except his boxers. Those arms might be my favorite part of his naked body.

I bite back a grin as I realize how much of a farmer's tan he has. I should have figured the color of his torso doesn't match the rest of him. I think it's cute. And it reminds me of what a hard worker he is.

Once he's naked, except for his tented boxers and the wolfish grin on his face, he narrows his eyes at me. "How come I'm the only one taking my clothes off?"

I laugh at this unexpected question. "Sorry. I was enjoying watching you so much, I forgot." Kicking off my flip-flops so they drop on the floor, I hold eye contact and reach down to unbutton my shorts. His breath hitches at the sound of the zipper going down. It makes me feel sexy and shameless. And gives me confidence as I shimmy my shorts over my hips and down my legs and then flick them at him when they get to the end of my toe.

He snatches them out of the air. "You trying to end this before it even begins? Because I'm feeling remarkably like a first-timer again, watching you do that."

"Oh...I'm sorry." I stop my movements and widen my eyes innocently. "Should I stop?"

His eyes roll in the back of his head. "Hell, woman. You're gonna kill me, aren't you?"

"I'll try to be gentle when I do it." Slowly, I sit up and peel my shirt over my head. Jack groans as my lacy blue bra and matching panties are bared to him.

It's been a long time since I've been naked in front of a man. You'd think it would make me shy or even embarrassed, but I'm not. Jack knows I'm not young, tight, and toned. He knows I'm going to be soft in certain places, and I'm sure he figured out long ago my breasts aren't larger than a handful. But if the way he's looking at me now is any indication, all he's seeing right now is *me*.

And possibly enjoying the anticipation of a really good orgasm.

I watch his Adam's apple bob as he swallows, before he finally speaks again. "Take off your bra," he demands, and I know I'm going to like this side of him. This is that Viking I was looking for. The one who can command in the bedroom while being respectful of my needs. Even if those needs are as quirky as keeping his shoes off the bed.

Reaching around my back, I unhook the clasps. As I slowly slide the straps down my shoulders, preparing to bare myself to him, Jack's patience runs thin.

"That's it," he bellows as he pounces on top of me, tossing the bra aside, "playtime is over." He latches onto my nipple, making me squeak.

But he's wrong.

Playtime has just begun.

CHAPTER FOUR

Jack

I wake with a start. Why? What woke me up? And where the fuck am I?

It takes a few seconds for my brain to pull out of the early morning muddle, but when it does, I remember everything.

The way Joie's soft, dark skin feels when I run my hands over it. The way her breath tickles my ear when she heaves with passion. The soft sounds she makes when I thrust deep inside her. I never thought I'd have that connection with someone again. But here it is. Here *she* is. Everything about her, about us, seems magical to me.

Or maybe I'm only a man who hasn't been with a woman in a very long time. Either way, my brain has barely woken up, but my dick is wide awake and ready for more of her.

Joie begins to stretch and, by the way her ass is squirming up against me, I think she might have the same idea.

"Good morning," I mumble, my voice still gravelly with sleep. "Did you sleep well with me here? I didn't take up too much room, did I?"

"Mmm," she responds and snuggles back down under the covers, and closer into me. "I haven't slept so well in forever." I can hear the contentment in her voice, and I swear it makes my dick twitch. Or that could just be morning wood. Either way, I move her hair out of the way and begin kissing a path down her neck. She smells faintly of sweat and sleep and left-over sex. "Did we stay tangled up like this all night?"

"I think so," I mumble against her skin. "It's because you're comfortable." She wiggles her ass back against me again. "And a little horny, aren't you?"

She chuckles huskily, her voice still not completely cleared of sleep. "Maybe a little."

Grabbing her hips, I grind against her, making her gasp. "Well then, what are we waiting for?"

"We need to brush our teeth," she whispers, reaching over her head to grab my hair and tug. The feeling increases my need to be inside her.

"Nope. No time for that," I respond and roll her over to face me, giving her a very quick, very closed-mouth peck on the lips before lying on my back and pulling her on top of me. "Ride me, baby, and our mouths won't get anywhere near each other."

I waggle my eyebrows, and she smiles at my ingenuity. But she also complies. Fortunately, we never put any clothes on last night, so we don't have to waste any time. Sitting up on her knees, I situate myself underneath her. We groan simultaneously when she slides down on top of me, until she's fully seated, hip to hip. Then I watch as she begins to move. Her hair is still mussed from sleep. Her skin glows in the morning sunlight. Her small breasts bounce slightly as she moves to and fro.

"You're so beautiful like this," I whisper and reach up to play with her nipples. She gasps and her eyes roll into the back of her head.

Suddenly, there's a quick knock and her bedroom door flies open.

"Ma, it's late. Why are you still in...?"

If this was a movie, people would be laughing at the ridiculousness of the scene. Because all of a sudden, everyone is yelling and moving at a frantic pace. Joie is screaming while jumping off my lap, trying to cover herself but exposing my hard-on in the process. Stevens is screaming and looking back and forth between his mother and me, and sometimes at my dick, which keeps showing itself every time Joie moves.

But this isn't a movie, so someone has to get this situation back in control, and I suppose that's gonna have to be me.

Propping up on my elbow, I go into coach mode and yell, "Okay, everyone shut up!" Surprisingly, it works. All the screaming stops. "Stevens, cover your eyes!"

"Yes, sir," he shouts and brings his hand to his face, slapping himself so hard, the sound echoes off the walls.

"Now get out," I command.

"Yes, sir," he shouts again and turns to leave, running into the wall a couple of times since he refuses to take his hand off his face.

"Close the door behind you."

The only response is the slam as he complies with my request.

Flopping back down on the bed, I let out a deep breath and look over at Joie. She's wrapped tightly in the sheet, face down, hands covering her eyes.

"You can open your eyes now. He's gone."

She shakes her head and her voice comes out muffled as she speaks. "Maybe if I don't look, it'll all go away."

I chuckle and roll to my side, running my hand down her back in comfort. "I don't think that's how it works, babe."

Her body raises and lowers as she inhales deeply, before turning to look at me. "This is not the way I wanted him to find out about us."

"I know. I don't find it ideal either." I continue rubbing her back, trying to help calm her.

"It's been just him and me for so long, ya know?" She bites her bottom lip and stares off into space as she talks. "I don't think I've ever introduced him to anyone I've dated before. Not in his whole life."

"Not even that guy from when he was in middle school?"

She shakes her head slowly and rests her chin on her arms. "Not that I can remember. Maybe once in passing, but other than that, no. I guess I was never serious enough with anyone to bother."

The room goes quiet as we both get lost in our thoughts. What a weird mess we're in. If her child were younger, I would understand being careful with him knowing about her dating. A child can attach to an adult pretty easily, and that would be really bad for him if the relationship didn't work out.

But this situation seems different, somehow. Stevens is an adult. He lives on his own and has his own life. No matter what happens between his mother and me, he'll never call me dad. He's too old for us to bond like that.

But I am still his coach, which puts me in a position of authority over him. And he did get an eyeful of his mother making like a rodeo star. Hmm. Maybe this situation is more convoluted than I first thought.

"You think he saw too much?" she finally asks. "Maybe he didn't really see anything. Right?"

She looks so hopeful, I almost don't want to tell her the truth. Instead, I raise an eyebrow at her, making her grimace. I don't need to say anything. She knows. "Babe, he saw his mother practicing her bull riding skills on his coach. We could have been fully-clothed and he still would've seen too much."

She groans and buries her head her pillow. "I was hoping you'd say we were covered up enough that he didn't get an eyeful. Or that he was looking at the ceiling or something."

I grab her hand, kissing her knuckles. "Sorry, baby. Not only is he traumatized by seeing you, I'm sure he's not going to get the image of my full erection out of his head any time soon."

Her head pops up. "You were totally naked?"

Chuckling, I say, "You were so busy trying to cover your-self, you kept *un*covering me."

She groans again. "This just keeps getting worse."

"Do you want me to talk to him?"

She sighs and looks up at me, her big brown eyes set in resolve. "No, I will. Assuming he's still here. Maybe I can butter him up with some pancakes or something."

"Eggs. He needs protein. He's in the middle of a season."

She snickers. "Yes, coach. I'll be sure to make him a healthy omelet full of vegetables and meat. No carbs."

"Good, girl," I say my lips quirking up as I try my best to ignore the unsettled ache hanging between my legs. "So I'm guessing rodeo practice is done for the day?"

She snorts a laugh before climbing out of bed. "I think we'll have to save that for another time." She flashes me a nervous look, and I brace myself for what she's about to say. "I hope this doesn't sound terrible, and I really hate to say it, but I think I need to talk to Isaac alone."

Relief floods through me that it's nothing more serious than that. "Of course. He's your son. As much as I was hoping to spend the day with you, this is more important. You guys need to have a private conversation without me hanging out, listening."

She leans over the bed and kisses me quickly. "Thank you." I run my hand down her cheek, glancing over her features one more time before clamoring out of bed.

Joie wraps herself in a pink fluffy robe and walks into the attached master bathroom while I put all of yesterday's clothes back on. I chuckle to myself as I realize I'm about to do the walk of shame in front of one of my kids. Usually it's them coming into the locker room in day-old duds. Talk about turnabout.

When she's done brushing her teeth and I've popped a piece of my spearmint gum in my mouth, she wraps her arms around my waist. "Thank you for an amazing night."

"It was the best milk I ever tasted," I remark, making her laugh against my chest as I rub my hands down her back.

"As long as you still want the cow, too."

"For as long as she'll have me."

She pulls away and I lean down to kiss her gently, sweeping my tongue in her mouth once, twice, three times before pulling away and rubbing my hands up and down her arms.

I can read the nervousness on her face. "Are you sure you want to do this alone? I don't mind staying if you want me as your moral support."

She gives me a shy smile and nods. "Yeah. I'll be okay. It's just going to be an awkward conversation."

I nod once and clasp her hand, intertwining our fingers. "All right. Walk me out?"

"Of course."

We make our way down the short hallway, past the kitchen and small eating area. Stevens is sitting at the table, his hands wrapped around a steaming mug of what I assume is coffee. I could really go for a cup myself, but when we pass by, he looks up and glares at me. If I was in coach mode, I'd tell him to wipe that look off his face and give me some laps for being disrespectful. But since I'm in boyfriend mode, I say nothing, instead mentally calculating how close the nearest drive-thru coffee shop is.

We reach the front door and I turn to Joie, cupping her face and giving her another quick kiss. "I'll call you later, okay?"

"Okay." She tries to smile, but she looks nervous. "And I'll let you know how it goes. Wish me luck."

I kiss her one last time and pull the door open, leaving Joie behind to clean up a mess I helped her make.

CHAPTER FIVE

Joie

I shut the door behind Jack and rest my forehead on the wood, taking a deep breath. This is not the type of conversation I wanted to have with my son. But it's time to face the music, so to speak.

Turning, I pad my way to the kitchen, the sound of my slippers brushing against the carpet breaking through the silence. The house is quiet. Too quiet for when Isaac is home. I don't like it.

Grabbing a cup of coffee, I doctor it with milk, sugar, and a little bit of the peppermint flavoring I got in my Christmas stocking last year. Isaac still doesn't speak. My boy always has something to say. He's a chatterbox. It's unnerving when he's quiet.

Turning to lean against the counter, I realize the washing machine is going. "Is that your laundry in the washer or the towels that were on the floor?"

"The towels," he responds. That's progress. But he still doesn't look up from his mug, which is bad. He's been staring at it since I walked into the room.

"Thanks for doing that."

The only response I get is a slight nod to his head. This is going to be harder than I thought. Taking a deep breath, I place my mug on the counter before speaking. "So are we going to just sit here in silence all day or are we going to talk about this?"

His eyes snap up to mine. "Which part do you want to talk about, Mom?" he spits out. "The fact that I now have visual images of you I can never unsee? Or the part about me now knowing how big my coach's dick is?"

"Isaac Gregory Stevens! I understand you're shocked after walking in on something you never should have seen. But you will not disrespect me. Ever," I berate, and his anger appears to deflate just a little. "I understand no one cares about privacy when you're living with a bunch of football players in a dorm. But when you knock once on my bedroom door and come barreling in before getting the go-ahead from me, you're libel to see something you shouldn't. And that part isn't my mistake. That's yours."

He throws his shoulders back against the chair, stretching his legs out in front of him. He's obviously frustrated, but he knows I'm right about that. Picking up my coffee from the counter, I walk to the table and sit across from him. His eyes are still avoiding mine, but I refuse to be deterred. This needs to be sorted out.

"Isaac." I sigh when he doesn't respond. "Yes, you are my child, but you are my *adult* child. So we're going to discuss this like adults. I'll answer any question you have. Except about what you saw, of course."

He grimaces, and I realize reminding him of the scene in my bedroom isn't a smart idea. But now isn't the time to apologize for the misstep, so I ignore it and move on.

"So," I settle in and clasp my hands together, resting my elbows on the table. "What do you want to know?"

He takes a few seconds before finally giving in. "Are you dating, or are you just fucking him?"

"Isaac…" I warn. I'm glad he's talking to me, but there are still boundaries.

"It's a valid question, Mom," he says when he finally looks up at me. "I have to work with Coach Pride every single day. I need to know what this"—he waves his hand around, like he can't quite find the word—"this…*thing* is. Is it a relationship? Is it a"—he grimaces—"a one-night stand?"

I nod in understanding. As much as I want to scold him, he's right. This information could very well change his on-field relationship with Jack.

"We're dating."

"Is he your boyfriend?"

"I don't know how to answer that."

He scoffs. "Seriously, Mom? You're sleeping with him, but you don't even know if he's your boyfriend?"

"I don't know how to explain it, Isaac," I rebut. "Boyfriend sounds very juvenile for a man in his forties. We're dating exclusively. Does that answer your question?"

"Yes," he says quietly and rubs his finger over his lip while he thinks. I wait until he's ready. There's no reason to rush his thoughts. "How long have you been dating?"

"A couple months."

His eyes snap up to mine again, and I can see that particular answer is only leading to more questions. "A couple months? But the donor banquet was less than a month ago."

I clear my throat before admitting the truth. "We were already dating the night of the banquet."

"But…" He looks around, trying to make sense of the memories he has of that night. "But you met that night. I introduced you."

I shake my head, and his shoulders drop. I lied to Isaac that night, and I never lie. I've always tried to instill in him that his honesty was his most important character trait. Now I've been caught doing exactly what I've always warned him against. Once again, I'm ashamed of Isaac seeing me this way. I know I'm only human, and none of this is anything I should be apologetic for, but part of me never wanted Isaac to know that I'm as flawed as everyone else.

Oddly, he seems to gloss over the lies part, as he continues to try and figure this all out. "If you were already dating, why did you pretend you didn't know each other?"

I slightly squirm in my seat. Isaac has always been protective of me, as is the case for many only-children of a single mom. And this is the part that could set him off again. "We were fighting. Instead of making a scene in front of the donors and boosters, when you came up and introduced us, we just went along with it."

He runs his fingers through his hair, clearly irritated at this news. "So let me get this straight—you've been dating my coach, the man I've talked about looking up to, for a couple of months. You've already had a major fight, so you pretended not to know each other. And you don't know if he's your boyfriend or not."

I cock my head at him. "Factually, yes. But that's really twisting my words to make it sound different than it is."

"Then how is it? And why didn't you tell me?"

"I didn't want to tell you until I knew this was serious. I didn't want you involved."

"Didn't want me involved?" He pops up from his chair and begins pacing, emotions heightening again. "You're dating my *coach*. That automatically makes me involved."

"Which is why I was going to tell you, but before I could" —I point down the hallway—"that whole scene happened."

"Jesus Christ, Mom…"

"Don't you dare cuss in my house, young man…" I challenge, pointing my finger at him, but he ignores me, continuing his rant.

"What happens when this goes south, huh? Will I lose my scholarship? Will I lose my place on the team? Will he just bench me to get back at you?"

"Oh yes, I'm sure that's what will happen. To get back at me, he's going to bench his best offensive lineman, lose a few games, risk his salary bonus, and possibly not get a contract extension, just to get back at me." I stand up and walk to him, trying to talk him down. "And who says this is going to end anyway?"

"He's *married*!" he yells.

"His wife *died*, Isaac!" I yell back.

He scoffs. "Even better. You're his rebound."

I look to the sky and beg for help to calm down before I say something I regret. "Jack's wife died three years ago, Isaac, after her third battle with cancer. If there was going to be a rebound woman, it would have happened years ago."

"Whatever." He throws his hands in the air and stalks to the laundry room. I follow right behind him.

"I'm sorry you found out this way, Isaac. That was very, very unfortunate," I maintain. "But until last night, I didn't know how serious this was." He snorts a humorless laugh and throws his dirty clothes back in his giant laundry bag. "I've always kept my dating life separate from you for this very reason. There was no reason to get you involved, or force you into a relationship if I didn't see a future with that person. Now, I finally do."

He stops what he's doing and stands up straight to look at me. "Wait, you mean you've kept this kind of thing a secret before?"

I have the sudden realization that Isaac genuinely and honestly has no idea I have a life outside of being his mother and my former job. "Do you really think I've been a hermit since your father left?"

His jaw clenches and he throws the last of the clothes in his bag, pulling the drawstring tight. "Whatever," he says and throws the bag over his shoulder. "I'm going to a laundromat."

I follow behind him as he storms toward the front door, pleading with him as I go. "Isaac, just stay. We need to talk about this."

"Nope. No talking," he refuses without a backward glance. "I know too much. I've seen *way* too much. I'm out of here."

Slamming the door behind him, another important man in my life leaves me alone in silence for the second time today. And it's not even noon yet.

CHAPTER SIX

Jack

"Come on, ladies! We're playing football, not dancing in the fucking ballet!" Hank yells and bangs on his clipboard as he paces next to me. I'm standing in my usual position, arms over my chest, chewing my gum.

I'm supposed to be paying attention to Anderson's hand placements, but instead I'm watching Stevens. He's off today. Way off. And if I were a betting man, I'd make some good money guessing why.

He hasn't spoken to Joie since he walked in on us over a week ago. She's called. She's texted. She even sent an email, but he refuses to respond. His silence is really hurting her. And that's hurting me. Not only because I want to make it better, but because I haven't spent the night with her since, just in case he shows up unannounced.

That's a lot of wasted nights when I could have enjoyed being with her.

Sure, we've gone out. But when it gets late, I've gone home and slept alone, waiting for this pansy-ass to pull his shit together and act like an adult. Instead, he's pitching the world's longest temper tantrum, which has been fine until now. Okay, not fine. But instead of his anger dying down, it seems to be getting worse. So, not only am I worried about how many times I'm gonna have to spank the monkey before I get to be with my woman again, now I'm worried Stevens is gonna get himself injured.

This is the part of the job I hate. When these kids think they've been wronged, they can hold onto a grudge for-fucking-ever.

Last weekend was our off week, so we didn't have a game. This weekend, we're traveling to Wisconsin. Texas may be known as a football state, but Wisconsin is no joke. They grow some big kids up there with some fancy skills. If we need to take any team seriously, Wisconsin is it.

"What the fuck is wrong with that kid?" Apparently, Hank is finally zeroing in on Stevens, too, who has multiple false starts during practice. It's like he's not paying attention.

I shake my head. "That is a little boy pitching a hissy fit." I rub my hand over the back of my neck. Dammit. I forgot the sunscreen again.

"Over what?" Hank demands. "He's got a full ride, a prominent career ahead of him, and as much pussy as a twenty-year-old kid could ask for. What the ever-loving hell does he have to be pissy about?"

I look over at Hank, eyebrows raised. "Sounds like someone else has his panties in a twist today, too."

He sighs and runs his hands down his face. "I just got the call about the ticket sale issue this morning."

"University is trying to take part of our budget to offset the new third-party fees?"

"Yep."

"What did you tell them?"

"That without new gear, we stand to be libel if someone gets injured."

I nod my approval. "And did they understand how much more money a lawsuit will cost them than giving us the same cut?"

"They said they'd get back to me."

"At least it wasn't a no."

We watch as another play unfolds in front of us. This time, Stevens launches at the wrong time. Plus he's still not all-in and gets run over by a defender.

Hank slaps his clipboard on his thigh. "What the fuck is that kid's problem?"

I take a breath and lean closer to him, so no one else overhears. "He caught me and his momma in a compromising position."

Hank looks over at me, his lips twitching like he's trying not to laugh. "Seriously?"

I raise an eyebrow and turn to look at him. "Do you think that's something I'd kid around about?"

A low whistle comes from between his lips. "How long ago?"

"Last weekend."

"That would explain his attitude for the last week or so."

"And how he's gonna get his ass hurt if he doesn't get his head back in the game." I uncross my arms and stalk toward the field when Stevens takes another hit wrong, landing on his back with his arm at a weird angle. He's not hurt, but if we were in a real game, he would be. "Stevens," I yell, which makes the entire team take notice since I never raise my voice. "Get your ass over here right now!"

Hank chuckles. "You stole my line."

I shake my head. "He's pissing me off for so many reasons. This shit needs to stop."

"Good luck," Hank says, patting me on the shoulder and then turns back to the field. "Get back in position, ya pansies! No one said to stop! Reynolds—stand in for Stevens!" he yells as he walks away, leaving me to a very uncomfortable conversation with my girlfriend's son. Especially if he keeps moseying on over, instead of running, like he should be. I bite my tongue from calling him out on it. Right now, the most important thing is for him to be safe on the field. Fuck the rest of it.

When he finally reaches me, he rubs his lip with his finger, looking anywhere and everywhere except at me. So this is how it's gonna go. I tried, but it looks like all bets are off now.

Taking my normal stance again, I lower my voice. "What's going on, son?"

He looks up at me, glaring, but doesn't say a word.

I raise my eyebrows and turn my entire body toward him. "You got a problem?"

"I'm not your son," he says with malice in his voice.

I take one step forward, arms still crossed. I've been nice. I've given him space, but this shit stops now.

"Let's get one thing straight," I threaten. "I may be dating your momma, but I don't give a shit about you beyond what you can do out there on that field. I get that you saw something you never should have seen. But if you don't stop with the thirteen-year-old-girl drama and quit crying in your helmet, you're gonna get yourself hurt out there."

He looks back down at the ground, but I continue, "I don't give a shit that you're angry with your momma. I don't give a shit that you're angry with me. But when we are on this field, I am in charge, and I will damn well call you whatever I want, do I make myself clear, *son*?"

He nods but says nothing.

"I asked you a question, boy, and you better answer me unless you want to do up-downs until you puke. So I'll ask again, do I make myself clear?"

Stevens takes a breath and looks up at me, eyes narrowed, but recognizing he has a lot to lose if he continues with this bullshit attitude. "Yes. *Sir*."

"I'm serious, Stevens." I point a finger right in his chest. "You get your head back in that game. We have a very big, very strong team coming up this weekend. Unless you want to run the risk of being injured and ruining your entire career, you better figure out how to get your brain to compartmentalize and think only about this game. You're pushing off too soon, you're not using your upper body, and you're not anticipating your opponent's moves. Figure this out."

For the first time since this conversation began, his shoulders seem to relax, like he's finally hearing what I'm saying, and he nods once.

"Good. Now get back on that field and get your head back in it. Go."

As soon as the play is over, he runs back on the field, relieving Reynolds. Getting in position, the QB calls the play, and they get back at it. Stevens pushes off at exactly the right time, and everything goes off without a hitch.

Hank bangs his clipboard and yells in victory as it all goes exactly like it was designed. "Damn, Pride, what did you say to that kid?"

"Nothing you wouldn't have said," I answer, although we both know Stevens is probably on-point because he's imagining it's me he's tackling.

Whatever works.

CHAPTER SEVEN

Joie

"I think I like doing Bunco on Sunday nights." Amanda plunks a load of dirty dishes down on the counter for me to wash. She's the last one here after a couple hours of games with our friends. We used to do it on Friday nights, but that didn't give me much time to clean house and cook after classes all day, so we tried something new. "We start earlier so everyone can get home a little earlier before the week starts, which is awesome...Oh hey! Drea left the last of the cake balls!" she exclaims and pops one in her mouth.

I smile and shake my head at her. When it comes to desserts, Amanda has no shame.

"I was thinking the same thing. I studied all weekend, so it was really nice letting my brain relax for a while, too."

"We didn't have any major disasters today."

"That's because you and I don't play at the same table anymore." Unplugging the drain, I grab a hand towel to dry what I've washed. I'll do the rest later. "No one is as competitive as the two of us."

Amanda tosses another cake ball in her mouth and covers the leftover dip with plastic wrap. "I don't get that. The whole point of Bunco is to get the dice. You're supposed to go for it. Not sit there waiting for them to roll into your lap."

"If it's too boring we could always go back to playing at the same table." I move to stack the clean plates into the cabinet. "But you'll have to start bringing your own card tables. I can't afford to keep replacing them."

She chews while she thinks for a second. "As tempting as that is, I think I'll have to suffer through a game with less action."

"Not willing to spend that much money on broken furniture?" I ask with a smirk. The last two times we played at the same table, we both launched ourselves at free dice. Needless to say, when we landed on the table, its legs broke under our weight and we ended up falling on top of each other in a heap. It was painful. It was also hysterical in hindsight.

"Oh, I don't care about that," she says with a shake of her head. "I don't want to end up with another dice-shaped bruise on my boob."

"A what?" I laugh.

"I didn't tell you about that?" I shake my head and snatch up some silverware to sort in the drawer. "Oh yeah. Apparently, I fell right on top of at least one die. When I woke up the next morning, I found a square bruise. You could see the outline and the shape. In case you were wondering, you rolled a four."

We both burst out laughing at the visual image. "Oh my gosh, that is so funny!"

"It's funny *now*. But it wasn't then. Jeff is a boob man. I can barely keep his hands off the girls at night and with a giant bruise? That shit hurts!"

Laughing uncontrollably, I give up on the silverware. I'm having too much fun talking with my best friend. "Poor, Jeff."

"Poor, Jeff? Poor me! Don't tweak my nipples when I'm all bruised up!"

I shake my head at her ridiculousness. Amanda is such a great friend, but she is also a nut. You just never know what is going to come out of her mouth.

"Speaking of tweaking nipples..."

Like that. I knew the conversation would end up back on me at some point.

She raises an eyebrow at me, waiting for me to say something. I shake my head back at her. "What? Why are you looking at me that way?"

Crossing her arms, she leans against the counter and stops cleaning. No surprise there. She always stays to help me get things back in order once game night is over. And by *help me,* I mean she talks to me while I clean. Apparently, this time she wants me to talk back.

"You know exactly why I'm looking at you this way. I wanna know more about Jaaaaaack," she singsongs.

Turning to the sink, I put the plug in and begin the process of filling it with soapy water for the second time. These ladies eat a lot of food to leave this many dishes behind. "What do you want to know?" I ask without looking at her. I can feel my face blushing, even if my skin doesn't turn pink.

"How was it?"

"What?"

"You heard me. How was *it*? The last thing you told me was Isaac walked in while you were riding the Pride Pony," I snicker, "but then we got distracted by Drea and these amazing cake balls." She grabs another and pops it in her mouth.

I sigh and drop the last of the dirty dishes in the water to soak, before grabbing the hand towel again and drying off.

Before I can say anything, Amanda's face registers understanding. "Wait, you still haven't heard from Isaac?" I shake my head sadly. "But you've tried to contact him, right?"

"Amanda, I've called. I've texted. I even sent an email. And I know he's gotten them. I can see that he's read them."

She crosses her arms, chewing slowly while she thinks. "He'll be back. He can't ignore you forever. Eventually he'll want his Christmas presents."

My lips quirk at her attempted joke. "I don't know what to do. I mean, I get that he needs space. He saw something no child ever wants to see, ya know?"

"And I sympathize with that part. But I gotta say, Joie, he's kind of being an asshole now."

If anyone else called my child a name like that, I'd be really mad. But in Amanda's case, it's not offensive. It causes me to sit up and listen.

"Just hear me out. I get that he's all traumatized from seeing you in the throes of passion. I get that it's only been the two of you, so this is something he has to get used to. But it's been how long since he's responded?"

"Ten days."

"Ten days?" she says incredulously. "That's not being surprised or even stunned anymore. That's being a dickhead. And I know. I have a dickhead for a son."

A giggle escapes me. "Dylan is not that bad."

"Don't try to defend him. He must have horrible parents for all the shit he pulls."

I laugh a bit harder at her ridiculous statement. "Stop," I say through my chuckles. "You guys are great parents. He's just...stubborn."

"And strong-willed. And refuses to grow up."

"Well, he is his own person," I defend. "Even if he acts like he can't function without some sort of intervention."

"I told you about his latest academic probation, right?"

I think for a minute about the details of it. All I know is that his GPA was so low last semester, he was warned he'd be kicked out of school if it didn't improve.

"Just that he was on it." I shrug. "I didn't know there was anything more to it than that."

"There's so much more." I look at her quizzically. "We finally found out exactly how bad his GPA was." She turns to face me, a dramatic look crossing her face as she leans in for effect. "Point- one-five." My jaw practically hits the floor. "Not one-point-five. Less than one. *Point*-one-five."

"How did he manage a grade point average of almost zero? That's not even possible." I run the math over in my head and can't figure it out. He must have failed almost everything.

"Oh, it's possible. He was taking thirteen credit hours. Twelve of them were in classes he quit going to, but he never dropped them. Just stopped going so those calculate in as F's. That last hour was bowling." She looks me dead in the eye before deadpanning, "He got a C."

"How do you get a C in bowling?"

She shakes her head in exasperation. "I have no idea. All I know is it ended in the lowest GPA, probably in history, and a strongly-worded letter from the dean's office about changing his ways."

"He's doing better now, though, right?"

"Oh yeah," she exclaims. "We told him if he didn't get his shit together, we weren't paying for school anymore, and since he's an adult, he could get a job to pay his own way. The little shit pulled a three-point-two over the summer."

"That's great!" And really, it is. I know she was stressed about what would happen if he flunked out of school.

"It is," she agrees. "It also goes to show he can man up if he really wants to. Just like Isaac can if he wants to."

I sigh. "You really think he's throwing a college-sized temper tantrum right now?"

She nods slowly. "I do. And I hope you're not just sitting around here, putting everything on hold while you wait for him to pull himself together."

I crinkle my nose and bite my lip. She knows me too well sometimes.

"I'm gonna guess by the grimace you're sporting, that's exactly what you've been doing."

"I didn't want him to accidentally find Jack over here again and the whole thing blow up even more than it already has."

She leans against the counter and crosses her arms. "Honey, I love you. But you have to stop putting him ahead of everything else in your life. If he was having a major life event or something, yeah, of course. But he's not. He's just throwing a fit. You deserve to have a life. Don't let him stop you."

I absorb her words as I think about the last ten days. It's true. I'm in a new relationship with a man I enjoy so much, he's all I can think about sometimes. But I've pushed Jack aside while I wait for my adult child to get over himself. Why? Why can't I put myself first this time? Why can't "Joie" and "Isaac's mom" be the same person? Why do I have to separate things out anymore? Isaac's not just grown up. He's been gone for two years. He has his own life. It's time I had mine, too.

A soft knock at the door startles us both. Amanda and I look toward the door before looking back at each other.

"Are you expecting someone?" she asks me.

I shake my head. "No. You think maybe Isaac is here?"

"Would he knock?" I quirk an eyebrow at her as I walk past her and round the corner. "Oh, I guess he'd be overly cautious now, wouldn't he?"

Looking out the peephole, my heart speeds up. It's not Isaac, but I open the door anyway. "Jack," I breathe, my face beaming.

Holding up his take-out bags in offering he says, "I found authentic Mongolian."

Grabbing the front of his shirt, I pull him to me and kiss him with everything in me. He gasps in surprise, but soon enough, he's got one hand around the back of my neck while we explore each other's lips with gentle kisses, small bites, and nibbles. I didn't realize how much I genuinely missed him until right at this moment.

A voice clears behind us and I realize Amanda is still here. Pulling away shyly, I clear my throat and turn to face her. "Um...yeah. Sorry, Amanda. I forgot you were here."

"I can see that." She pushes off the wall where she's been leaning and walks toward us, hand extended. "It's about time I finally met the famous Jack Pride."

"You follow football?" he asks, sporting his fake game-face smile and reaches out to shake her hand.

"Nope," she replies. "I follow Joie's life." A real, genuine grin crosses his face. "I'm Amanda. Nice to meet you."

"You, too."

"Well, now that you have company, I'm gonna get out of your hair." She reaches over the side of the couch and grabs her purse. "You guys have fun tonight. And you"—she points at me while walking past us to the door—"don't forget what I said."

I nod at her, appreciative that she helped me refocus myself.

Once the door locks behind her, I turn to face Jack again.

"I hope it's okay that I came by unannounced," he apologizes. "I know Stevens's got an eight o'clock tomorrow morning, so I figured it would probably be safe by now."

Walking up to him, I kiss him gently again. "I'm glad you did. I missed you. Did you have fun in Wisconsin?"

"We won, so it was a great time." He pulls back and looks into my eyes. I can tell he's making sure it's okay that he's here. "You want to try this new cuisine with me?"

"More than anything," I say, and guide him farther into my house. Where he stays all night long.

CHAPTER EIGHT

Jack

She shifts under the sheets, waking me from a good night's sleep. It's been ten days since I've been with Joie this way. I missed it more than I realized I would. After last night, I'm hopeful we won't go another ten days.

As my eyes begin to focus, I take in how fucking pretty she is. Dark skin that covers her from head to toe, unlike my farmer's tan that boasts lily white under my clothes. Dark, wavy hair that's fanned out behind her while she sleeps. Dark pink lips that are just slightly pursed. She looks nothing like my blond-haired, blue-eyed late wife.

Not that there's a comparison. They are their own individuals with their own strengths and weaknesses. Their own dreams and motivations. To compare them would be to do a disservice to both women. But I can't deny it's different to lie next to someone who is so dark to my light. I like the contrast.

And I like Joie.

And I really like being inside her.

"What are you looking at" she asks sleepily, eyes still closed, making me chuckle.

I reach out and roll her over, pulling her toward me so we can spoon. "I didn't know you were awake."

"I'm not. Not really." She yawns so big, I'm almost afraid she'll break her jaw. "What time is it?"

"About six." I kiss her neck and snuggle back into her.

"Mmm. That means I'm late. I should probably get up." Her words hold no real conviction when she doesn't make any move to get out of bed. Not that I'm complaining.

And as much as I don't want to, a few minutes later, I play the role of responsible adult and bring up the time again. "When do you have to leave for class?"

"In a little less than an hour." She sighs but I'm not sure if it's with contentment or of reservation. "I'm trying to decide if I can get away with missing a day of class. It's just one day."

I chuckle lightly. "You know you would be pissed at yourself later if you skipped."

"Stop being the voice of reason," she reprimands playfully.

"How about this?" I suggest. "I'll get up, run us a hot shower, wash you from head to toe, maybe dirty you up just a bit"—I feel a giggle from deep in her chest at the suggestion— "and I'll even spring for coffee at Starbucks on our way into town."

"That sounds like a fantastic idea," she replies. "But I'll help you run that hot shower. If I wait for you to tell me it's ready, I'll fall back asleep."

"Deal."

We take our time, peeling ourselves out of bed and heading toward the bathroom. She's still asleep enough that I have to practically drag her as she shuffles behind me. When I turn on the spray, she folds her arms across her chest and leans into me so I can hold her up while we wait for the water to get hot. Fortunately, we never bothered to put clothes back on last night, so we don't have to mess with getting undressed. I'm not sure Joie has enough balance yet to do it without injuring herself.

"You're not a morning person, are you?"

She shakes her head, making me chuckle.

Even when the water is warm enough to climb in and stand underneath the spray, we stay just like this...her snuggled into me with my arms wrapped around her back, the warmth of the steam billowing around us.

Unfortunately, a few short minutes is all we can spare, so once again I play the role of responsible adult and grab her loofa sponge and some shower gel, soaping it up so I can soap her up as well. Okay, maybe I'm not *that* responsible.

"I'm glad you stayed last night," she admits, as she leans back into the water, getting her hair wet while I wash down her neck, over her small breasts, down her stomach to her mound, where she finally bats my hands away and grabs the loofa out of my hands and trades places with me.

"I was surprised you wanted me to stay."

"I always want you to stay, Jack."

Wiping the water out of my eyes, I smile at her, loving the intimacy that watching her shower brings. It's such a mundane, everyday thing to do, yet I feel so honored that it's me she chose to be with when she does it. Not surprisingly, watching the water sluice down her curves also turns me on. I can't help but kiss her neck when she turns away from me. She groans her approval.

"I wasn't sure what would happen since Stevens is still being a piss-ant."

Her fingers run through my hair and my hands begin exploring the front of her body—pinching her pebbled nipples, down her soft stomach, through her private curls.

"Can we not talk about my son when your finger is"—she gasps at my touch and moves her legs farther apart—"right where I want it. Jack, we're gonna be late."

I hmph. "I'll be quick, baby. That's why it's called a morning quickie."

"Okay," she breathes, still tugging on my hair.

I smile against her skin and turn her to face the wall. "Put your hands on the tile, baby. This is gonna be fast."

She complies and even leans forward a bit so her ass is sticking out, perfectly positioned for my hands to rub up and down her cheeks. But I know we have a time limit and I want to maximize my efforts, so I quickly line my dick up to her and push inside. We both groan at the feeling and are soon lost in each other.

Of course, a dirty shower means having to scrub down all over again, but it's a small price to pay for that kind of wake-up call.

"So what's on tap for today?" I ask once we maneuver to the middle of the large bathroom to get dressed. It's funny how we haven't been dating that long, but we still instinctively move around each other, almost like a well-coordinated play. She shifts when I reach for a belt here. I lean when she extends for a bra there. Both of us move when we stretch for a toothbrush over there.

"I have a quiz in my lit class," she answers as she puts on mascara. I have no idea how she can talk with her mouth being that wide open. "I should get my grade back from my biology test today. And that's the most exciting thing happening."

"What time are you finished?"

She sighs. "Not until late. I have my study group tonight at eight-thirty."

I don't look up as I thread my belt through the loops of my jeans. I'm glad I had the foresight to bring an overnight bag. It would suck to have to go home to change. But it would be even worse to show up at work wearing the same thing I left in last night. "I hope you have someone walk you to your car. You are done way too late at night to walk by yourself."

"Aw, are you nervous for me?"

I shoot her a look that says, "Duh." "I know Flinton is a safe town, but it's still easy to find victims on a college campus. Haven't you heard how high crime rates are at universities?"

"I concede," she jokes, but I know there's truth in the statement. "I will make sure someone walks me to my car. I'm sure Brian won't mind."

I narrow my eyes at the thought. "You tell him to keep his shitty little hands off you, or I'll condition him until he can't move those hands again."

"Yes, Jack," Joie says through a laugh. "I'll make sure my son's friend knows this cougar is off limits."

"You'd better." I slap her on the ass, making her squeal.

"Anyway," she continues while packing up her makeup, "what do you have planned for today?"

"Mostly a light workout at practice. We have game tapes to watch, so Hank and I will go over them before we rake them all over the coals for all the mistakes that were made at the game this weekend."

Joie rolls her eyes. "I watched the game. There weren't any mistakes."

"Maybe they weren't mistakes as much as there are things that could have been done better."

"I can agree with that. Give 'em hell, baby."

I gasp, eyes widening. "Did you just say h-e-double-hockey-sticks? The prim and proper Joie Stevens just...just cussed?"

She giggles. "And don't you forget it, mister. And also, don't tell anyone."

I snort a laugh. "Your secret is safe with me."

Glancing at the clock on the wall, she gets visibly agitated. "Crap. I don't have time to blow dry my hair. I'm gonna look like a mess today."

"Wear it back in that bandana thingy you have."

She furrows her brow at me. "You mean like when I'm cleaning the house?"

I shrug. "Sure. I think it looks cute on you." Smiling, I pull her to me and give her a chaste kiss. "Like a pinup model."

She wiggles her eyebrows. "You think that's what I look like?" I nod. "Like I came straight out of a different time." I nod again. "When wearing a bandana was an everyday thing because all women were supposed to do was clean house and take care of their man?" I smile...

And then frown. "How the hell did that just turn on me?"

Joie bursts out laughing and pulls away, grabbing the aforementioned cloth and some bobby pins. "I'm just kidding. But you set yourself up for that."

"I suppose I did." Leaning against the wall, now that I'm ready to go, I watch as she situates her hair exactly like I like it. "I'll have to watch myself around you. First the cow comment, now this."

"I may look nice and motherly, but I'm a sneaky one."

"I like being kept on my toes."

She catches my eye in the mirror, smiling at me and finishes getting ready. Despite sleeping in and a morning quickie, we walk out the door, hand-in-hand, only five minutes late. I even make good on that Starbucks run.

CHAPTER NINE

Joie

My brain is fried. I mean, break-me-open, scramble-me-up, throw-me-in-the-pan, and cook-for-five-minutes fried.

That may be a slight exaggeration, but we've been studying identity theories for the past hour-and-a-half straight, and I'm pretty sure my brain is turning into mush. Don't get me wrong, I love my educational psychology class. It's interesting, and the professor is fun. But with three classes, two observations, and a study group every single week, not to mention the massive observation project due next month, it's exhausting.

I suppose I'm grateful for the reminder that this is nothing compared to teaching two dozen kindergartners every day. I'm just building up my endurance. But on nights like tonight, it's hard to remind myself that knowing all the parts of James Marcia's Identity Status Theory will actually be important someday. Especially since Isaac was in grade school, I've been planning to teach early childhood education and not adolescents.

Brian practically groans in my ear as he takes a second bite of a pumpkin-spiced muffin. I stare at him, thinking, *On second thought, maybe I'll have more interaction with adolescents than I initially believed.*

He catches me staring and his chewing slows while he shifts his eyes back and forth, looking around. "What? I thought you brought these for us to eat."

"I did," I admit, slightly embarrassed that I got caught gawking at him. In my defense though, he eats a regular-sized muffin in two bites. It's kind of fascinating to watch. "Sorry. Just lost in thought. Can I ask you a question?"

"Sure." He swallows his bite and take a long drink of his water before focusing his attention on me. Well, part of his attention. He's still shooting gazes at the rest of the snacks. "What's up?"

"You guys have a home game Thanksgiving weekend, right?"

He makes a face. "Don't remind me. Coach keeps bitching about it."

Which coach? Surely Jack would have said something if he was upset. Wouldn't he? "Why is he mad?" I ask. "Don't you guys play that weekend every year?"

He shrugs and finally caves, grabbing another muffin and peeling the paper away. I guess my special recipe is a hit. Okay, fine. I got it off Rachel Ray's website and prayed really hard they wouldn't end up being a Pinterest fail. But I make a mental note to bake them again, just for him.

Brian and I haven't necessarily become close. But being in the same class and study group, we've developed a relationship of sorts. He reminds me of Amanda's son, except more motivated and successful. And knowing his family is so far away makes my mom-heart ache a bit. I find myself wanting to do the little things to make him not feel so homesick.

Hence, sneaking more baked goods into the library.

"All I know is he keeps grumbling about having to put up with his in-laws for an extended period of time because it's a home game this year, and they want him to get box seats or something."

Ah. That must be Hank, who I haven't met yet, but I know he's married.

"If you can't go home, what are you going to do on Thanksgiving Day? Where do you eat?"

He shrugs again and crams the rest of the muffin in his mouth, chewing slowly and clearly enjoying it before finally answering me. "We'll probably see if a Chinese food place is open. Or maybe get some pizza."

My jaw drops open. "You mean the school doesn't have some sort of dinner for you?"

"Not that I know of. From what I hear, they used to have a real Thanksgiving dinner for those of us who couldn't make it home. Someone would cater in turkey and dressing and all the fixings. That's what I've heard. I don't know if it's actually true or why they stopped."

I furrow my brow as I take in all the information. I wonder why no one ever thought to feed these boys on Thanksgiving. Was it too expensive? Did they not think it was important enough to factor into a budget?

"How many of you are staying in town over the holidays?" I ask, the wheels in my brain turning rapidly. I don't know if anyone would be opposed to me hosting something at my house, but I know who to ask.

He looks up as he thinks. "Uh…five or six of us, maybe? Not that many." He side-eyes me like he can see the ideas racing through my head. "How come you're so interested in this?"

I flash him a bright smile and feign indifference, while grabbing for my phone. "No reason. Just curious is all." Turning to my phone, I begin typing out a text.

"Uh huh," Brian replies. "I don't believe you, but these muffins are too good for me to care right now."

I snort when he grabs for a fourth helping while I text. Good thing everyone else already ate one before stretching their legs on what's turning into a very long break. They may not get another at the rate he's going.

> **Me:** *Hey. How come no one provides Thanksgiving dinner to the players who are stuck in town over the holiday?*

> **Jack:** *Is that pansy ass complaining about not getting fed? Tell him he's gonna have a hard time chasing down a running back if he packs more on around the middle.*

> **Me:** *Lol. No. He's completely happy with the muffins I smuggled into the library. I'm just curious why no one does it.*

> **Jack:** *Actually, Sheila used to be in charge of putting together a dinner. I had forgotten until now.*

My eyebrows shoot up. Jack's late wife used to coordinate this event? No wonder they stopped doing it. Now I feel bad for asking. But not bad enough to drop it. There goes my mom-heart taking over again.

Me: *Would it be weird if I hosted something at my house?*

Jack: *Why would that be weird?*

Me: *Because Sheila used to do it. Is that stepping on her toes or something? I don't want it to seem like I'm moving in on her territory or anything.*

Jack: *Considering you're the mom of one of kids who would take advantage of the meal, it doesn't feel like it to me. Who gives a shit what it looks like to anyone else?*

Me: *So it's okay with you if I start making plans? I feel really bad for these kids. Brian's talking about eating Chinese. That's just sad!*

Jack: *You mean like they did in A Christmas Story? Fa ra ra ra ra? Man, I love that movie.*

Me: *Lol. Focus, Coach.*

Jack: *Sorry. Yeah, it should be fine. Let me hook you up with Renee, Hank's wife. I know the dinners used to go through the boosters, and they had a bunch of it donated by local businesses. So if you're not opposed to having a few extra athletes from other sports at your house, they'll pay for it and then we can be 100% sure it doesn't violate some weird NCAA rule.*

Me: *That would be great! Thanks, babe. Gotta run. We're about to start again.*

Jack: *No problem. Learn well. And bring some muffins home with you! I could eat your muffins all day every day.*

Me: *Don't be dirty.*

Jack: *gasp I can't believe you think I had my mind in the gutter! Okay, fine. I did. You win. Bring the muffins anyway.*

I snicker as I shut my phone off, but when I see Brian sitting back in his chair, the stunned expression on his face directed at me, I'm immediately on alert. "What? Why do you look like that?"

Leaning forward, he whisper-yells, "You're dating *Coach?!*"

I shush him, looking around to make sure no one else heard him. "What do you mean? What are you talking about?"

"Oh please. Don't even deny it. I saw your phone."

I gape at him, trying to change tactics. "What are you doing looking over my shoulder at my phone? That's very rude, ya know."

"I didn't look over your shoulder. Your background picture caught my attention when you picked up it. And then the name 'Jack' in giant grandma-sized letters at the top was a dead giveaway."

I grimace. So that tactic change doesn't work. And suddenly, using the selfie Jack and I took on our last date as the home-screen picture doesn't seem like such a good idea.

"Just because there is a picture on my phone doesn't mean we're dating. Maybe…well…maybe…You know this is football country. Maybe I have a picture of myself with the famous Jack Pride because he's like a celebrity."

That doesn't even sound like a plausible excuse to my own ears. Clearly, Brian agrees with how ridiculous it is.

"Joie," he says quietly. I look over sheepishly, quirking my lips to the side, not quite sure what to do now that I've been outed. "Does he treat you right? Like he's respectful and all that?"

I smile and nod. "Yes. So, so much yes."

"Good," he says, relaxing back into his chair. "Then I have no problem with it."

I pat his arm. "Thanks, Brian. It's not a secret. We just don't want it to turn into this huge public deal. We like the privacy."

"Understood." He turns to point at me. "But you tell him, if he hurts you, I'll take it out on his ass."

I throw my head back and laugh. "Ohmygod, I am not passing messages back and forth between you two Neander-thals."

"Fine." He grabs yet another muffin. "At least tell him to keep his hands off my baked goods. I'm a growing boy."

I snicker and grab a pen as Nick calls us back to order again, so we can debate the merits of Social Identity Theory until the librarian finally forces us to call it a night.

CHAPTER TEN

Jack

"How do you think Brickmore's looking?" Hank taps his pen on his desk as we review some tapes of practice. We do this in the afternoon almost every day, while the earlier practices are still fresh on our minds. "Think he'll be ready to step into the starting position next year?"

I rub at the mild sunburn on my arm. Only in Texas do you still need sunscreen in late October. And only I forget it every single day, despite its necessity. "He's been really solid as the second string QB. I know he's young, but it sure would be nice if we could start him for three years. Right now, I don't see anyone ready to come up after him."

Hank nods absentmindedly. "I'm right there with you. We finally have momentum on our offensive line, but that's not gonna mean shit in three years if we don't have a QB."

"I just hate scouting the high schools for fresh meat so far out." I lean back and stretch my legs when he turns off the screen. "Those fourteen-year-olds are such scrawny little shits when they first hit high school."

"I'm not sure we have a choice at this point. We don't have to start tossing names around yet, but make a mental note to look when we start scouting in a couple months."

Rubbing my hand down my face, I sigh. "Yeah. And I'll put in a call to my buddy, Ryan Lennox. See who his competition is this year and if anyone is standing out."

"He still coaching high school 5A?"

"6A now," I correct him.

He whistles through his teeth, clearly impressed. "Holy shit, that's a big school."

"Yep." I stretch my arms over my head to relieve some of the tension from sitting in this chair. I wish Hank would upgrade to something beyond the metal-folding variety. But he never does. My guess is because these make a lot of noise when they're thrown, and Hank's all about being loud when he gets riled up. "Chicago area keeps growing. Pretty sure three thousand kids per school isn't unusual over there."

"Three thousand high schoolers? I'd put a bullet in my head," he snarks, making me chuckle. "College freshmen are hard enough to deal with."

"Speaking of college freshmen..." Hank groans before I finish my sentence. "Now don't start that. I'm just reminding you Randy Whitman from the boosters will be here soon to go over the preliminary numbers for next year's scholarships."

He shakes his head at me. "Don't scare me like that. You know I can wine and dine with the best of them, but I like to dumb down my brain cells before candidates get here."

"Those are our future starters you're talking about." I chuckle. "You're such a dick, you know that?"

He looks back at the screen, treating my dig like a compliment. "It's what makes me a good coach. Now watch Reynolds's footwork on this next play."

Before he can start the video again, a noise from outside the office catches our attention. "What the hell?" We both jump up when we realize what we're hearing sounds an awful lot like a scuffle. As we race through the door, sure enough, we find Stevens and Anderson being pulled apart by a few other players, while they continue to spout shit back and forth.

"I didn't even do anything, asshole!" Anderson yells as two other players pull him back and force him to sit on one of the benches. "I said I *like* her. What the fuck is the matter with you?"

"What the hell is going on in here?" Hank bellows, and the room goes silent, except for the sounds of people shuffling around. No one answers so he yells again, "Someone wanna tell me why there's a fistfight happening in my locker room?"

Still no response.

"Stevens?" Hank challenges, but all the kid does is look at the floor, two of his teammates still flanking him in case he charges again, which it looks like he wants to. So Hank turns his attention to the other half of this clusterfuck. "Anderson? Wanna tell me what the fuck is going on here?"

The kid spits some blood onto the floor and wipes his split lip. "All I said was that I thought it was cool that his mom was dating Coach, and he fucking charged me." My eyebrows shoot up, and my body runs cold. I glance around the room to see what their reaction is about to be, but no one even looks my direction. Either they all already knew about Joie and me or they just don't care.

Until I catch Randy Whitman's eye. Well, isn't that fantastic timing on his part? But I don't have time to worry about what he's thinking. We've obviously got bigger issues right now.

"*That's* what this is about?" Hank hollers, turning to look at Stevens, whose machismo suddenly seems to deflate. "You're throwing down with one of your teammates because your mother might have a sex life?" Stevens winces but doesn't say a word when a few people snicker in the background. No one has the balls to actually laugh, though. Smart move.

"Well, get over it, son, because I'm pretty sure everyone on this team has a sex life, except maybe that weird looking water boy. What's his name?" He snaps his fingers as he tries to remember. "Peter? Is that his name?"

"I can hear you," an irritated voice yells from across the room, but Hank isn't done with his rant.

"Pretty sure that boy is still a virgin."

I stifle a laugh as I hear "Hey!" come from where Peter is standing. Hank doesn't even notice.

"Hell, I myself got a piece of ass last night. Twice." A few of the guys grimace at Hank's proclamation. "But what the fuck does any of that have to do with football, huh?" He looks at each player individually as he speaks. "Nothing. Not a damn thing. We are here for one reason and one reason only— to win football games. And I will not have some stupid shit about who your momma is dating tear this team apart." He stalks over to Stevens and gets right in his face. "And you ever attack one of my players again, your ass will be benched so hard you will waddle when you walk. Do I make myself clear?"

"Yes, sir," Stevens says quietly, never looking up from the floor.

Hank backs up and turns in a circle as he calls out commands. "Now that you pussies have done your best to piss me off, get those running shoes back on and give me a mile."

"Aw, Coach. I already showered," someone complains.

"Then you're gonna smell pretty for the clean-up crew when you run by," he counters. "Now get out there before I change my mind and make you suit up first."

"You stay." I point to Stevens, who sighs and drops to the bench, the room clearing out quickly with Hank's threat looming. This shit needs to be hashed out, and I will stay here all night if that's how long it takes to come to an understanding with this kid.

Once the door closes behind the last person, I begin. "How long until you plan on letting this go?" He shrugs. "That's not good enough. You have let a personal issue cause you to lose focus on the game. You damn near got yourself hurt on the field this past weekend. And now you're attacking your teammates. You can be angry at whatever and whoever you want, but the minute you step into this room, you better check that attitude at the door."

He continues looking at the floor, elbows on his knees.

"As your coach, I'm telling you don't ever pull this bullshit again. This is not your team. This is not your locker room. This is not your field. I am responsible for it, and there is no room for people who cause problems. Do you understand?"

"Yes, sir." This time, when he speaks, it's with humility. Looks like we're finally getting somewhere.

"Now since you started this whole mess, you're about to suit up. And you're gonna give me five hundred up/downs and two miles. *With* pads. Got it?"

"Yes sir," he says again without hesitation.

"But before you go, you need to know a few things." I walk over and sit down next to him on the bench. He doesn't look at me and that's fine. It's time to stop pussyfooting around the elephant in the room and lay it all out on the line. "Your mother spent seventeen years putting her life on hold for you. Seventeen years. You seem to think she was happy just being your mother and working, and yes, she's always been happy. But she's also had dreams and goals of her own that she set aside. For you. And now, when you're finally an adult, when she can finally have a life of her own, you pull this self-centered, entitled bullshit."

He winces, but I'm not done.

"I have talked to her every single day for the last two weeks, and you know what she's talked about more than anything? You. How much she misses you. How many times she's texted you and called and has gotten no response. I've watched her suck back tears because of how much your silence has hurt her, and as your mother's boyfriend, it makes me want to take your ass down to the floor. But let's get one thing clear, for as much as you're worried I'll break her heart, take a look in the mirror. The only one hurting her is you. You think you're the shit? A big deal because your driver's license says you're an adult? Then man up and let her find happiness. You hear me?"

"Yes, sir," he says, surprising the shit out of me. Maybe he's scared he's gonna lose his starting position. Or maybe I'm finally getting through. Either way, this is progress.

"Good. Now when you're done with this practice, you're gonna take your happy ass to the store and get your momma the biggest bunch of flowers you can find." He nods. "You're gonna drive over to her place, hand them to her with a smile on your face, and thank her for giving birth to you and for every day since that moment. And your gonna apologize sincerely for acting like a spoiled jackass. Got it?"

"Yes, sir."

"Good. Now suit up."

I stand up and start to walk away, but before I make it across the room, he calls after me. "Hey, Coach?"

I turn to look at him, surprised he's finally speaking to me, but pleased he seems to have snapped out of his attitude problem. "Are you just sleeping with her or do you really like her?"

I take a breath as I figure out how to put my feelings into words he can understand. "I like her more than I've ever liked anyone. And I never thought I'd say that again after my wife died."

He nods and rubs his lip as he looks away and turns toward his locker.

CHAPTER ELEVEN

Joie

Everyone has a favorite chore. You know, the one you always pick first over every other task that has to be done around the house. Mine is laundry. Something about the monotony of shaking out a fresh piece of clothing, still smelling of laundry detergent and cleanliness, folding it carefully and sorting it all into piles is almost soothing. That and the fact that I can do it while watching TV and still consider myself productive.

Unfortunately, once Isaac moved out, the vast majority of our laundry went with him, so my favorite, most cathartic chore is over way too quickly. One load of clothes to fold and a few towels does not take an entire episode of *Riverdale*.

Instead, I'm sitting on the couch, watching a very wrinkly Luke Perry reprimand his teenage Archie for being a dumb ass once again, while the few clothes I have are piled in nice neat stacks around me. If I was actually watching this on the CW,

I'd put everything away during the next commercial break. But no. I prefer to binge watch, which means no breaks. It also means no ability to pull myself away once I get sucked in. This is how I ended up sitting in this exact spot for the last three hours. The episodes just keep going once you start.

Not that I want to turn it off at this point. This twisted version of the Archie comics is giving me a much-needed brain break before my long day tomorrow. When I set my schedule, I opted to take all five of my classes on Mondays, Wednesdays, and Fridays so I could work the other days. I still think it was the right decision, and I know I'll do it the same way next semester. But it makes for a lot of sitting and concentrating all in a row.

Plus, the added emotional stress of Isaac's behavior and my decision to wait it out instead of trying to force the issue, still makes my brain spin. It's hard letting your children go their own way. Especially when it's impacting your relationship.

Yes, sometimes mindless television is welcome.

I watch as my former celebrity crush instructs his on-screen teenager, the latest celebrity heartthrob, to get into the truck on screen, still berating him for finding yet another dead body. Seriously? How does anyone survive in that town? They're all a bunch of sociopaths. It's fascinating.

A knock at the door brings me back to the present, and the pile of clean underwear some poor, unannounced visitor is about to be subjected to. Oh well. If it's Jack, he's seen my panties before. If it's not Jack, I'm not letting them in the house anyway.

Another quick rap sounds just as I turn the knob and open the door partway.

"Isaac," I breathe.

He's standing on the stoop, looking abashed and barely able to make eye contact with me, but holding a giant bouquet of flowers. I think I recognize some version of small sunflowers and maybe stargazers, but I can't be sure. I'm too busy looking at my prodigal son, grateful he's finally come home. And yet, not quite sure how to handle the fact that he's here.

"Hi, Ma. Can I come in?"

I realize I'm still standing in the doorway, blocking his entrance. "Oh!" I blurt, moving out of the way and pulling the door all the way open. "Of course you can. Why didn't you just use your key?"

He twists his lips and crinkles his nose, like he's embarrassed I would even ask. "I, uh...I didn't know if he'd be here."

"Ah." I nod in understanding. I don't bother telling him sex in the living room is not really my style. I'm not opposed to it. I just have had a child for a long time. When it comes to protecting little eyes from things they shouldn't see, old habits die hard. Not that my habits ended up protecting anyone, obviously, since his eyes, that aren't so little anymore, were still traumatized. "Are those for me?" I ask, gesturing to the bouquet.

He looks at them, like he forgot they were in his hand. "Uh, yeah. I don't know what they are, but I thought you'd like the colors."

"I do." I take the flowers from him when he offers them. My fingers graze over the purples and creams. "They're very pretty. Thank you."

He nods and digs his hands in his pockets, but doesn't make eye contact with me. I shift my stance to try and get him to look at me. "Isaac?" Finally, he glances up. "I'm glad you're here."

His shoulders relax, proof of just how hard it was for him to come over. I'm still not sure how this conversation is going to go, but what I do know is pride makes it really hard to say you're sorry sometimes. Especially when you're not totally sure what you're sorry about. And I suspect Isaac isn't positive which part I'm still upset about...the way he left, his two-week silence, or the fact that he hasn't wanted to accept that I can have a life, too.

I stand in my spot, waiting for him to initiate the conversation. Obviously, he has something on his mind and I don't want to make any assumptions on what it could be.

Finally, he speaks. "Can we talk?"

I smile at him and cup his cheek. "Of course we can."

Without another word, we head to the couches. He sits on one, I sit on the other, still surrounded by clothing. Isaac looks from the clothes to the TV and back. "I guess you needed a brain break?"

He knows me so well.

"I did. Educational psychology is killing me slowly, and my biology vocabulary was starting to blur together."

"Are you sorry you went back to college?"

His question is completely unexpected and throws me for a loop. "Not at all. I'm tired, and there are times my brain feels like mush. But I'm having the best time. I love learning and meeting people. And I can't wait to be a teacher, you know?"

He nods and clasps his hands together, resting his elbows on his knees. I wait for more questions. I'm sure he has many. When he takes a deep breath, I know he's finally ready.

"How did you meet him anyway?"

I know the happiness of the memory is written all over my face as I stroke some of the petals mindlessly. "We ran into each other. Literally. I was walking to class and he was, actually I don't know where he was going. But neither of us were looking, and we crashed right there on the sidewalk."

"And that was it? Love at first sight?"

"Oh no." I shake my head. "We ran into each other a couple of times before he asked me to coffee. You need to know, I didn't go because he was *the* Jack Pride, your coach. I went because he was nice. He was attractive. We just kind of clicked. So we went out again. And then again. And he called and we texted." I shrug. "It was just dating."

He snorts humorlessly. "Didn't look like *just dating* to me," he grumbles.

I raise an eyebrow at him. "Did you come over to fight with me or to make amends?"

He closes his eyes, and I can tell he's trying to stay focused on the task at hand. But this is uncharted territory for him. For us. And I know he's not quite sure what to do.

"Isaac," I say gently, "I've never not dated. Not ever." His head snaps up, and he gapes at me as I talk. "As a mom, my job has always been to protect you. That meant protecting you from my dating life as well. There was no sense in bringing someone around if I wasn't sure the relationship was going anywhere. That would have been really hard on you...to attach and then separate. It wouldn't have been healthy. But my mistake was not at least letting you understand that I was, in fact, dating. It probably wouldn't feel so jarring if you had always known."

"I always…" He rubs his thumb over his bottom lip, something he always does when he's trying to find the right words. "I guess I thought it would always just be you and me."

I love the fact that he may be a six-foot-something grown man, but in some ways, he's still just a little boy. "Isaac, what did you think would happen when you found the woman of your dreams and got married? Would you move in here and have two women to take care of you?"

He snickers. "No. I guess the reality of my own life never connected with the reality of yours. Like, why would you be lonely? You have me. Without really thinking about the fact that I'm not here anymore."

"And it's always been you and me against the world." He nods sadly at my statement. "Isaac, it'll still be you and me. We have a unique bond, just by virtue of you growing up as an only child to a single mom. We have a stronger connection than many parent-child relationships out there. But that doesn't mean either of us should or even wants to cut out love interests."

He sits up and for the first time since he got here, he seems to relax. Really relax. Like he's not uncomfortable being here anymore. Like it feels like home again.

"I had a nice long talk with Coach." Those are not the words I was expecting, but I roll with it. "I asked him if he was just sleeping with you or if he really liked you."

I want to be irritated with my son for discussing the significance of my relationship with Jack before I do. But instead, I'm nervous about the outcome. "And what did he say?" I ask quietly, hoping the answer isn't a bad one.

"He said he hasn't liked anyone as much as he likes you since his wife died."

I can feel my cheeks stretch when I grin. Isaac rolling his eyes at my reaction confirms how wide my smile is. It feels good to know Jack likes me that much. I like him that much, too.

"Don't read too much into it, Mom." His face is turned up in a grimace as he thinks about me being in love. "It's not like you're marrying the guy. Wait"—his eyes snap over to mine—"you're not marrying him right?"

I cover my mouth, trying to stifle a giggle but failing.

"It's not funny," Isaac complains. "I don't wanna accidentally find out something like that by walking in on you during your honeymoon or something."

I'm not even trying to not laugh at his ridiculousness now. "Oh my gosh, Isaac, I'm not getting married. And if I do, I'll tell you long before it happens."

"Uh huh," he deadpans.

"I'm serious," I protest. "I was planning to tell you we were dating, but I didn't have a chance before you—" Isaac scowls before I even finish my sentence. "Well, you know. But it really wasn't a secret. More like a missed opportunity."

"I'll have to take your word for it." He smiles shyly at me and I smile back. All of a sudden, everything feels right again. "Anyway, Mom. I just want to say I'm sorry. For everything. I shouldn't have disappeared like that. I was being an entitled little brat, and it was wrong of me."

I reach over and clasp his hand. "It was. But you are so, so forgiven. I've missed you."

He tugs on my hand and pulls me to the couch he's on to hug me, causing me to squeal and drop the flowers on the floor. It still surprises me sometimes that my baby boy is big enough to manhandle me. "I've missed you, too. And I guess I should start calling before I come over."

Pulling away, I pat him on the cheeks. "You don't have to do that. You can use your key. I promise you, as long as you don't barge into my bedroom, you will never catch me in a compromising position."

"Yeah," he says, obviously getting uncomfortable again. "You guys weren't exactly quiet." I gasp, mortified that not only did he see us, he heard us. And yet, I'm baffled as to why that wasn't his first clue he shouldn't come barreling in that day. "So I'll make sure to have my earbuds in if his truck is in the driveway."

I giggle and lean over to pick up the flowers. "Come on." I pat his knee and stand up. "Help me put these clothes away, and we can watch a couple episodes of *Riverdale* before I hit the sack."

"Isn't that the Archie and Jughead show with all those nineties teen stars as the parents now? Why would I want to watch that crap?" he argues as he picks up some towels and heads toward the bathroom.

"Because it's a good brain break."

"If you say so," he calls over his shoulder.

Despite his objections, he stays and watches for a while. And much to my delight and his mortification, he's now hooked.

CHAPTER TWELVE

Jack

"Well hey there, gorgeous! Fancy seeing you here."

Joie's jaw drops open in delighted surprise. "What are you doing here?"

I saunter over, really wanting to kiss her, but knowing that's not possible right here, right now. Instead, I admire how little wisps of her hair blow in the breeze. Good god, I've turned into a love-sick sap.

"I'm headed over to the administration building. Thought you might need an escort."

She narrows her eyes at me playfully. "Need one? No. But I would love the company."

"Noted."

We begin a slow meander toward the orange brick science building, me giving half-hearted waves when random students greet me. We're in no rush. She'll make it to class with plenty of time, and I'm avoiding my destination anyway.

"How was your lit class?" I ask.

She immediately scoffs. "The class itself is fine. It's Mia I have the most trouble with."

"Mia?"

"Chatty Cathy."

"Ah," I chuckle. "She's still chatty?"

Joie's head falls back like she's begging the heavens above for mercy. "I know she's young. I know she's immature. But if she could just shut up for one minute, that would be great. I really don't need to be kicked out of this class because she has no filter. I mean literally. None. There is no shutoff valve."

"You won't be kicked out," I reassure her.

"Oh yeah? How do you know, Mister Smarty Pants?" She bumps me with her shoulder, which does nothing at all to knock me off balance. She, however, loses her step. I grab her by the arm, steadying her. "You'd be surprised how much a student's reputation precedes them in the world of academia."

Her eyebrows shoot up. "Oh yeah? Even you know about the famous Mia?"

"Know all about her. And not because she's a partier, but because she's not the only chatty one. You should see an entire university's worth of professors at an open bar Christmas party."

She laughs, which makes me happy. I love that she's so lighthearted and free. Joie doesn't worry about the same crap most people stress over. She has no interest in keeping up with the Joneses. She just wants a good life filled with good people.

"I want to thank you, Jack," she says, turning serious. I look at her quizzically even though I suspect I know what she's talking about. "For convincing Isaac to make amends."

"Bah," I say, dismissing her claims. "I had nothing to do with it. He was getting ready to come around all on his own."

"He may have been getting ready to, but I know you were the push he needed." I don't bother telling her it was actually a locker room brawl and an ass chewing by Hank that shook him out of his hissy fit. Some things a mother doesn't need to worry about. And I know her. She'll worry. She may have handled Stevens like the adult he is, but she's still Isaac's mom. If she's anything like mine was, she'll never stop worrying about her child. "Anyway, just know it's all sorted out and in a weird way, we sort of have his blessing now. Although he and Brian both may have threatened to kick your butt if you ever hurt me."

"Anderson, too?" I need to have a little talk to these ass wipes.

Joie giggles at I what I assume is an agitated look I'm sporting. "Relax. I think it's sweet they plan to fight for my honor if you don't."

I give her a look that makes her giggle again. Yes, she has a point, but I'll never admit to it. They've become far too comfortable with talking shit in front of my girlfriend. I may have to add some drills, where they play the role of the tackle dummy. We were going to do it anyway, but they don't have to know that. Might as use the extra conditioning to my benefit.

"What time are you done tonight?" I ask when we finally reach the front of the science building.

"Um, my last class ends at three, so I'll probably leave around six after I study for a bit. Why?"

I cock one eyebrow at her. "Are you expecting Stevens at home tonight?"

She smirks back at me, knowing what I'm getting at. "Even if I was, he doesn't plan on barging into my bedroom again. Ever."

"Does that mean you're up for company?"

"Always," she says and turns away to walk up the stairs.

I know she's about to be late, but I can't help myself when I yell, "Hey Joie?" She turns to look at me, one knee bent having stopped mid climb. It makes her hip pop out and her ass look amazing. "When you see Anderson today, don't ask him about his lip, okay?"

"Brian?" she asks quizzically. "What happened to his lip?"

"Trust me." I raise my hands up in front of me as I walk backward. "You don't want to know."

"That wasn't nice, Jack Pride," she calls after me. "Now I want to know."

I wave over my shoulder and chuckle to myself. Now I'm off the hook from having to tell her about Stevens's meltdown, and Anderson is on it. Serves that little punk right. But he's still doing the drills.

Accelerating my pace, I head to the administration building. My appointment is in five minutes, and I don't want to be late. Even though I wouldn't mind not going at all.

When I got the call from Human Resources about thirty minutes ago, I was shocked, to say the least. But the more I thought about it, the more I realized I should have seen this coming. I'm dating a student. Not only that, I'm dating the mother of a scholarship recipient. As innocent as it is, I'm sure there are red flags all over this situation. I'm less surprised by the need to call me in, and more surprised that it took this long.

Taking the stairs two at a time to the second floor, I reach Patty Strause's door right on time. Before I can knock, she calls for me to come in.

Patty has been a fixture of Flinton State University for as long as anyone can remember. She's well past retirement age, but swears she's going to outlast us all. With her sharp-as-a-tack hearing and quick wit, I don't doubt it. But her ability to keep up with all the changing human resource laws is what has me running scared right about now, too. If I've done something wrong, she'll know and there won't be any way to talk myself out of it if she thinks it puts the university at risk in any way.

"Have a seat." She gestures to the red chair in front of her desk. Briefly, I wish Hank would splurge for some fancy chairs like this. But then I remember how sweaty we get on a daily basis and realize a cloth chair, no matter how comfortable, would eventually smell like funk. We have enough of that already.

Turning from her computer, she faces me, placing a small recording device on the desk. This does not look good for me at all.

"Thanks for coming in on such short notice. I want to get this over and done with so we can all move on."

My heart rate ratchets up a notch. "Move on? Why are we moving on?"

She waves me off like I'm being ridiculous. "It's a figure of speech. You can relax."

I take a deep breath and sit back in the chair. "Okay. So why am I here?"

She leans her arms on the desk, hands clasped in front of her. "Because it's come to my attention that you're dating a student. And now I get to investigate."

"Shit," I mumble as I rub my eyes with the heels of my hands. "Randy Whitman called?"

She bobbles her head side to side. "As well as a few other rumblings I've been hearing lately."

"I was afraid you were going to say that."

"So you knew it was a violation of university policy when you began dating her?"

"Yes. No. I don't really know." I shake my head to try and clear myself of the confusion and sudden fear I have that I'm going to have to choose between my job and my girlfriend. Neither is one I want to give up for the other. "I assumed that policy was more about professors dating students or coaches dating players."

She stares at me for a few seconds, like she's trying to make a decision. Then she speaks. "Between you and me, and completely off the record, I agree with you."

I feel my eyes widen as she waves me off again, clearly not impressed by my reaction.

"That policy was put in place years ago and was for the exact intensions you mentioned. We didn't want anyone to be able to use their position of authority to manipulate the young adults they were in charge of. In contrast, we didn't want the young adults to be able to ruin the reputation of the people in charge of them. It was a quick and easy solution."

"Wait, you were here when that policy went into place?"

She looks at me like I'm not the brightest bulb. "Of course I was. It was my idea. Preventative measures if you will. But back then, colleges were run more like high schools.

Coaches did double duty and taught in the classroom. Things have come a long way, and clearly, not all our policies have kept up."

"So then why am I here?"

She gives me a look that reminds me of the cat that ate the canary. "Because you found a loophole. I like it when people find loopholes. It means I get to fill them. So we're going to clear the air before anyone even cries foul."

"You mean Whitman wasn't pissed?"

"Angry? No." She grabs a piece of paper off the printer and places it in front of her. "Curious about what it could mean for the program? Yes."

I don't really know what she's getting at, but at this point, I don't have to. I just have to go along with whatever she's talking about and pray my job and my relationship come out of this fully intact. I watch as she reaches over and presses the record button on the small tape player. Once it's rolling, she begins the inquisition.

"I'm speaking with Jack Pride, Assistant Football Coach for the Flinton State University Vikings. Jack, can you please verify that the information I have just provided is correct."

I furrow my eyebrows for a second but then shrug. This isn't my rodeo, so I'll just have to go along with it. "Yes. That is correct."

"And you are currently dating Joie Stevens, a student at Flinton State University. Is that correct?"

"That's correct. However," I add, "I think it's worth noting, she's not a regular student." I expect Patty to be angry about the addition to my answer. Instead, she nods, like she's encouraging me to continue. "She's a forty-two-year-old non-traditional student, who I have no authority over whatsoever."

Patty smiles conspiratorially at me and continues, "Jack, when you began dating Ms. Stevens, were you aware of university policy that prohibits faculty from dating students." I look up her and see her nodding her head at me, like she's encouraging me to agree with her statement. So I take a chance.

"Yes."

A thumb's up is flashed my direction. Now I'm thoroughly confused, but I trust her.

"When you began dating, did you think it was a direct violation of the aforementioned policy?" She shakes her head at me. Now I know she's guiding me through this, and I feel myself relax into the questioning.

"No," I say. "Because I do not, and will not, ever have any authority over her. I did not believe it would be in violation of that policy."

Another thumbs up my direction.

"When did you first meet Joie Stevens?"

I chuckle, eliciting a frown from Patty, which immediately dries up any laughter. Patty can be scary if she wants to be.

"I believe it was the first day of class."

I stop, expecting another question, but Patty moves her finger in a circle, telling me to continue.

"I was on my way to speak to the advisor of one of our players who isn't doing so hot academically. I was looking at my phone and I ran into her."

"Like ran over her?"

"Yep." I chuckle at the memory. "Her bag flew open and spilled everything everywhere. So I helped her gather her things and gave her directions to her next class. Didn't see her again for another week."

"What happened the next week?"

I clear my throat and rub my neck. "I'm almost ashamed to admit, I ran into her a second time."

For the first time since I've met her, Patty looks somewhat stunned by my admission. "You...you ran into her *again*?"

"Yeah. It wasn't my finest moment."

Patty shakes her head, trying to refocus, and looks at her notes. I assume it's a list of questions to make sure she doesn't forget anything. Even though we both know she won't. "Let's go back to the first time you, well, ran into her. At that time, did you know her son, Isaac, was a scholarship recipient on your football team?"

My automatic reaction is to grimace, but Patty waves it off, the look on her face indicating I need to stop thinking so hard and just answer the damn question. She really uses her hands a lot when she talks. Or when she's not talking, as is the case right now.

"No. I had no idea."

"And when did you find out?"

"The night of the booster's fundraising gala."

"And tell me how you found out."

I close my eyes tight, hating the memory, but realizing that whole debacle might be my saving grace in this situation.

"I put two and two together when she showed up as her son's date." Patty leans her head toward me so I'll continue. "And then I, uh...I accused her of being a stalker, and she sort of put me in my place."

Patty's jaw drops open, just for a split second. I know she's silently judging me for that whole situation. Truthfully, I still judge myself for it.

"I'm actually quite ashamed of the whole thing," I continue, looking at Patty and recognizing the look of victory on her face. My clusterfuck is what makes this whole situation seem less shady, which works to our advantage. "At first, I was upset she hadn't told me, but we worked it out. It was basically a miscommunication."

Patty reaches over and pauses the tape recorder. "You really accused her of being a stalker?"

This time, she doesn't react when I chuckle. "Remember when that crazy woman used to show up in the stadium screaming at Matthews about how much she loved him and she'd never let him go."

"I couldn't forget that if I tried." I believe her. Patty had to be directly involved in that mess, which ended up in a lot of paperwork and stress for everyone involved.

"Hank and I had been talking about it right before I ran into Joie at the gala."

"Ran into her…?"

"Yeah," I admit. "Ran into her a third time."

Patty shakes her head at me. "You need to start paying better attention. I would expect a football coach to be fancier on his feet than the next guy."

"Hey, I never let her fall down," I defend. "I always caught her."

Patty quirks an eyebrow at me. "Enough chit chat. Let's get this done." Turning the tape recorder back on, she begins her line of questioning again. "You can understand why it's hard for anyone to believe you didn't know she was the mother of one of your players for that long."

This is the question that has plagued me for months. And Hank. And my sister. And pretty much anyone who knows the story. How did I not know? All the puzzle pieces were right there in front of me, and I never put it together. So I give her the only answer I've been able to come up with.

"It just didn't click." Patty cocks her head in my direction as if saying *Ya think*? "I'm responsible for coaching seventy-five players a year for the last decade. I don't talk to Isaac Stevens every day. I talk to him when I'm working with the offensive line. And I don't call any of them by their first names. It gets too confusing when we have a dozen Jasons and Ryans. And never once in the entire time I've coached college football have I ever met a student who doubles as a football mom. Ever. So my mind didn't go there."

Patty nods slowly like my explanation has some merit.

"Plus, I may have taken one too many hits to the head way back when I wore a helmet."

The scolding look she shoots me has me regretting my lame attempt at a joke. Clearing my throat of my sudden discomfort, I wait for her next question.

"Has your relationship with Joie Stevens influenced your on-field relationship with her son in any way?"

I open my mouth, then close it. I'm not sure how to answer. Finally I pull myself together. "Yes and no." Patty raises another eyebrow at me. At this point, I'm pretty sure that's her answer for just about anything during this inquisition. "Yes, in that I know on a more personal level when something is bothering him, so I have been able to remind him to get his head in the game. But no, in that I've threatened to bench him several times in the last couple of months if he doesn't get his ass in gear so he doesn't hurt himself."

Patty nods, seemingly pleased at my answer. We continue with the questioning for another fifteen minutes or so, her nodding when she feels confident in my answers, and shaking her head if she needs me to downplay something. It's clear she's guiding me to give her the right answers, but I don't care. If it allows me to keep the two most important things in my life, I'll do whatever it takes.

Finally, the tape recorder is turned off and Patty sits back in her chair. "There. That wasn't so hard, was it?"

I cock my head and purse my lips. "I was just asked to prove I haven't taken advantage of a poor single mom whose son is in my program. Hard? No. Brutal? Maybe."

Patty smiles at me. "After everything you've told me, I have a hard time believing Joie Stevens could ever be taken advantage of."

She's got me there. "Yeah. She's pretty great. She put her whole life on hold to raise her son, so it's kind of fun seeing her go for her own dreams now, ya know?"

Patty just stares at me, lost in her own thoughts. It's a little disconcerting. She's such a bulldog in the boardroom, and she's my mother's age, so she demands respect. But having her just stare…what do I do in a situation like this? I'm not sure so I wait it out until she finally speaks. "I've always liked you, Jack."

"Thank you," I say with way more confidence than I feel. I have no idea where she's going with this.

"And I always liked Sheila."

Ah. Now I see. I think. Really this conversation could go any which way, but I understand better how she got lost in her thoughts. Besides Hank, Patty was the only other person who I worked closely with to make sure all our needs were covered during my sabbatical before Sheila died. That whole time frame is such a blur, I forgot she was an integral part in making sure we had everything we needed, financially and with our medical insurance. In hindsight, she went above and beyond what most HR departments would do in that situation.

I don't speak, just let Patty get out whatever she needs to say.

"But I've always hoped that you would find someone special again," she says gently. It's a stark contrast from the blunt way she normally speaks. "This Joie Stevens must be a really amazing woman to have captured your attention."

I can't help but nod my agreement. "She is. She really is. She's so different from Sheila, and yet, in the ways that are important, she's so much the same. Did you know she wants to work with the boosters to re-implement a Thanksgiving dinner for our athletes that are stuck here over the holidays."

Patty flashes a huge smile, bigger than I think I've ever seen on her face before, clearly pleased with this news. "Just make sure she goes by the books. Just in case someone gets their panties in a twist."

"I will. I've already hooked her up with Renee to make sure it's done right."

"Good man," she says, and I watch as casual acquaintance Patty turns back into Human Resources Director Patty. "Well. Thank you for stopping by and answering all my questions. I feel better knowing we're being pro-active."

Recognizing my cue to leave, I stand up out of the most comfortable chair I'll probably sit in for a while. "Thanks, Patty. I really appreciate you helping me out with this."

"It's my job." She turns to face her computer again. I've officially been dismissed.

Before I reach the door, however, she speaks.

"Hey, Jack." I turn to face her. "I'm really glad you found her. Don't screw it up again."

I bark a laugh because, no, I did not see that one coming. I salute her and walk out the door, closing it quietly behind me. I feel strangely victorious. Not only do I get to keep my girl-friend, I get to keep my job. I can't ask for much more than that.

CHAPTER THIRTEEN

Joie

As far as houses in Texas go, this one isn't that big. But as far as houses in *Flinton, Texas* go, I'm sitting inside of what many would consider the equivalent of a mansion. In a gated community on the edge of town, and at roughly four thousand square feet, the red brick veneer boasts sharp angles and points. The circle driveway contributes to giving it the feel of a small castle, as do the wide, concrete steps you have to climb to get to the front door.

The inside features a beautiful foyer, complete with a curved staircase and a chandelier. Beyond that, it's all open concept, with a formal living room, as well as a den off the giant, eat-in kitchen, where I'm currently enjoying coffee with Renee, Hank's wife. Family pictures pepper the walls and football memorabilia take up most of the shelf space. A blanket is heaped on the couch, like someone was taking a nap in front of the TV and didn't bother to fold and put it away. A few dirty dishes sit on one side of the sink, waiting for someone to have time to wash them.

Despite its size and amenities, nothing in the house seems pretentious. Not even Renee, who is sporting yoga pants and a messy bun.

The only thing I can't figure out is where the ground-level window I saw on the outside leads to. Is there a crawl space underneath the first floor? A basement? Really, it's completely irrelevant, but my mind still won't let it go.

Focusing on the layout of the space we're in, I do what all good guests should do...I compliment my hostess. "Your home is beautiful."

"Thank you," Renee replies kindly and holds up the cream and sugar in question. I nod and she plunks them down in front of me to serve myself. A giant steaming coffee mug has already been provided. "Originally I thought it was too big, especially since I'm the one that gets to clean it. But it's definitely comes in handy for entertaining, and with Hank's job, I feel like we're always entertaining."

Hoping she doesn't feel like I forced my way into her private space by asking to meet, I admonish, "Renee, we could have met somewhere else. I didn't have to come to your home."

She waves her hand in dismissal as she plops down in the chair next to mine. "Oh Joie, meeting here is totally fine. As long as you don't judge me on the dishes in the sink," she says with a laugh. "This is me in my normal, homebody state."

I relax into my seat, more comfortable knowing I'm not imposing. "You don't seem like a homebody. You seem very outgoing."

"I am. But years of having to be the center of attention by default in our social circle makes me enjoy my private time even more."

"By default?"

"Hank is always the star," she explains, no malice or resentment in her voice, just matter of fact. "Our entire life revolves around Vikings football, and Flinton is a small town. Outside of church, we don't do much else. There's not time. And even then, the Sunday after a winning game, you can bet the preacher is going to mention it from the pulpit. And the Sunday after a losing game, it's all pats on the back and 'Better luck next time.'" She shakes her head quickly like she's shaking off the memories. "There's not a lot of places to go and get away from having to shake hands and kiss babies. This is my sanctuary."

"Well, it's a lovely place to call home," I reply. "But can I ask a random question? I noticed the ground level windows outside, but I can't figure out what rooms they go to and it's driving my poor brain crazy. Do you have a basement?"

"Mmm." She responds with a nod as she swallows her sip of coffee. "It's more like a half basement because about a third of it is above ground. But yeah, when we built, we specifically asked to add it on."

"I was wondering about that. You don't see many around here."

"There really isn't a need for them," she laughs. "We're not in tornado alley or anything. But with three boys, three football players at that, Hank thought we would need the extra room as a kid's area. Oh boy did we fight about that. I thought it was a waste of money, but Hank dug in his heels. Now I'm glad he did. Do you know how loud it gets when all my kids and grandkids are here?"

I laugh and shake my head because I really don't understand. "It was only Isaac and me until he left for college, so the noise level at my house has always been pretty low."

"It gets so loud it's almost deafening." It's clear by the look on her face that, despite her complaints, she loves the chaos a big family brings. "It's really nice to have the downstairs playroom for all the kids to congregate in over the holidays. They can stay down there for hours playing pool or video games. Cuts down on at least half the people up here with me at any given time."

"Speaking of holidays…" I segue, knowing her time is valuable and not wanting to overstay my welcome.

She sits up and crosses her arms. "Ah, yes. The Thanksgiving dinner. How can I help you with this?"

"Jack said you worked with Sheila on this in the past?" I pull a notebook out of my black bag, along with several different colored pens, placing them next to each other, one right after the other. "I was hoping you could direct me to any of the businesses that donated some of the supplies. Maybe the turkeys or drinks or something."

She reaches over and picks up a couple of my pens. "Oh wow. Think you have enough colors here?"

I bite back a grin. "Yeah, I'm pretty particular about my organization. I'm sure after I take notes here I'll go home and turn them into note cards and spreadsheets that can be laminated and put in a binder."

Renee's eyes go wide. "Laminated?"

"Well, yeah." I shrug. "Isaac is only going to be around for a couple more years. I'm sure it'll be helpful to leave the information for the next person who feeds these kids."

She furrows her brow at me, but I don't quite understand why. Did I say something wrong?

"I guess..." she begins and then stops to think about her words. "I guess I assumed you and Jack were kind of *it* for each other."

I gape at her. "We are...I mean...I don't know if we are ...we, um..." I stumble over my words, unsure how to respond to this change in conversation, or even how to define our relationship. Up until this point, we've just been exclusively dating, but we've never really talked beyond that.

Renee recognizes my unease almost immediately. "I'm sorry. I didn't mean that like it sounded. Let me try that again. I assumed that even after Isaac graduated, this would still be a project you'd like to spearhead."

"Oh." That makes sense. "I guess I didn't realize you would want me to. I thought once the child is gone, the parent isn't needed anymore."

"Nothing could be further from the truth," she argues. "The boosters can always use help getting stuff done. I just assumed you were taking on this role because Jack asked you to."

And therein lies the problem I was afraid would surface. That those who have been around for a while, who have worked with Jack for years, will think I'm trying to take over the life Jack's wife left behind.

The idea hadn't crossed my mind until Isaac's hurtful words a few weeks ago. And even then it was only a niggling in the back of my brain, wondering if he was the only one who thought Jack was using me as a replacement. Funny how one small conversation turns into a giant elephant in the room. I realize I need to nip this potential issue in the bud quickly.

"No, I went to Jack and asked about it. I had heard from another player, a guy in one of my classes, that it had been done in the past, so I thought if I could coordinate it, it could be implemented again. That's all. It wasn't until I asked Jack if it was even allowed that I found out Sheila used to be in charge."

"Oh honey," Renee says quickly, "I don't mean to make it sound like you're taking over something that was Sheila's."

"I just don't want anyone to think I'm...that I'm..." I fumble with what I'm trying to express, but Renee seems to understand immediately.

"That you're stepping right into the life Sheila left behind?"

My shoulders fall and I nod my head.

"For the record," Renee says, "I don't think that at all."

"You don't. But I think this conversation proves some people will."

"So? Yes, Jack and Sheila had an epic love story. Like a relationship you'd see on one of those cheesy movies I love. Part of the reason he loved her so much was because of how well they worked as a team. She was organized, willing to step in if she saw a need she could fill, and really understood how important it was to Jack that his players were taken care of when they were so far away from home." She sits back and crosses her arms. "So the way I see it, it's no wonder the next time Jack found a great love of his life, she would have those same traits. Because that kind of character, that kind of thought process, is important to him. And that's what makes you guys fit."

My lips quirk to the side in appreciation of her words. "You make it sound like he found someone exactly like her."

She shakes her head quickly, adamant that I'm wrong. "Oh no. You are nothing alike. You know how it goes in football. We're one giant family."

I nod because I do know. Even in high school, other football moms become your best friends, merely because you see each other so often and volunteer together so much.

"Sheila and I were really close. She was like a sister to me, so I can confidently say you are nothing alike. First of all, she was tall and blond, so that doesn't match. She was also really, really quiet. Almost to the point of being shy, until she got to know you. She had a law degree and was very matter of fact. Really straight forward. She was wonderful, and I miss her terribly sometimes. Her death was a huge blow to our little tribe. *Huge*. But as far as being alike, with the exception of those traits I already listed"—she shakes her head—"not even close."

Hearing her say it out loud makes me realize how much I actually needed that confirmation. I don't think I ever felt *un*-comfortable with Jack's and my relationship. But knowing without a shadow of a doubt from Sheila's best friend that we're practically polar opposites is kind of comforting.

"Jack told me about the trip they took right before she died."

"Oh!" Renee leans forward, clearly excited. "Isn't that amazing? I was so jealous of that trip. I mean, I know it was because of a terrible situation that I wouldn't wish on anyone, but why can't Hank find a way to take me on an extended vacation overseas somewhere?"

I appreciate her exuberance and how thinking about her friend makes her happy, even if they are sad circumstances. "Maybe you should start pushing for a trip after the season is over."

She snorts a humorless laugh. "I have been pushing for it for years. That man is a bigger homebody than I am! More coffee?"

I nod and we enjoy chatting about the college and what exactly it means to be romantically involved with a football coach. Apparently the words "silver fox" are thrown about freely on university's social media pages whenever the coaches show up in a picture. I'm almost positive it embarrasses Jack, so I make a mental note to look some of the comments up for future conversations.

Then we get down to business, planning a Thanksgiving dinner. Several hours, and multiple phone calls later, my notebook is full of organized information, and our plans are set in motion, neatly displayed in multi-colored ink.

CHAPTER FOURTEEN

Jack

Thanksgiving

It's amazing how small a four-thousand-square-foot house can feel when you cram a few dozen people inside it.

Originally, when Joie brought up the idea of hosting Thanksgiving dinner, she wanted to do it at her house. But then she realized a dinner provided by the boosters meant more than just football players. If I'm counting correctly, this year, it means seven football players, eight basketball players, a couple wrestlers, four or five baseball players, three softball players, three swimmers, and a cheerleader. There may be a couple golfers downstairs on the Xbox. No way that many people would fit inside Joie's tiny bungalow.

Instead, we convinced Hank to provide the location. At first, he wasn't thrilled about adding almost three dozen people to his holiday, especially when he already had a full house. But he agreed it was better than having the kids drive all the way to Joie's house. He was even more convinced when I reminded him it would add an additional buffer between him and his in-laws. Yeah, he picked up the phone and discussed it with Renee immediately once I reminded him of that.

Joie still did all the cooking. Said there was no reason to spend extra money on catering when she could learn everything she needed to know on the Internet. I was skeptical, but boy did she pull it off. Three days ago, her entire kitchen table was covered in color-coordinated binders with highlighted recipes that had been laminated "for easy cleaning" is what she told me. It looked overwhelming to me, but considering the meal we had today, it worked for her.

Renee seemed happy to get in on the hosting duties, as well. With as long as she's played hostess to just about all the football events at Flinton, I figured she'd be pissed about having another party at her house. But she and Joie have been flitting around the kitchen all day, talking and laughing and shooing anyone out who tries to help. Except for Renee's mom. She was recruited for cooking duty when Joie found out she makes an award winning green bean casserole. I wouldn't know if the awards were warranted or not. The athletes ate it all before I got any.

Assholes.

Now that dinner is over and dessert has yet to be served, I'm sitting on the couch in a tryptophan coma. Or it could be exhaustion from staying up all night eating the dessert between Joie's legs. Thank fuck, Stevens decided to crash at a friend's overnight since the dorm kicked out everyone who didn't have special permission to be there for the holidays. With our away game, this is a gonna be a long weekend coming up. I was gonna be with my woman whether he liked it or not.

"Go. Go. GO. GO!" someone chants next to me, deeply engrossed in the game on the TV we're all crowded around. Actually, considering it's a giant projector screen that drops down from the ceiling, we're pretty spread out.

My eyes are glued to the screen. I'm not really that interested in the outcome, but since football is my life, I tend to watch it no matter who is playing. Today, it's the Giants versus the Cowboys, so the loyalties in this room are deeply divided. It's Cowboys' fans against Anyone-but-the-Cowboys' fans. Right now, the Anyone-but-the-Cowboys are in the lead.

As we watch the wide receiver sprint for the end zone, several of the guys stand up, still yelling. The white jersey with a big blue star dodges left, then back right, avoiding several tackles. The kid is quick, but I knew that already. At about twenty-six years old, we played against him several times when he started for A&M. It's not a big surprise he's done as well as he has since he went pro.

I would never tell Joie, because I wouldn't want to get her hopes up, but Stevens has a real shot of being a star in the NFL. I'm hoping a couple of years from now, he'll be a first-round draft pick. He's gotten that good. Hank knows it. I know it. I think Stevens might suspect it. But until it happens, we'll keep our noses to the ground.

"WHOO!"

Speaking of the devil, Stevens jumps off his seat on the couch, throwing his hands in the air when the running back crosses into the end zone, scoring for the Cowboys.

"That's what I'm talking about!" he yells, gloating in Anderson's face, who is clearly on the Anyone-but-the-Cowboys' side of this match up. Anderson shoves him playfully, and they begin wrestling, legs and arms flailing as they roll around.

"Hey!" I bellow. "Knock it off, ladies! You're guests in someone's home, so act like it."

They immediately pull themselves apart, big goofy smiles on their faces as they run fingers through their disheveled hair and straighten their clothes.

Renee takes this exact moment to hand me a huge piece of pumpkin pie with a heap of Cool Whip on top. "Leave them be, Jack. I raised three boys in this house. There's nothing in this room that hasn't been broken before and nothing that can't be fixed."

"That's nice of you, but they know better than to act like little heathens. No reason to break your house." I glare at both boys who conveniently pretend they're engrossed in the game, which is currently in a time out.

"Don't worry," she says with a pat to my shoulder. "If it's anything major, I'll get a reimbursement from the boosters."

"The hell you will," Hank hollers from the other side of the room. "I'm already working with a tight budget for new gear." He turns his heated glare back on the two troublemakers. "You two break anything that needs reimbursement, and I'll have you mucking the porta-potties in the parking lot after the tailgaters leave, you hear me?"

They both grimace and nod their heads with a "Yes, Coach."

"What are they 'yes, coaching'?" Joie plops down next to me, phone in hand.

I turn to her and just take in her essence, wishing I could lean over and kiss her. If it was just us at Hank's house, I'd do it. Hell, I'd even do it in front of Stevens, just to show him I could. But neither of us feels comfortable with much PDA in front of these kids. Yes, they're young adults, but we're old enough that they're still kids to us.

"Nothing. Just boys being boys." I shift over, making room for her and putting my arm on the couch above her. My arm isn't exactly around her, but it's clear I'm staking my claim. Glancing up, I see Stevens watching. I can't tell if he's upset or trying to get used to it. Either way, he has lots of time to wrap his brain around it because I'm not going anywhere.

"So what are you doing the first weekend in April?"

I furrow my brows at her. "Uh…probably in the middle of recruiting, but nothing's been scheduled yet. Why?"

She holds her phone up in front of her. "I just got off the phone with my brother Greg. He's getting married, and I was hoping you'd go to the wedding with me."

"Uncle Greg's getting married?" Stevens interrupts.

"Yep." Joie is beaming. Apparently she likes whoever he's marrying. "Remember Elena?"

"The lady he lives next door to?"

She nods. "That's the one. They're finally making it official."

Stevens turns back to the game, shaking his head. "I hope she's not as psycho as his first wife. That bitch be crazy."

"Isaac!" Joie admonishes while Hank and I snicker. "Anyway, I know it's still far out, but I thought I'd ask you early, so you can make plans or whatever."

I lean into her so I can look directly into her eyes. "I'd love to go. I'll have to get the exact dates on the calendar."

She smiles at me, clearly relieved that I plan on being around then, just as Stevens yells, "Thanks for the invite, Mom. Looks like you've replaced me as your plus one."

Before either of us can respond, Anderson jumps in. "Aw. Did your girly thong ride up your butt too high? Your mom has a boyfriend now. I'm sure Uncle Greg will let you come as her plus two," he chides.

"You did not say my mom has a boyfriend," Stevens jokes back and quickly grabs Anderson in a headlock, making them roll around on the floor again. "Say uncle!" Stevens yells.

"I already did! I said Uncle Greg was going to invite you," Anderson yells back as he punches Stevens in the ribs. His angle is off, so no one is getting hurt. "I'll be your plus one if you're so hard up for a date you need to go with your mommy."

"Knock it off," I yell. This time, though, they ignore me. Hank finally steps in, using his head coach voice.

"That's it! I want three laps around my house. All of you," he points around the room. "Even you wrestle people. I know you're used to running in leotards and shit, but make it quick or you'll miss the first play after the commercials. Go, go, go!" he yells and not surprisingly, everyone obeys. They do it with groans and complaints, but they start running.

I chuckle when I think about what his neighbors must think, seeing a bunch of college students running around the property.

As soon as the door closes, I take advantage of the alone time and lean down for a kiss. Joie immediately wraps her arms around my neck, like she's just as desperate to make out as I am. After several seconds of tangling my tongue with hers, I pull away. "I've been wanting to do that all day."

"Me, too." Her eyes are bright, and she's breathing heavily. "But I think we should stop."

"Why? They won't be back for a few minutes."

She's still staring at my lips like she's trying to resist temptation. "Because it's reminding me of that thing you did with your tongue last night, and those aren't really appropriate thoughts to be having at this particular time."

I chuckle and kiss her lightly. "I love your humor, you know that?"

She blinks rapidly a few times. "You...you do?"

I nod and smile shyly. She knows where this is going and so do I. "I do. Your humor. Your energy. Your ability to talk to anyone no matter what the situation. The fact that you're going for your goals and dreams and nothing is going to stop you. Not even an old meathead."

"You're not old," she whispers as she lightly runs her fingers down my cheeks.

"I'm old enough to know what I want," I respond. "And I want you. I love you, Joie," I whisper back to her. "So, so much."

She closes her eyes and swallows hard. When she opens them and looks up at me, tears are glistening. "I love you so much, too."

Unable to resist anymore, she reaches up and presses her lips to mine. We're so caught up in the moment, we don't hear the door fly open until the sounds of catcalls and whistles surround us.

"Ugh! Do you guys really have to do that?" Stevens complains, and Joie buries her face in her hands to hide her embarrassment. "That's my *mother* you're kissing."

I open my mouth to lob a one-liner his direction, maybe something about being respectful or he can do some more laps, but close it when he winks my direction, a smile on his face.

Looks like he's finally gotten over his aversion to me dating his mother. It's a good thing, too. Otherwise, it'll be a long ass holiday season.

PRIDE
&
JOIE

FINALE

CHAPTER ONE

Joie

"Joooooooooooie!" my brother's voice bellows from across the house. "Where is your Mary Poppins bag?"

Jack, my boyfriend, snickers behind me. I told him my propensity for giant purses that have the same function as a kitchen's junk drawer is a well-known and much chided fact in my family, especially with my brother. Greg is three and a half years younger than I am and is as annoying as little brothers come. At least he used to be. He grew up into a nice adult, but he still pokes fun at me because of my bags.

Greg comes racing through the doorway of the guest room, breathing heavily. "Please tell me you have the giant monstrosity with you and somewhere inside it is a safety pin."

Rolling the biggest bag I own to the middle of the floor, I begin opening compartments. "You think I would come to your wedding without my baby? Someone has to be prepared around here, and obviously it's not you."

Jack snickers again, staring at himself in the floor-length mirror as he situates his tie. Jack Pride and I began dating several months ago after meeting at Flinton State University. He was the assistant coach for the football team, and I was a returning, non-traditional student when we ran into each other. And I do mean *ran* into each other. Like, barrel-me-over, drop-everything-on-the-ground, butt-bruised-for-days, ran into each other.

It wasn't love at first sight, but neither of us really believes in that junk. Instead, we've been building a solid relationship. I love him, which is a nice surprise since it's something I had given up finding long ago. And he loves me, which is something he never thought he'd find again after his wife lost her battle with cancer. Now, here we are on my baby brother's wedding day, and they're making fun of my strong organizational skills.

They all think they're a bunch of funny guys.

At the sight of my black, fold-up rolling case, chock-full of all of life's necessities, Greg visibly relaxes. "I never thought I'd be so grateful for your magical abilities to stuff a suitcase so full of crap, but today, I really am."

"Hey!" I exclaim as I find my box of pins. "How dare you call this a suitcase! This is a ZÜCA pro-travel with an alloy aluminum frame, five zippered pouches, including four that pull out like drawers, and is designed to double as a chair for anyone up to three hundred pounds." I spin around and smirk at him as I open a tiny container in his face.

One of Greg's eyebrows raises ever so slightly. "Working really hard to break that old English nanny image that you hate so much, aren't you?"

I slap him playfully on the arm and Jack belly laughs behind me. I vaguely hear him mutter "nailed it," but ignore him in favor of more important things.

Greg hands me his boutonniere to attach to his lapel and takes another deep breath.

"Wow. I've never seen you nervous like this. Not even when you married Libby."

"I'm not sure I cared so much when I married Libby."

Briefly, my eyes flicker up to his and then back down, as I try not to push too hard through the material and poke him. Libby, his ex-wife, was nothing but trouble. Still is. From the beginning, I didn't like her. Thought she was just looking for someone to take care of her so she didn't have to work, which still seems true. That part I could deal with, as irritating as it was. What I couldn't deal with, or I should rephrase...what I was forced to bite my tongue about was how she treated Greg. She was never kind to him unless she wanted something. She was constantly putting him down and emasculating him in front of people. Using him as a target for her nastiness. They weren't married for long, but over the years it wore him down. I hated it.

When he finally pulled his head out of his ass and let their marriage dissolve, I cheered. Not in front of him, of course. But I'm sure Isaac has stories of the big ole smile on my face when I got the call that the divorce was finalized. Since then, Libby still tries to use Greg's daughter, my niece Peyton, to get her way. Ever since he started dating Elena, though, his backbone has grown back.

I'd like to give Elena all the credit for the confidence I see in Greg again, but I don't think it's just her. I think when you have two people who love each other so much that their focus is always on making the other one happy, they can't help but both be built up. It makes the romantic side of me swoon. Even if it is my brother.

"For what it's worth," I say quietly, "I think this one is forever."

Greg flashes me a lopsided grin. "I *know* this one is forever. But I also know we have five kids in this wedding who are remarkably well-behaved right now. That means at any moment, all hell is going to break loose."

I giggle because he's right. Between Peyton, Elena's three girls, and her friend Callie's son, Christopher, they'll be lucky if everyone makes it down the aisle. "There." I pat his lapel. "All finished."

He exhales another deep breath and kisses me on the cheek. "Thanks, sis. I'm gonna see if we're ready to get started before Libby gets a stick up her ass and shows up raising holy hell."

"Is she still drinking all the time?" I ask with a roll of my eyes. It's really hard to remember she gave birth to my sweet niece sometimes.

"Now more than ever." My jaw clenches at the thought of her being drunk around Peyton. The only reason I'm maintaining this much control is because Peyton is currently safe and sound next door with my mother, and because when she's not here, they live with Libby's mother, who seems to do a nice job with her granddaughter, even if she lets her daughter get away with whatever she wants.

Greg struts toward the door, pulling his phone out of his pocket. I assume he's texting his bride-to-be to see if it's go time. "Don't worry. Full custody is next on the family to-do list."

"What?" I screech, his only response is laughter coming from down the hallway.

I pivot towards Jack and know I look insane. Obviously, the bomb Greg just dropped temporarily paralyzed my eyes and jaw because I can't seem to close either. "Did you hear what he just said?"

"I did." Jack wraps his arms around me and kisses me on the temple.

"He's finally going to fight her for custody." I'm stunned by his admission and giddy with delight.

"I know."

Wrapping my arms around Jack, I nestle into his chest and get comfortable. I didn't mind being single for as long as I was. I was busy raising my son and working full time during those eighteen years. But when we stand like this, I remember my favorite part of being in a relationship. I love the physical touch. Not the sex. Although I like that, too. I just like the intimacy of holding onto Jack and breathing him in. Of feeling like we're more solid together. Like we're a team, and we protect each other. I had no idea I missed it until Jack showed up in my life. Now, I only hope I never lose it. I have a bad feeling it would be like losing my left limb if he was gone.

"Can you guys *not* do that in here? I have to sleep on that bed tonight." Pulling back, I shoot my son Isaac a mom-glare. He ignores me and stands in the doorway. "Uncle Greg says it's time to get a move on. Something about nap time after a sugar crash."

Over the months, the tension between the two most important men in my life has dissolved a bit. Somehow, someway, Isaac and Jack have fallen into two separate roles. When they're at the house, they interact like acquaintances—they're polite, talk about sports, and don't get in each other's way. Jack doesn't push Isaac to be friends. And Isaac doesn't try to one-up Jack. When they're on the field, they slip right back into coach/player mode. Jack is in charge and Isaac does what he's told. It's a balancing act, but they make it work because they both love me.

"No more couch for you tonight?" Jack asks my son as we pull apart, the three of us heading through the house and out the back door.

"Nope. Since Greg and Elena are going to a hotel tonight, I get the guest bed." Isaac stretches his arms out like his back hurts. "I'm glad, too. I'm too big for that tiny little couch. I slept like shit last night."

"Watch your mouth," I reprimand. "You know I don't like hearing that language."

When I hear Jack chuckle, I don't have to look over to know Isaac is rolling his eyes at me. Mostly because Jack cusses like a sailor, but I never reprimand him. Maybe someday I'll lay off Isaac, too. But not anytime soon.

My men hold the door open for me, and we step out into a beautiful scene of white folding chairs, the nice wooden kind, white lace, and white flowers strung from tree to tree. There's a white archway covered in the same floral arrangements in the corner of Elena's yard. Because Greg and Elena live next door to each other, they removed the privacy fence in between to open up the space. It works. Greg's side is ready for the reception. Elena's is ready for the ceremony. And the groom, well…

he looks equally nervous and excited as he chats up Elena's mom.

We make our way to the chairs, sitting on the second row —me between the men I love most in the world. There aren't many people here. My parents, Elena's parents, a few people from each other's jobs. It's small but intimate. Only the people who love them the most are here to share in the celebration. Only the people who know how hard the road was until they found each other. It's hard to describe how happy I am for my brother. He deserves this. He deserves Elena.

"You ever thought about getting married again?"

Jack's question surprises me, but doesn't freak me out. I can tell by the look on his face he's not proposing, just making normal wedding conversation.

"I don't know," I answer honestly. "I guess I never thought I'd be in a position where I'd want to, so I haven't put much thought into it. What about you?"

"Same thing, I think. I always assumed I'd only get married once. Never really thought I'd meet someone I wanted to spend my life with again."

Isaac leans across me. "If this is your way of proposing to my mother, you're doing a terrible job. Even Peter the water boy has more game than that."

Jack shoots him a look while I giggle. "I wasn't proposing, Stevens. I was making conversation. You just sit over there and look pretty."

Isaac opens his mouth, no doubt with some form of witty comeback, when music begins piping through the outdoor stereo system.

It's time.

As everyone takes their seats, Jack grabs my hand, recognizing before I do how emotional I feel. My baby brother, who I have loved since he was a tiny, bald baby, is getting married to a woman I feel privileged to know. Just as my eyes begin to water, Isaac hands me a tissue.

Greg takes his place at the front with Dave from the gym, his lone best man. A few seconds go by and finally the back door to Elena's house opens, her friend Callie marching down the aisle first.

Callie's wearing a lovely teal dress which complements her skin tone. She's carrying more of those beautiful white flowers, a huge smile on her face. When she gets to the front of the aisle, she takes her place on the opposite side of my brother and eyes the door she just came out of. It's odd. And it makes me wonder what's going on. I'm curious enough that my eyes keep darting back and forth between her and the door, but no one comes out. Finally, my beautiful niece and Elena's daughter Max come out holding hands. Each of them is carrying a basket of flowers, but at three and four years old, they're not interested in dropping petals as much as they are at staying together.

Once they make it halfway down, Elena's two older girls follow, wearing the same beautiful white dresses their sisters have on. As I watch the older two sprinkle the aisle with flowers, it occurs to me, I now have *four* nieces. The thought brings a giant smile to my face.

The girls all take their places at the front and once again we wait.

And wait.

And wait.

Finally, we hear a high-pitched shriek, and Christopher comes running out of the house like his pants are on fire. He races down the aisle, throws the pillow with the rings right at Greg's head, and runs past everyone to the playscape.

Callie, who seems to have anticipated this move, is just a few steps behind yelling, "Christopher, you get over here right now! We talked about this. You get no cake if you climb up there, do you understand me?"

But it's too late. He shimmies his way to the top. Not to the top of the slide. Oh no. To the very top of the roof of the little fort where no one can reach him without a ladder.

I swivel my head and catch Greg's eye. He's just laughing and shaking his head, completely unconcerned that his ring bearer has just gone AWOL. As I watch, he reaches in his pocket and pulls out the rings that should have been on the pillow.

Elena wasn't kidding when she said Greg is a child whisperer. Apparently he's good with anticipating their every move, too. I should have known better.

"Please tell me you don't want any more children," Jack whispers into my ear. "I'm too old to handle this kind of shit."

I laugh quietly into my hand and shake my head. "No way. This shop is closed, buddy."

"Thank Christ," he mumbles, making me laugh even harder.

Before he can say another word, the music changes again, and we all rise as my soon-to-be sister-in-law steps out of the house.

Elena is gorgeous in a short, A-line sundress. It's white, of course, with an intricate lace overlay. She's wearing teal shoes, the same color as Callie's dress, and she's carrying an identical flower bouquet. Her long, dirty blond hair is half up-half down, boasting big, soft curls. But what makes her the most stunning is her smile.

Well, that and her legs. If that's what spin class does for everyone's calves, I may need to reconsider my stance on regular exercise.

She can't take her eyes off my brother as she walks toward him, which of course makes my eyes water. Jack squeezes my hand tightly when I sniffle, understanding why I'm so emotional. He has a younger sister who has been through rough times. He gets how happy I am that my brother has finally found his happiness. Greg can finally blossom into a good man with a good woman by his side.

As the ceremony goes on and Greg and Elena vow themselves to each other for as long as they both shall live, one stray tear makes its way down my cheek.

Greg and Elena make me believe in true love again. And when it's right, it's a very beautiful thing.

CHAPTER TWO

Jack

A s Joie stumbles into our room, I grab her by the arm to steady her.

"You okay, there, babe?" I ask as I right her. "I didn't realize you drank so much."

Holding on to me for balance, she says, "I didn't. My feet are killing me." Sure enough, she doesn't wait until the door closes before taking off her shoes and tossing them aside. "I've gotten soft from wearing flip flops to class every day."

"Wearing five-inch spikes on your heels don't help your comfort any, I'm sure."

"Don't make fun of my heels. They're the only way I can feel anything other than short next to you." She smiles at me while she reaches for the zipper on the back of her dress. "Besides, it was kind of nice not having to reach all the way up on my tiptoes when I wanted to kiss you."

Spinning her around, I attack her zipper to help her out of her clothes. "You don't need to go through that much effort anyway. If you ever want a kiss, all you have to do is ask. I'll lean over for you."

Her dress practically floats to the floor, landing at her feet in a puff of dark blue chiffon, leaving her in just her bra and panties. They're black. And lacy. And giving her a chaste kiss is no longer a priority.

"My eyes are up here, Pride."

My eyes snap up to hers as she smirks. Busted.

"Weddings make me horny."

"They do not," she argues, and she's right. They really don't, but every time she throws her head back and laughs, my mission is accomplished anyway. I love making her happy, and it doesn't take much. A bouquet of purple flowers. A funny meme. A cheesy joke. It all makes her laugh, and her laughter makes me feel like I'm doing my job as her significant other.

I shrug and toss my tie and jacket onto the freshly made bed. "Must be that sexy lingerie you're wearing then. Care to join me in the bath?"

She narrows her eyes at me, putting her hands on her hips. Her pose makes me want to strip the lace right off her body, but I have more important plans. "Are you offering me dirty sex in the bathtub?"

"I was offering you a nice, relaxing bath. But since you mentioned dirty sex, I'm game."

She rolls her eyes, but takes my hand anyway and follows me in the bathroom. For a hotel, the bathroom is good sized. We didn't spring for anything fancy when we booked the reservation. Just some local franchise place. The room is pretty standard, but the bathroom was a surprise for both of us. Double vanity with granite countertops. Separate glass shower with a garden tub. I've never seen a bathroom like this in a hotel before, but I'm not complaining either. I just plan to take advantage of it.

As I set the water to the perfect temperature, Joie uses her fancy shower gel to make giant bubbles. Then we strip down to our birthday suits, and I help her climb in with me. As much as I'd love to sit her on my lap and have her ride me until the waves spill over the side onto the floor, just relaxing is nice, too. It's been a long day for both of us.

We practically melt into each other, Joie running her hands up and down my arms lazily and playing with the bubbles.

"It was a nice wedding," I finally say, kissing her gently behind the ear and nuzzling into her more.

"Mmm," she replies noncommittally.

This right here. This is what I like about being in a relationship. Knowing someone well enough, trusting someone deeply enough, that we can be together without expectations of keeping the other entertained. That we can talk about our day without it making it all dramatics and emotional hoo-ha.

"Elena seems really nice."

Joie sighs. "She's really great. Perfect for Greg. I'm so glad he found her."

"I'm so glad I found you."

She reaches up and cups my cheek, stroking my scruff gently before going back to playing with the bubbles.

"Do you ever feel like you're cheating on Sheila?"

I freeze at the unexpected question. "Because we're together?"

"Yeah." Her shoulders shrug slightly. "I've never been in your situation, so I'm curious. I wanna know about your feeeeelings," she singsongs with a giggle. I pinch her in the rib gently in response, making her squeak.

One thing I've always liked about Joie is she's never seemed intimidated by a ghost. She doesn't mind talking about my late wife. Doesn't seem to mind that a part of me will always love her. She just accepts that part of me. I have tremendous appreciation for her respect of my feelings and that relationship.

Wrapping my arms tightly around her, I respond, "Actually, no."

"Really? I've read about so many people who say they feel guilty about stuff like that."

"I think it's because it wasn't sudden. It wasn't like she fell overboard on a cruise ship and I'm left with all those 'what ifs.' It was a long, long process. I watched her wither away and was there when she died."

Joie stiffens. "I'm sorry. I didn't mean to imply anything …"

"No, no," I reassure her. "I'm not trying to put you in your place. I just think when it's sudden, like a car accident or heart attack or something, it must feel different. Jarring. We had a lot of time to prepare. There wasn't anything left unsaid, and one of the things Sheila told me was to find someone else. Someone who would make me happy." I lean my head back against the tub as a thought occurs to me. "Wow. It almost sounds like she broke up with me."

"No, breaking up would be a choice. She didn't have a choice." Joie intertwines our fingers and kisses my knuckles. "She let you go so you could be happy."

"Yeah. Yeah, that's it. I guess that's why it doesn't feel like cheating. It feels like she gave us her blessing a long time ago."

"Hmm."

I know that kind of response. There's more on her mind. "Okay, spill it," I demand. Here I was thinking she wasn't intimidated by a ghost. Maybe I was wrong.

"But if she hadn't died, or if she came back somehow, would you be able to choose between us?"

It's the question no widower ever wants to answer, because, how can you? "There is no way I can answer that correctly."

"It's not about answering correctly," she says calmly. Okay, maybe my original assessment is still true. "Call it morbid curiosity. Which actually might be the wrong choice of words in this context."

I chuckle. "I don't think it's a valid question. Having to choose between both of you means comparing you against each other, and that's not a fair assessment."

"It's not?"

"Nope. She was the love of the first half of my life. You're the love of the second half. Equally important. Equally loved. Equally as good. But only one of you is here rubbing your slippery, soapy ass all up and down me."

I guide her to shift in my arms until she's straddling me, her core right where I want it.

"What's with all these deep questions anyway?"

She shrugs and begins rubbing herself against me. "Just my mind wandering. It started with the wedding and how they're both on their second marriage and how we'd be on our second marriage if we got married someday…"

I open my mouth to respond but she cuts me off with her finger on my lips.

"...don't say anything. It was only wandering thoughts. But I was thinking about the difference of marrying after a divorce versus after a death. That's it. No big deep emotional crisis happening or anything."

"Good," I say as I begin kissing below her jaw. She lifts her chin to give me better access. "Because I don't ever want you to think I love her more than I love you. I love you different, but the same."

"I know," she breathes, her head falling back further as she grinds down on me. "And I love you way more than I ever loved my ex."

I smile against her soapy, smooth skin then pull back to look in her eyes. She's beautiful like this—a sheen of sweat from the heat of the water, her mascara smudged under her eyes from the steam, the glow of pending sex. I rub my thumbs into her shoulders, watching as her eyes close, and she relaxes even more into my touch.

"Wanna move in with me?"

The question catches her off guard, but not so much that she reacts quickly. It's more like she takes a few seconds for it to register. When it finally does, her eyes look up at me lazily.

"Yeah, I do."

I try not to grin because I feel like there's a "but" coming. "But?" I coax.

"No but." I start to relax until she says, "except..."

"That's the same as a but." She grimaces, which makes me feel bad because I wasn't trying to embarrass her. Wrapping my hand around the back of her neck, I encourage her to continue. "Tell me. What's on your mind?"

"I'm trying really hard not to let this influence my decision…"

"Isaac."

She nods and bites her lip.

For eighteen years there was no husband or father to protect or provide for Joie and her son. The asshole ditched them. Joie's parents were around, but Joie was young enough and too stubborn to admit she needed help. So it was her and Isaac against the world.

In some ways, I think they have a much stronger bond than parents with multiple kids. They act a lot like best friends versus parent/child. Granted, he's a grown man, so laying down the law is long since over. But when we first started dating, it was hard for Joie not to take Isaac's feelings into consideration. For a while, it seemed she was willing to sacrifice our relationship, so he wouldn't be uncomfortable. So much so that I had to put him in his place and remind him of what a selfish bastard he was being.

But Joie powered through the struggle and eventually realized she deserves to be happy, too. Still, her old patterns of insecurity sometimes rear their ugly head, and she has to think through the implications before making a decision. Now is one of those times.

"Baby, look at me." She focuses through her lashes. Damn, she's beautiful. "Be really, really honest with me." She nods and takes a breath. "You're worried he'll be mad and won't approve, right?" She nods again. "But after everything we went through before, don't you think, even if he has concerns at first, he'll eventually get over it?"

She sighs and leans into me, looping her arms around my neck and resting her head on my shoulder. "I know he'll be okay with it. He'll be more than okay. I think maybe I'm more anxious about telling him than about his reaction. Like the anticipation being worse than the outcome."

Rubbing my hands down her naked back, I try to validate her concerns. I don't totally understand them, but that doesn't make them any less real. It's no different than my desire to win football games. She may never understand the gravity of that desire, but she would never disregard it. And for all her independence and strength, the one thing that can bring her to her knees is the worries she has as a mom. I have to respect that.

"Would it help if I asked for his blessing?"

A giggle erupts from her. "What?"

Laughter is good. That means her anxiety is dissipating. "You know, man to man. To make sure he knows my intentions."

She pulls back to look at me. The waves keep dropping so her nipples peek out above the water line before disappearing again. It's very distracting.

"I don't think that's necessary." Her hands come to my cheeks and she scratches my scruff. "But I appreciate it. And I'd love for you to be there so we can tell him together."

I break out into a smile. "So is that a yes?"

"Of course it is. Was there really any question?"

I pull her to me, crushing her lips to mine, no more confirmation needed.

CHAPTER THREE

Joie

Breaking the news to Isaac wasn't as hard as I thought it would be. Yes, his jaw clenched for a few seconds when the words "Jack is moving in with me" registered. And yes, he took a deep breath, probably to calm himself. But then he said, "I'm glad you found someone who makes you happy."

Yep. I was shocked.

As it turns out, the hardest part was deciding where we were going to live.

Jack has lived in Flinton for ten years, so he wanted to stay close to campus. Staying close to campus, though, meant either me moving into his tiny apartment, or us going through the process of selling my house and buying a new one. That meant a bunch of income verifications I would never pass as a full-time student who works only six hours a week.

Granted, the idea of not having a forty-five-minute commute each day is appealing, but coming home to my house is gratifying. It's my little slice of paradise away from the rest of the world. It reminds me of how far I've come from the party-hard teenage girl I once was. Plus, giving up the equity, especially since we have no idea where I'll end up working in a few years, seemed like a poor choice when we discussed our options.

In the end, we made a compromise of sorts. Jack gave up the apartment and decided to move into my home for the next few years. Once I graduate, and we know if I'm going to get a job in San Antonio, Austin, or one of the small towns like Flinton, we'll discuss our living arrangements again.

At least, Jack wants me to believe it's a compromise. I think the deciding factor was his realization that moving to the outskirts of San Antonio opened up a lot of options for hole-in-the-wall restaurants to try. It's been a while since he's found something new and authentic.

Regardless, now my house is being overrun by boxes and bags. So many bags. You'd think it would excite me, but Jack seems to only have two kinds of carryalls—black, carry-on suitcases with wheels and Vikings duffle bags. That's it. It's very disappointing, not to mention non-functional for the modern-day traveler.

Jack laughed when I told him that.

With the exception of a few odds and ends still being brought in, I think we're finally almost done with the moving part. It's taken us most of the day, despite how little he brought with him.

Since my house was already furnished, Jack was able to take most of his stuff to Goodwill. A few pieces here and there came with him, like an old wooden trunk that Sheila had jokingly called her hope chest. It's a beautiful piece of woodwork that looks very rustic and Texas. It's also where Jack stores all their old photo albums and the mementos he had of their life together. No way was I making him get rid of it. It's too important. With a piece of specially-cut glass placed on top, it now sits in our living room and acts as a coffee table. It's like part of Jack's past is here, welcoming him into his future.

Yes, I know that sounds ridiculously cheesy, but there's no other way to explain why it's important for me to have it in our line of sight all the time.

Other than that one beautiful piece and a few odds and ends, all the rest of his furniture is gone.

I look up from the box I'm unloading when the front door bangs open and Hank practically falls into the room, carrying . . .

Oh no.

"What is that doing in my house?" I practically screech. "It's...it's..."

"It's fucking heavy is what it is," Hank exclaims. "Can you grab the cushion? I think it got stuck in the door jamb."

"Oh!" I hustle, realizing he's going to injure himself at any moment if they don't get it inside and put down. Seeing Jack holding up the other end, grimacing, I work as quickly as I can.

A few tugs and twists later, I have the cushion out of the way and the two big bad football coaches come staggering in, trying their hardest to place the recliner gently on the floor.

Pointing my finger at the monstrosity, I try very hard not to sound as appalled as I am. "Uh, what is that?"

Jack either doesn't notice or doesn't care about the look of disdain on my face. He's smiling like it's Christmas morning. "It's my chair."

"Yeah, I got that. Why is it in my living room?"

He looks dumbfounded. "Because it's my chair."

Hank snickers from the other side of the room as he plops down on the couch so he can lean back and close his eyes. "Hasn't even unpacked yet and the honeymoon is already over."

We ignore him as we continue to stare at each other—him with a big, goofy grin and me looking like I smell something bad. Come to think of it, I might be. There's an odor in the room now that wasn't here before. I'm not sure if it's the men or the monstrosity.

"Jack, I know the chair is important to you, but, um, it doesn't really, you know…match the décor of the room."

I'm trying to not sound like a horrible controlling person, but I don't do well when other people get in my space and start moving it around. Which is a terrible thing to say since we're moving in together and, technically, this is *our* space. But it's going to take a bit for me to adjust.

My attempts at being polite are obviously not working, since Jack crosses his arms and widens his stance, blocking my way past him. I'm not sure where he things I'm trying to go, but clearly he's defensive about his recliner. And here I thought men had a weird relationship with their cars.

"Are you saying my chair is not welcome in your home? In *our* home?"

I can tell by the look on his face that he's not really irritated, but I also know he isn't going to back down because he has a point. It's just been so long since I've had to share a space with anyone other than my son, I'm not sure where my hard limits are. I don't think the chair is one of them, but... *wow, is that thing ugly.*

Choosing my words carefully again, I look him in the eye, cross my own arms, and try a different angle. "I'm saying there is an underprivileged person out there who needs it more than you do."

My eyes narrow when he begins laughing at me. I knew he wasn't really irritated, even though I'm headed that way.

"Really, Joie? You're pulling the starving-kids-in-China tactic?"

"I would never do that!"

He quirks an eyebrow at me. "I think you just did."

Huffing, I blow my bangs out of my face and cave. "Fine. I did. Did it work?"

"No."

"Come on, Jack," I plead. "It's just so...so...it's so ugly."

His jaw drops and covers his heart like I've wounded him. "How dare you?! I have had my chair since I was a junior in college..."

"I can tell..."

"It has been with me longer than most of my friends. Longer than my niece and nephew have been alive. It's a part of me."

"Literally?" I ask, crinkling my nose. "Because it kind of smells like BO."

Hank barks a laugh, his eyes still shut so he misses the glare Jack shoots his way. He spins back to me, and I continue with my argument.

"I mean really, Jack. What color is this anyway?"

"It's green."

I scoff. "Hardly. If anything, I might call it puce, and that's being generous."

"I call it diarrhea brown," Hank tosses out.

"You stay out of it," Jack chides before looking back to me. "Come on, Joie. I only brought a few things with me. This chair and my dead wife's hope chest are the only two pieces of furniture I own anymore."

I gape and him and point my finger. "Don't you dare use Sheila as a sympathy card. That's so inappropriate."

"Oh come on. She would have used it against me."

"It's true," Hank pipes up, eyes still closed. "She used to joke about her death all the time. She had a wickedly morbid sense of humor. You know she got me to open my fifty-year-old bottle of Johnny Walker Black, telling me she was gonna die? She was in remission then, and I fell for it."

"See?" Jack says victoriously. "If Sheila wouldn't be offended, you're not allowed to be."

Staring at him, my mind starts spinning. Despite his wildly inappropriate humor, I love this man with all my heart, and I want this to be his home, too. I want him to feel like he belongs here with me. Like he can't wait to come home to me. And darn him for playing on my sympathies, because it works. I hate that Sheila's gone and all that's left of her is in that trunk. As ridiculous as it sounds, the more I've learned about her, the more I know I would have liked her, and I have no intentions of ever disrespecting her. Even if Jack has a morbid sense of humor sometimes.

My face must show everything I'm thinking because he's trying really hard not to smile.

"Please? For me?"

Throwing my hands in the air, I give up with an "Argh! Fine!"

"Thanks, babe!" He leans in for a kiss, but his lips end up on my palm instead when I hold up my hand.

"Wait."

"What?" he asks, looking confused.

"Here we go," Hank mumbles under his breath. This time it's me shooting daggers at him.

Swiveling back to Jack, I give him my idea. "The key to a healthy relationship is knowing when to compromise, right?"

Jack shrugs. "Yeah, I guess."

"I think it should go in the third bedroom."

He gapes. "How am I supposed to use it when I'm watching TV if it's not in the living room?"

"I was thinking about that. I know we were talking about replacing my TV with yours because it's a bit newer. Instead, what if we make that third bedroom into a man-cave, of sorts?"

His eyebrows shoot up at the idea and I know I've got his attention. But I can also see the gears shifting in his brain. "A man cave, huh?"

"Yep. I use it as an office now, but the only thing I really need is the desk and maybe the book shelf. And there's plenty of space to put your memorabilia and stuff up."

He scratches at the scruff on his jaw. "I'd get my chair and the TV and be able to hang up some of my sports stuff?"

"Yep," I say again.

Rubbing the back of his neck, he tosses out his own compromise. "Can I get a mini-fridge for beer?"

"Done." I throw out my hand so we can shake on it. He takes it and flashes me a huge grin.

"We're nailing this living together thing already."

Then he pulls me into his arms and kisses the living daylights out of me, while Hank keeps his eyes closed and pretends not to notice.

CHAPTER FOUR

Jack

Driving fifty miles to and from work isn't my idea of a good time. But over the last few days, I've learned there are a couple of advantages to it.

First, sports radio. Before I get to work now, I've heard all the highlights, which saves me time once I get to the office.

Second, I've scoped out at least three new restaurants Joie and I are going to have to try. One of them specializes in Mongolian food, which I'm not sure is actually authentic, but I could eat the hell out of some spicy Szechuan beef, so it may be worth it.

Last, I have lots of time to talk to my sister. And after months of encouraging her, she's finally decided to move her family down to this neck of the woods.

"So plans are still on track to get you here next month?" I ask, as I maneuver my truck into the private parking lot by the stadium.

"So far, so good," she says with a yawn. That's not good. If she's already tired at ten o'clock in the morning, it usually means she's having a rough go of it with Oli, my nephew. "We're still scheduled to close on the morning of the nineteenth. I may need you to hang out with the kids that morning, so I don't have to keep Oli with me while I'm signing a bunch of legal documents."

"What day is that?"

"A Monday. We'll drive in the day before and stay at a hotel. I hope I can sign all the papers before eleven, so you guys can just hang out at the hotel until I get done. Then we can go straight over and start unpacking."

Climbing out of my car, I slam the door behind me, my skin immediately breaking into a sweat. You'd think late April would have spring-like temperatures, but not in Texas. Here we have four seasons: almost summer, even hotter summer, still summer, and Christmas. I neglected to remind Greer of that bit of trivia when making plans for the move.

"I still can't believe you're driving the U-Haul and towing your car," I say with a chuckle. "You're a Texas woman already, and you haven't even gotten here."

She laughs quietly. "No, I'm just a single mom. Comes with the territory."

"Yeah, I suppose so." The blast of the air conditioning when I walk in the athletic center immediately cools me off and actually makes me a bit chilly. You never know what the inside temperatures are going to be like in these buildings. I swear the maintenance faculty get a kick out of making us guess every day. "I can't wait for you guys to get here. And I think that program is going to be really good for Oli."

Oli, my seventeen-year-old nephew, had some brain damage at birth due to oxygen deprivation, so he's more of a handful than most teenage boys. He has all the hormones, hygiene issues, and physical changes with the brain capacity of an eight-year-old. Plus, his impulse control is basically shot. It's been a long haul for Greer, especially once she got divorced and her ex went to jail. But being closer to me means I can help out more, so Greer can have a break sometimes.

"I'm really excited about that program," she says. "I've already talked to the special ed director, and we're going to get all his paperwork done immediately so he can start this summer."

"You mean like summer school? That kind of sucks."

"Not really. If he takes a summer off, he loses all the social skills he gains over the year. Plus, it gives me consistent time to work, even if it is shortened hours."

"Just be prepared for more fights about taking a shower," I say with a chuckle. "He's gonna come home smelling like cows every day."

"Can't be worse than him smelling like teenage boy."

Taking the short cut through the locker room to my office, the overwhelming odor proves her point. We're not even in season, and these kids still don't wash their lucky socks. "You got me there," I admit. "If he smells anything like this locker room, you have my sincerest apologies."

Greer's laugh comes through the receiver, and I can't help but smile, knowing she's going to be okay. I worry about my baby sister. She's dealt with a lot over the years, and none of it was deserved.

"I don't think it's that bad. But I'm not going to try to prove you wrong any time soon. You can keep that stinky room to yourself."

"Wimp," I mutter, making her laugh again. "Hey listen, I'm at work now so I need to let you go. But you'll call me if you change your mind about me flying up there to drive you down?"

I can practically hear the roll of her eyes. "Yes, Jack. I'll call you."

"Don't make fun. It's my job to take care of you."

"No, it's *my* job to take care of me. It's your job to be supportive. And you do it very well, so quit worrying."

"Yes, ma'am." That's a lie, and we both know it. I'll never stop worrying about her.

After pulling up my schedule and making the few phones calls I need to make, I start going over some tapes from potential recruits. For the most part, we've got next year's lineup all ready to go. We'd be running behind at this point if we didn't. But there's always someone who surprises us last minute, and we don't want to miss out. That one late bloomer could get away if we aren't watching.

I look up when I hear a knock at my door.

"Stevens? What are you doing here?"

"I was hoping I could talk to you for a minute...Jack."

Immediately I'm on guard. Stevens has never called me by my first name unless we're at Joie's house. "I take it I need to change out my coach hat for my boyfriend hat?"

He nods sheepishly. "Is that all right? It can wait. I just didn't want to talk about it in front of my mom."

Now I'm really on guard. He and Joie don't keep many secrets, and I'm certainly not close enough to him to be included in them. "I've got time. Have a seat…Isaac."

He smirks knowing we have an understanding now. This conversation is personal. I'm not sure if that's an improvement on our relationship or if I need to watch my back. Whatever is going on, it must be big.

Leaning back, I clasp my hands behind my neck. "It's a little late to say your piece about my moving into the house."

"Nah. That doesn't bother me."

"It doesn't?"

"No. I actually feel better about you living there."

Well, color me surprised. I never expected that reaction.

"I know we've lived there forever, and we have great neighbors," he continues, "but I never liked her living alone. It makes me feel better, knowing she has security detail there."

I snicker. "Is that your way of conveniently forgetting I'm her boyfriend?"

He looks amused that I've caught on. "Hell, yes. No way I wanna think about what goes on in that house when I'm not there."

"You don't have to worry. It's all very respectful."

Isaac makes some gagging noises, making me laugh. It's nice to joke around with him a bit. I don't think we'll be best friends or anything, but mutual respect and understanding works for me.

Still, he's here for a reason and now that I know it's not about me, I'm even more concerned. "So what's going on? It must not be good if you're tracking me down in the middle of the day."

He rubs his bottom lip, elbows resting on his knees, before he speaks. "My dad called me."

I try to contain my composure. Isaac's dad left Joie high and dry with a toddler years ago. He never helped. Rarely showed up. Even if he had a solid relationship with Isaac, I'd be pissed about the way he treated Joie. But as far as I know, there's never been a relationship. That makes this so much worse. So I go with the noncommittal response.

"How long has it been since you've seen him?"

He shrugs. "Twelve, thirteen years at least. I was like ten or something."

I have a bad feeling I know what's happening here, but I don't dare tell him my initial assessment. This isn't the first time I've seen a deadbeat dad come out of the woodwork once his long-forgotten kid becomes a star.

"Is this the first time he's contacted you?"

"A few months ago, I noticed he was following me on social media. He'd like some of my posts or make small comments. Nothing big." He shrugs.

"But?"

"The timing was suspect."

"How so?"

Isaac blows out a breath and rubs his hand over the top of his head. I already have an idea what he's about to say. He looks uncomfortable, which I understand. Saying it out loud makes it more real. "He didn't find me until after I got my scholarship."

I nod in understanding, still waiting for him to come to his own conclusions before I say my piece. "And you think it's because he saw all the press on it."

He shrugs again. "Awfully coincidental, don't ya think?"

I nod but let him continue. It's a lot to process.

"I was hoping you could tell me what to do. Or at least what to make of this."

Choosing my words carefully, I say, "Well, I'm sure he's proud of you."

He laughs humorlessly. "Of course he is. I'm on the starting line for his favorite football team. That's not what I'm asking."

"What are you asking?"

"I figure you've been doing this for a long time, and you've probably seen this before. Are they, the dads that just show up, are they ever for real, or is it just more games?"

I was hoping we could avoid this question, but I would be doing him a disservice if I didn't tell him the truth.

"You're right. I have seen this before. It's not an uncommon thing."

"And?"

"And I'm sorry to say, but I've never seen it end well."

"Never?"

I shake my head. "Don't misunderstand. I don't know your father from anyone else on the street. I don't know if he's a recovering alcoholic and he's making amends, twelve-step style. Or if he's had a come-to-Jesus moment and is trying to atone for his sins. But if nothing else, I'd be leery. And if you choose to let him into your life, I'd make him prove it's for the right reasons before trusting him. Not at this stage in your career."

He nods and bites his bottom lip as he thinks over what I've said. "Any advice on how to handle it?"

"What do you want to do?"

"I want to tell him to go to hell and then beat him to a pulp for what he did to me and my mom."

I can't help but chuckle at his response. "I can respect that. Wouldn't mind throwing a punch or two of my own on your mom's behalf."

Isaac smiles. "See? Security detail."

The fact that he can make a joke in the middle of all this means he's gonna be okay. He has a lot to process, but is still handling it better than most of the kids I see who get starry-eyed at the idea of having a relationship with their long-lost father. It's sad to watch because no matter how long it's been or how angry they are, there's a part of each of them that still wants their dad to want them. When it doesn't work out as planned, it causes a lot of turmoil. We help them channel it appropriately on the field as best as we can, but it doesn't make it any easier on them emotionally.

"I think I just want him to go away. Or at least not contact me during the season. If he's interested in me at all, it better not be about football."

"That's understandable. Maybe talk to him a couple more times. Feel him out when he calls. You'll know what he's after at some point."

"Okay. Yeah." He goes silent for a few minutes as he absorbs our conversation. I watch him. I don't have anywhere to be. "I have to get to class," he finally says, grabbing his backpack and heading for the door. "Thanks for leveling with me, Jack."

"Hey," I call out, "is there a reason you didn't go to your mom about this?"

He grabs the doorknob and pivots around to look at me. "It's not that I don't want her to know. I kind of wanted to know what I was going to do about it before having that whole discussion about loving her the most even if he's back. Also, now that you're involved, it's better if it comes from you first." He flashes me a shit-eating grin.

"You're a little shit, you know that, Isaac?" I jest.

"Yep," he says, waggling his eyebrows. "I'm sure you guys are all in the 'no secrets' stage of your relationship or whatever so have fun with that conversation."

I roll my eyes. "Get out of here. You're gonna be late to class, and I don't wanna bench your ass for ineligibility."

Snapping his legs together, he salutes me. "On it, Coach." Then he turns on his heel and leaves.

Stevens no more than rounds the corner of the hallway when Hank saunters in and leans against my desk, crossing his ankles. "Should I pass out the congratulatory cigars or something?"

I don't bother looking up from the email I'm opening. "What are you talking about?"

"You just became a daddy today! That was some great fatherly advice."

"What?" If he was trying to make me look at him, it worked. He has my full attention. "How did you hear that? Were you standing outside the door with a glass pressed up against it?"

"You don't know these walls are paper thin?"

"No."

"Oh yeah. I can hear everything," he says with a wave of his hand. "Remember that time you were banging that blonde over your desk?"

"I have never had sex in my office. Ever."

"Huh. Maybe that was me and Renee." I grimace and immediately back my hands away from the desk, running through my memories of any unknown substances I may have accidentally touched in the last ten years. "Anyhoo, the walls are paper thin."

"Now you tell me." I begin searching through my file cabinet, looking for the anti-bacterial wipes Joie made me bring one day. "I could have been talking shit about you all these years."

"But you weren't. So tell me, how are we going to handle this Stevens situation?"

Aha. Found them. Now if I can only get the loose wipey thing through the damn hole at the top of the canister...

"You don't think it's a coincidence his daddy called." I push Hank off my desk as I begin the tedious process of de-contaminating.

"Nope. Look what was posted yesterday morning." He hands me his phone with an article pulled up. Holding it with the wipe still in my hand, all I see is the title before it all makes sense.

Scouts List Flinton State's Isaac Stevens as a Potential Draft Pick.

The article straight out of this morning's Austin paper mentions some interview, in which Stevens's name was mentioned as a potential prospect. It lists all his current stats and even compares his first year pics with now. It's amazing how much he has not only grown, but improved in just a couple years. I already knew that, but it seems that others are starting to notice as well. Including his elusive father.

"Well, that explains it," I mumble.

"What are you going to do?" Hank pockets his phone and leans against my desk again.

"Nothing I can do. In the end, it doesn't matter what I think. It matters what Stevens thinks. I'm here to help guide him if he wants it, same as all the others."

"If he's in here using your first name, sounds like he wants it."

I nod and put the wipes back in the cabinet. Suddenly, imaginary germs don't seem as important as all the other shit happening.

CHAPTER FIVE

Joie

I honestly wasn't sure how living together would go, but so far, it's pretty good. Yes, Jack leaves dirty clothes everywhere, and I don't know when the last time was that he washed a dish. But it's nice having him here. Just the simple things like leaving me leftovers so I have something to eat when I get home from my study group confirm this is right for us. Plus, I feel so much safer than I did before, which is weird because I never realized I felt *un*safe. Something about his presence just calms me. He balances out my desire to constantly be moving. And I hope I balance out his desire to constantly be sedentary.

Now, if I could only get him to leave the toilet seat down. I almost fell in a few minutes ago. Fortunately, I didn't scream obscenities and wake him up. Not because he doesn't deserve it, but because I need to finish getting rid of my lady 'stache, and I'd rather him not see me like this.

Putting the last of the bleach on my upper lip, I set the timer so I don't lose track of time. I like to multi-task, and there's no better time to clean a bathroom than when you have to be close to a wash rag anyway so you don't accidentally burn your skin off.

Squatting down, I grab some cleaning supplies from under the sink. Ajax for the tub. Toilet cleaner for the commode. Scrubbing Bubbles for the tile. I stand up and turn around just as Jack pads into the room, scratching his head, his eyes barely open.

"Morning." His voice comes out all sleepy and husky. Normally I love the sound, but right now, I'm mortified he walked in on me like this.

Whipping around so I'm facing the wall, I squeal. "Ohmygod, what are you doing in here?" The telltale sounds of him peeing answers that question for me. "Are you *peeing* in front of me?"

"Is that a problem?"

"Yes, it's a problem! You can't pee in front of me!"

"I'm not. I'm peeing behind you. Why are you facing the wall, anyway? I don't care if you see this."

Carefully, I place the cleaning bottles on the counter, one-by-one, trying not to drop them since I can't move my head to see where they're going. "Don't you think that's a little bit intimate?"

He snorts a laugh. "Really, babe? We have sex, but this grosses you out? And why are you still facing the wall?" The toilet flushes, and I brace myself for what's next.

Sure enough, he takes me by the elbow and spins me around, a curious stare crossing his features as he takes in my appearance. "Is that like that Nair stuff or something?"

"It's bleach. And you're not supposed to see me like this."

He looks so confused at that statement. "Why?"

"Because you're not supposed to know your live-in girl-friend has to bleach her mustache."

"Really? I had my tongue in your pussy last night, but I can't see a little goop on your face?"

I gasp and begin laughing, smacking him playfully. "Jack! I can't believe you said that! You're so crude."

"You love it when I'm crude." He pulls me into his arms, careful not to get my face near his chest, and nuzzles into my neck. "I know it makes you horny when I tell you how much I love your pussy and how good it feels on my dick when you come."

I suck in a breath. He's right. It turns me on, but I'll never admit it. "So crass," I murmur, as he kisses down my neck.

"Only for you."

"Lies. You cuss like a sailor."

He chuckles in my ear. "You've got me. But I only dirty talk for you." Kissing my neck again, he pulls away. "When does that crap come off? I wanna give you a proper good morning kiss."

"Here." I reach behind me, pulling his toothbrush out of the silver holder and slap it in his hand. "Brush first. I only have about two more minutes to go."

"That's it?"

"I've been doing this for years. It's just maintenance eve-ry few weeks."

A blob of toothpaste falls into the sink when he squeezes it onto his brush. He doesn't even notice, so I reach over the clean it up while he tries to talk and brush at the same time.

"Shee?" His words sound slurred around the bubbles in his mouth. "It waddn't sho bad telling me abou that, wight?"

The buzzer goes off, and I grab my wash rag, the one with other bleach stains already on it, and quickly clean up my face. "I suppose not. There are just some things a lady doesn't want her man to know about. Masculine facial hair is one of them."

He spits and wipes his lips on the hand towel—ew. Mental note to replace that every morning before using it on my hands—and leans over for a kiss. "Many a bearded lady made a good living in the circus off that facial hair. No judgement here."

I laugh while rolling my eyes at him. He's ridiculous. And messy. As he heads out of the bathroom to go throw some pants on, he leaves the hand towel crumpled up on the counter. Sighing, I remind myself leaving it in a heap almost guarantees I won't accidentally forget that it's dirty and use it.

Following a few seconds behind him, I toss the towels into their respective baskets—hand towel with the rest of the towels. Wash rag in with the whites that will also be bleached later. Pre-sorting like this has saved me a lot of time over the years.

"Come help me make the bed," I bellow over my shoulder as I toss all the pillows on the floor.

"That's my least favorite chore," he calls back, but he shuffles around the bed to help, dressed in some old sweatpants and a T-shirt. He's very careful not to walk around the house without being somewhat dressed. I'm not sure if he's always done that or if it's out of respect in case Isaac shows up unannounced. If it's for Isaac's sake, I hope he'll stop. This is his home, too. If he wants to walk around naked, I have no problem with it. None at all.

"You mean you have a favorite one?" I playfully scold while we fluff the top sheet and blanket, then pull it up at the same time, smoothing it out.

"Okay, true. I don't really like any chore. But making a bed seems pointless. We're just gonna undo it tonight and mess it all up again."

"What? A made bed makes the room look cleaner," I argue, tossing the pillows back on. "Plus there's nothing like the feeling of sliding your feet in between cool, tight sheets."

He raises an eyebrow. "Is the word *sheets* code for something dirty?"

I shake my head in amusement and snatch some yoga pants out of the drawer. "Always with the dirty mind."

"It's your fault. It started when you had that sexy-ass goop on your face while I had my morning wood."

"You wouldn't have seen that goop if you hadn't come in to pee in front of me."

He stops and looks at me quizzically. "Does it really bother you that much?"

I shrug because the way he's looking at me makes me feel embarrassed by my feelings. Is it really that weird? Am I just so set in my ways because I haven't had to share my space that normal things couples do don't feel normal to me?

"Joie, if it's really that big of a deal, I'll use the half bath next time."

"Well, now I feel bad for making it into a thing."

"Don't. I honestly don't get it. You literally watched me come all over your stomach that one time, so I don't quite see how this is different." I blush at the memory. That was a good night. "But if it makes you uncomfortable, I can adjust. I'm not gonna invalidate your feelings because they're different than mine."

I look up at him through my lashes and have this strange, overwhelming feeling in my chest, like I've fallen for him even more because of his goodness.

"I might make fun of you for them, but I won't invalidate them."

And now my regular Jack is back. Sometimes I have to remind myself it's a good thing I have the same crazy sense of humor he has. He never would have made it past the front door with me if I didn't.

"No," I sigh. "Don't stay out of the bathroom. I'll deal with it. I can't guarantee I'll ever pee in front of you, but I won't look when you do it."

He shrugs. "Okay, but if you change your mind, just tell me. And Joie"—I look up at him, not sure what to expect from him next; he's pretty ornery this morning—"just know, someday you're going to accidentally fart in front of me, and that's okay, too."

My jaw drops open. "Excuse you, Mister. Ladies do not *fart*. They whisper in their panties." I stick my tushy out, put my finger to my lips and make a "shhhhhhhh" sound. Jack laughs so hard, I legitimately think he's going to fall over. Walking past him to the kitchen, a smirk lights up my face for having gotten the upper hand.

He follows behind me, still chuckling and wiping his eyes. "That was so funny. I've never heard that before."

Snatching two mugs out of the cabinet, I grab the ready-made coffee and begin pouring us both a cup. Thank goodness for timers on coffee makers. "Never?"

"No." He sniffs and pulls himself back together. "It was great though."

I smile at him as I bring the mug of look-alive juice to my lips. This right here. This is what I enjoy so much. Bantering with him first thing in the morning. Enjoying a cup of coffee together. Getting ready for the day, side-by-side.

"So what's your day look like?" he asks between sips. "You ready for your biology test?"

I groan. "I hope so. I don't know what I was thinking taking Bio II this semester."

"As opposed to what? Chemistry?"

"Yeah. But chemistry has so many more labs, I thought it was more conducive to my time management to take the second part of biology. Plus, I figured it would just be a continuation of what I already learned. I had no idea it would be this hard."

Jack finishes his coffee in record time and drops his mug on the counter. Rounding the corner to kiss me on the top of my head, he goes right into coach mode. "You're going to be fine. You've worked hard for this. Take a deep breath and stay focused. You know what you're doing."

I can imagine him giving the exact same pep talk to his players before a game, which makes me giggle.

"What?" He pulls away, but keeps his hand on my neck and looks at me. "Why is that funny?"

I shrug. "I think it's cute that Coach Pride came out to play so early in the morning."

"What can I say? It's who I am." He kisses me again and turns away. "I'm gonna go take a shower now. Join me?" He waggles his eyebrows up and down. I really do love playful Jack.

"Maybe in a minute. I'm gonna start gathering my things. Maybe clean up the dirty coffee mug you left sitting on the counter." I poke fun at him for it, but it really does drive me crazy sometimes, and he knows it. Keeping a clean house isn't his forte at all. But I have to give him some grace as we get used to living together. Neither of us has to be perfect in this endeavor. I know I'm not. I can be way too set in my ways.

Still, he has the wherewithal to look apologetic. At my reminder, he grabs the mug and begins rinsing it out. "You're right," he says. "I need to be better about cleaning up after myself. Or maybe I need to spring for a maid."

Hmm. The thought actually makes me pause. I've always thought a maid would be a waste of money when there were able-bodied people living in the home. But I'm so exhausted from late night study groups, the idea has some merit.

"You like that idea, don't you?" he jokes as he, no doubt, sees my eyes light up at the prospect of never having to do windows again.

"We'll table that discussion for a later date." Slapping him on the rear, I say, "Go. Shower. I'll get this cleaned up and be there in a minute."

He follows my instructions and I make quick work of cleaning the kitchen. Neither of us are big breakfast eaters, which comes in handy. Just as I shut the dishwasher, I notice the light blinking on my phone. It's a text Isaac sent this morning.

Isaac: *So how pissed are you?*

About what?

Isaac: *About dad calling.*

My whole body runs cold. I haven't heard from Charlie in over a decade. Why is he calling now? What does he want?

What? When did that happen? Did you talk to him?

Isaac: *Uh...I take it Jack didn't tell you about it.*

Now I'm flushing hot. Jack knows about this? Before I do? And why didn't he tell me? My thoughts are racing as I try to stay calm for my child, when I'm feeling anything but.

Nope. So why don't you tell me. What did he say?

Isaac: *Nothing much. He left a message. Jack's seen this before so he kind of talked me through it. But I don't know if I'm going to call him back yet.*

I blink a few times as I get my thoughts straight. I'm so angry right now, but I'm not sure why. Is it because Charlie's back? Is it because Jack kept this from me? Is it because Isaac doesn't need me anymore? The only thing I know for sure is I have to stay calm for Isaac. Even if I'm furious, he doesn't need to know that. I've never been more grateful to hide behind a text message.

Well, keep me updated. If you need me to get involved, let me know.

Isaac: *I will. But I'm sure it'll be fine.*

You've got a good head on your shoulders. I have to get to class now. Have a great day, honey. Love you.

Isaac: *Love you, too.*

276

Gently placing my phone on the counter so I don't accidentally smash it into the granite, like my muscles really, really want to right now, I turn and stomp my way into the master bedroom, straight to the bathroom. I whip open the shower curtain, making Jack squeal like a pig. Which is what I want to call him right now because I'm so angry.

"You knew Charlie called?"

"Who?" Jack crossed his arms and rubs up and down his biceps, warding off the chill that is probably beginning to take over now that the steam is gone.

"Charlie! Isaac's dad."

"Oh, I never knew his name." He ducks his head under the water, droplets spraying all over the bathroom. I don't care about the mess right now.

"Jack!" I cry out stomping my foot. "Why didn't you tell me?"

He leans down and shuts the shower off, then twists to grab the towel off the rack to start drying off. If I wasn't so irritated, I'd probably be lusting over his chest right about now.

"I didn't tell you because it's not my story to tell."

"That's a cop out."

Pushing past me, he climbs out of the shower while wrapping the towel around his waist. "It's not a cop out. If I had told you, you'd be mad the information didn't come from Isaac, right?"

I crinkle my nose, knowing he's right but not wanting to say it out loud.

"Instead, you're mad at me because he *did* tell you. So are you really mad at me or are you just upset in general, and I happen to be here?"

In this moment, I don't know the answer. All I know is the man who left Isaac and me high and dry is coming around again, and I'm the last one to know.

"What did you and Isaac talk about?" I can't look at him, partially from my own embarrassment. Although I can hear the sounds of the shaving cream squirting out of the can and him rubbing it on his face.

"He came to me in my office to talk about it. At first, I thought he wanted me to move out of the house or something."

I catch his eyes in the mirror. I didn't realize he was worried about that.

"He assured me he actually feels safer with me here, which was nice to hear." He pauses to run his razor through the hot water for a few seconds. "He told me his dad had called. Knew I had dealt with other players whose absent parents showed up when they started showing promise on the field. He just wanted to know my opinion—did I think Charlie …Charlie?" I nod. "Did I think Charlie was really interested in Isaac or was he after something?"

Jack angles his head so he can clean off the hair growth under his chin. For whatever reason, I like the sound it makes. Yet another thing I'd like about living with him if I wasn't so full of emotion right now.

"What did you say?"

He cleans the razor off again. "I told him I didn't know his dad, so I couldn't say for sure. But that he needed to be careful. Make his dad prove he's trustworthy before blindly falling into a relationship with him."

I nod. "Okay," I say quietly. "Okay."

"Joie." I look up again to find Jack staring at me in the mirror. "I'm sorry I didn't tell you. I wasn't keeping it from you. It never came up, and as far as I know, there's only been the one message. I figured Isaac was still sorting his thoughts out and needed some space."

"I know. I don't think I'm mad at you. I think maybe I'm just surprised."

Jack's lips quirk up into an understanding smile. "I was surprised, too. I never thought Isaac would come to me for man-to-man advice. But this is a good thing, right? That means he's okay with our living arrangements."

I smile back, even though I'm not really feeling it. "Yeah. Yeah, this is good."

Walking slowly out of the bathroom to get ready for my day, my words don't match my thoughts. If this is so good, why do I feel like my entire world just shifted upside down?

CHAPTER SIX

Jack

Today was a shitty day. After the argument, or whatever that was Joie and I had this morning, it all kind of went downhill.

First, there was a major accident on the highway into Flinton, so I was late for a meeting with a potential recruit. The kid is a huge linebacker prospect from Alabama. We really want him, and I gave him the impression we have a lackadaisical program by not showing up on time. Not good.

Then we got a tip that one of our running backs may be juicing. A few mandatory pee tests later and not only did we find steroids, it looks like he's been snorting coke, too. We could have canned his ass, but instead we benched him and spent the rest of the day looking for a rehab that'll work with his parents' insurance. That's after I got tasked with calling the kids mama to tell her he's a druggie who might lose a full ride over this. The decision on his future as a Viking is still up in the air, but agreeing to treatment was a show of good faith on his part.

And to top it all off, because of the positive drug test, we had to call in everyone else for mandatory testing. The whole team. Fortunately, no one else popped positive, but the flip side is we may have a campus-wide problem and the athletic director now gets to take over. It's likely that I'll be doing my own pee test tomorrow and having drug dogs sniffing around my office. The kid got the drugs somewhere and the university doesn't take this shit lightly. They'll investigate everyone: players, coaches, and anyone in between.

At the same time, we spent all day making sure no unnecessary personnel found out about the whole mess. Last thing we need is it leaking to the press. Nothing pisses off the people who write checks more than bad PR about their team. Being on lockdown meant no cell phone usage until everyone had been tested and was gone. That meant no texting Joie. Under already strained circumstances, it didn't sit well with me. But what was I supposed to do?

I was finally able to text her at about seven when we got out of there. She didn't respond, but I didn't expect her to. Her biology study group was tonight. Yes, there was a test today, but she refuses to fall behind and the class is kicking her ass.

The house is quiet when I walk in. I toss my keys onto the side table and stretch my arms over my head after the long drive. The only thing on my mind is food; I'm starving. We still have some leftovers from that Filipino place we found in San Antonio. I'm pretty sure it gave me gas last time I ate it, but I'm the only one here. I'll use some air freshener before Joie gets home.

Dishing all the noodles and veggies onto a plate and popping it in the microwave, I lean against the counter and look around. I'm happy living here. Even with my chair shoved back in the spare room she pretends is a man cave, it already feels like home.

The dryer runs for a few seconds and then buzzes. I wonder how long it's been doing that. Joie and I left around the same time so it must have been all day. Making myself useful as I wait on the microwave, I pull the load of clean clothes out of the dryer and walk down to our bedroom, dumping all the clothes on the bed. I'd fold them now, but as soon as I hear the microwave ding, my stomach starts growling again. I need sustenance before anything else.

The food is steaming hot and smells delicious. The preliminary bite I take over the kitchen sink is amazing, too. So good that I almost grab and eat the wayward noodle that fell into the sink. Almost. I'm still a gentleman. Pulling a beer out of the fridge, I toe my shoes off and I carry my dinner to the man cave so I can settle in my chair and watch Sports Center.

Five big bites and a few swigs of beer later, my dinner is gone, the empty plate sitting on the table next to me as I relax and enjoy today's highlights.

A baseball game that went into eleven innings.

A basketball player arrested for what seems like a fist fight at a bar.

Another basketball player in a car accident in LA stopped to do CPR until paramedics got there.

So far, it doesn't seem like anyone has caught wind of our juicing scandal...

A noise startles me awake. Weird. I didn't realize I'd been sleeping. I must have been more tired than I thought. Rubbing my hand down my face, I look at the clock.

11:47 p.m. Joie must be home.

Sure enough, she walks by grumbling as she carries my shoes.

"Hey!" I call out. It takes several minutes for her to finally return.

When she does, she doesn't come in the room. Instead, she leans against the door jamb. "Hey." She's polite, but not her normal, happy self. "I see you left a noodle for me in the sink."

This doesn't sit well with me. I knew I should have left some for her, and now I look like a total prick.

"Yeah, I'm sorry. I was hungry. Do you want me to make you something? I think we have a frozen pizza."

"No thanks. I'm actually not really hungry. Maybe just cranky."

"Come here," I say, holding my hand out to her.

She hesitates momentarily, but finally makes her way toward me. She looks exhausted. Dark circles under her eyes and that messy bun thing on her head looks messier than normal. Grabbing her hand when she gets close enough, I pull her onto my lap. She snuggles into me, which I take as a good sign.

"How was your day?" I ask as I nuzzle her neck.

She clings to my shirt like she's trying to pull me closer. "Not good."

"How did your test go?"

She sighs a deep, tired sigh before answering. "I don't know. I either aced it or I flunked. I honestly don't know which one."

"How come?"

She unwinds herself from my grasp and leans her head on my shoulder, absentmindedly watching some beer commercial. "I couldn't concentrate. I kept thinking about Charlie and Isaac and what it all means and what I need to do."

"I'm not sure there's anything you *can* do. I think this is one time you have to let Isaac decide what he thinks is best for him."

She scoffs quietly. "That's easy for you to say. You haven't spent the last eighteen years watching Charlie make promise after promise, only to deliver nothing but disappointments."

Shifting, I run my hand down her thigh. As much as I hate that this situation is bothering her so much, I love sitting here like this in my favorite chair talking about our day. I could do it for hours.

"You're right. I wasn't here. But I don't think you're giving Isaac enough credit. When he came to me the other day, he seemed calm. Like he wasn't making an emotional decision. He wanted information so he could make a really good choice. Give him some time, but Joie"—I turn her to face me—"you have to be prepared. He may want Charlie in his life and that's not something you can stop."

"I know." She says she knows, but I can see the disappointment on her face. "I've always said if his father came back around, and Isaac wanted a relationship with him, I would learn to be okay with it. I guess it's just harder than I thought it would be." She sighs again and I can tell thinking about it is part of why she's so tired. "Anyway, how was your day?"

I drop my head against the back of the chair as I remember the fucking nightmare caused by one entitled little brat. "Shitty."

She crinkles her cute little brow at me. "How come?"

"Off the record?"

"Uh...yeah, since I'm not a journalist."

"I mean from telling anyone. Especially Weaver."

Her face drops, and I can tell she already understands the gravity of the situation. She nods and shifts her body toward me.

"One of our guys got caught using drugs. More than one kind."

Joie gasps as I tell her about the drug tests, the athletic director, and the looming PR nightmare if it leaks. It feels good being able to vent to her. To trust that it'll stay between us and she's supportive of me after a really hard day. It's different than when we would talk on the phone at night. Being able to touch her and feel her and watch her reactions takes that bond to a whole different level.

"So anyway, I'm expecting to have to do my own pee test tomorrow and will probably have my office searched. All because of one little punk."

"I'm glad you guys are getting him into rehab, though." My eyes drift shut as she runs her fingers through my hair. "You could have just kicked him off the team. I hope he learns a lesson from it."

"Yeah. Me, too."

"When did being an adult get so hard?"

Opening my eyes, I smile at her. "Remember when we were kids and we wanted so bad to be grown up? Were you like that, too?"

"Oh yeah," she says, her head nodding furiously. "I was going to have a fancy apartment in New York City and live the glamorous life of a super model because obviously my parents had no idea what living a good life actually meant. Clearly, my tiny stature was meant for a runway."

I chuckle. "You were quite the little shit, weren't you?"

"You have no idea."

Pulling her to me, I kiss her quickly. "I think we need a break from adulthood. What do you say we go out this weekend?"

The smile that lights up her whole face is back at those words. "Really? Where are we gonna go?"

I shrug. "I don't know yet. How about I call Hank and see if we can double date with him and Renee? You like her, right?"

"I do. She's great. And I think Hank's funny."

This time my laugh is more of a disbelieving snort. "Don't let him hear you say that. He'll try too hard."

"Noted."

Rubbing my hands up and down her back as she snuggles back into me, I can already feel some of the tension leave the room. All we need is some fun. A night out with our friends will be just perfect.

CHAPTER SEVEN

Joie

"**B**allroom dancing? You're taking me ballroom dancing?" The look on Jack's face when he finds out where Hank and Renee are taking us is priceless. He obviously didn't have much to do with the planning part of this date.

"You know how it is," Hank replies nonchalantly as he drives us through a small business area on the outskirts of Austin. "You tell your woman you're taking her on a date, and she decides she wants to go dancing no matter how much you try to talk her out of it."

Renee twists around in her seat next to him, shaking her head and giving me that look every woman knows. The one that says *That's not how it happened.* I press my lips together as I try not to smile.

"The way I figure," Hank continues to lecture, "if I have to suffer through this, next time I get to decide, and we're doing something more manly. We're Texas men, dammit."

Renee pats his arm condescendingly. "We're from Kentucky, honey." He ignores her and continues his rant.

"We've lived here for twenty-five years. We're Texans now, and next time, we're going to the shooting range."

I cover my mouth to stifle the laugh that really wants to burst out of me. The roll of Jack's eyes says he doesn't find this exchange as entertaining as I do.

"We most certainly are not," Renee argues. "The last time we went to the gun range, you nearly blew off your toe when you unlocked the safety while pointing that thing at the ground by your side."

Hank points his finger at her, but never takes his eyes off the road. "That was not my fault and you know it. Someone messed with my gun. The safety was too loose like someone had oiled it."

"You're the only one who touches that gun, Hank."

"Obviously not since it had been tampered with."

"*Any*way"—Renee turns around in her seat to continue our conversation—"our daughter is getting married in a few months, and she really wants Hank to know how to dance appropriately. So I promised her I'd make him taking dancing lessons. He's been resisting for weeks until Jack called the other day about going out."

"So I got suckered into it," Jack grumbles.

"Hell yeah," Hank admits. "I need to bring some backup testosterone in case one of those dancer boys in tights and ballet shoes decides this silver fox is right up his alley."

There's no hiding my laugh this time.

"How do you have any friends when you say stupid shit like that?" Jack asks, still sounding irritated.

Hank just shrugs. "I don't know. You're the one who called and asked me to get together, remember?"

"Oh my lord. Just ignore him," Renee advises. "The older we get, the less the filter between his brain and his mouth works."

"It doesn't bother me any," I admit. Jack stares at me wide-eyed, shaking his head frantically, like my admission is about to open Pandora's box. I'm not worried. "Frankly, I'm surprised he hasn't asked me about my ability to make tacos yet."

Jack drops his head in defeat. Hank, on the other hand, his eyes light up as he looks in the rear-view mirror. "Can you? Make tacos, I mean?"

"Sorry to disappoint. Except for Thanksgiving turkey and a couple staples, I'm not much of a cook."

"Dammit." He actually looks crushed. "I was hopeful we finally got a cook in this little foursome here."

"Why?" Jack's tone changes, and he sounds really irritated now. "Because she's Hispanic?"

"No, you racist shithead. Because she's a woman."

"Oh my lord!" Renee yells while Jack smacks his hand against his face. I'm the only one laughing so I guess I'm the only one who finds him funny. Inappropriate...yes. But harmless. "You are not allowed to talk anymore for the night."

Hank mimics zipping his lips and throwing the key away as he pulls into a parking space in front of the *Alexander Astaire School of Dance*. I highly doubt this Alexander guy is actually related to Fred Astaire, but props to him for making himself sound the part.

We all climb out of Hank's extended cab pickup—the vehicle of choice for any man living in the Lone Star State—and head into the building. It's one giant ballroom, complete with a massive dance floor and dark red drapes strategically placed around the room. A woman in a white flowing dress and a man dressed to match stare into each other's eyes as they glide around the floor, gracefully dancing a waltz.

I watch, mesmerized at how beautiful they look together. It's like they're two halves of a whole. They can completely anticipate each other's moves, and I have no doubt that, if one of them messes up, the other is there to keep them on track. It's beautiful.

As the music winds down and they end their dance, the patrons begin applauding, to the obvious delight of the dancers. He bows and she curtsies before breaking apart and going their separate ways. The man heads our direction.

"Velcome, velcome!" he says with a strange accent I've never heard before. That answers the question about his link to Fred Astaire.

Jack is obviously confused as well. "Is he from some random European country, or is he faking that accent?" he whispers in my ear. I *shh* him so I can hear what this odd man has to say.

"My name is Alexander Astaire, and I vill be your instructa this evening."

"My money is on faking it," Jack whispers. I smack him playfully.

"Let's get everyone zigned in and ve vill begin."

The next fifteen minutes is made up of people signing in and making introductions. This is followed by a series of stretches to warm up. I can't be sure, but I think I heard Hank whisper "My nutsack doesn't stretch this way" to Renee. Her hand clamped over his mouth pretty quickly.

An hour later, we've been taught some basic steps and the instructors are ready to set us loose on our partners.

"Remember," Alexander calls into crowd of a dozen or so couples, "Zee man alvays leads on zee dance floor. Ladies, you may lead everyvhere else, but vhen you are in his arms, let him be in control." He waggles his eyebrows up and down like he's made a joke, and sure enough, several of the women are giggling. Jack rolls his eyes for the umpteenth time and sighs.

"Oh come on." I hold my arms out in the correct ballroom dancing position. Jack does the same and pulls me to him, ready for the music to begin. "It's not that bad, is it?"

"I don't like dancing," he grumbles. "Didn't like it when my coach forced us into it at college. Don't like it now."

"Okay, Mr. Sourpuss. At least try to have some fun with me and your friends."

He hrmphs, but I ignore him, trying to enjoy myself despite his grumpy mood. The music begins, and Alexander counts us down. I take a deep breath and prepare to dance with my man, excited about the idea of us floating around the room gracefully. Before I can take my first step, Jack beats me to it.

"Ouch!"

"Oh shit, I'm so sorry. I didn't mean to step on your foot," he says apologetically, as I rub my toe. My cute flats are no match for his cowboy boots.

"It's okay," I say as I shake my foot out. "Let's try again."

We get back in position and listen to the music, waiting for Alexander to give us the correct count again. He does, and we begin dancing. It's not great, but we're moving.

Until I step on him this time.

"Oh my gosh. I'm so sorry."

Jack chuckles. "It's okay. I barely felt it."

Smiling through my discouragement, I raise my arms and we get back into position again. Third time is a charm and all that, right? Alexander calls out the count and we begin moving to the music. We make it all of ten steps before Jack steps on my foot again, making me cry out.

"No! No! No!" Alexander comes stomping over to us and we stand in the middle of the dancefloor while everyone else dances around us. "This iz not dancing. This iz...I don't know vhat this iz. But iz not dancing. This..." He waves his hands at us. "This iz a couple that iz completely out of sync."

I look at Jack and realize Alexander's not wrong. We are out of sync. And not only on the dance floor. Jack and I love each other, that hasn't changed. But with work, school, studying, football drama, Charlie drama, Jack's inability to pick up after himself, and everything else in between, moving in together is harder than we originally thought it would be. It's just the reality of everyday life, but I thought tonight would at least get us out of the chaos for a few hours so we could just enjoy each other like we used to. From the scowl on Jack's face, I can see that's not going to happen. At least not tonight.

"There. Look over there." Alexander gestures toward Hank and Renee who are, to my surprise, gliding gracefully around the room. Alexander folds his hands together and covers his heart. "You zee how they hold each other. How they caress each other? How they love each other? This iz how you dance with your partner. Like you are making love on the dance floor."

Jack puts his hands on his hips. "I am not making love to her on the dance floor."

Alexander ignores him and calls to the other couple. "Come. Come here. Ve'll svitch."

Jack scoffs. "What? I don't want to 'svitch.' I want to dance with Joie."

Alexander cocks an eyebrow at him. "You need to learn to not stomp on her toes first. Come now. My beautiful Renee." He grabs her hand and practically dances her over to my boyfriend. "You. Dance vith Jack. Show him how to treat hez lady."

Before Jack can respond, Renee grabs him and waltzes him away. Oddly, he doesn't seem to step on her toes. Does that mean I'm the problem in this duo?

As Alexander follows them around the room, calling out basic instructions, Hank looks at me and does a sort of bow. "May I have this dance?"

I smile at his chivalry and hold my arms out, getting us in the proper closed hold position. Within seconds, Hank is whisking me around the room. I'm shocked by how easy this seems to be. Looking over, Jack seems to be doing well. So why can't we seem to do it together?

"You're really good at this," I remark, feeling myself relax and enjoy feeling graceful.

"Yeah, well, don't tell anyone but my mother made me take ballet lessons when I was a kid." My eyes widen at his revelation. "I didn't take them for very long, but I was the best in the class. I've got very good rhythm."

"I'll say. I feel like I should be on *Dancing with the Stars* or something right now."

"Just don't tell Jack or I'll never hear the end of it."

I laugh as he twirls me. "Your secret is safe with me."

We continue to move around the room, keeping time with the music. Sometimes we spin so fast, I can feel a breeze on my face. I can't help my huge smile.

"You know I'm not really a bigot, right?"

The smile falls as I take in Hank's face. He seems really concerned that he's offended me. I don't understand why, since I've never given him any indication my feelings were hurt. But thinking back to our conversation in the car, I bet Jack's anger made him wonder if he'd crossed a line.

"I never thought you were," I reassure him. "Honestly, I think you like popping off because you like shocking people."

He responds with a broad grin and another spin. "You caught me. Their reactions are hilarious. Jack especially. Man, that boy falls for it every time."

"I think he's probably more amused than he lets on."

"Maybe. But he sure can be set in his ways." Suddenly the tone of the conversation changes, and I don't think we're talking about whether or not Jack offends easily anymore. "He driving you crazy yet?"

I look over at the other part of our group again as they show off some fancy footwork. Jack is smiling, and Renee has her head thrown back at something he's said. He's finally starting to relax. "I wouldn't say he's driving me crazy."

"Hogwash," Hank exclaims. "That man is the biggest slob I've ever known in my life. Has he started picking up after himself yet or are you still doing it for him?"

My shoulders relax more. Looks like I was suffering in silence, waiting for us to get into a groove, for no reason. "You mean it's not just at home?"

"Oh hell no. His office is a mess. That's why we always use mine for meetings."

"I guess I should have checked out his office space before I moved him in."

"Eh." Hank shrugs. "Just tell him they'll be no riding the Jack Express if he doesn't pick his shit up off the floor."

I laugh and roll my eyes at yet another comment designed to get a rise out of me. It didn't work.

"I can't shock you, can I?" he asks, seemingly perplexed at why I take everything he says in stride.

"Nope. My grandfather has no filter either. You've got nothing on a ninety-two-year-old man."

He narrows his eyes. "So you wouldn't be offended if I called you Taco Belle?"

"Only if you don't mind me calling you Ritz."

"Because I'm wealthy and powerful, right?"

"No. Because you're a cracker."

A belly laugh bursts out of him as we keep dancing... spinning and twirling until Alexander ends the class, handing us all a coupon for a discount on regular classes as we leave.

Somehow, I don't think Jack will ever let us cash it in.

CHAPTER EIGHT

Jack

I woke up with the biggest smile on my face. After years of hoping and praying and a whole lot of cussing, my sister Greer has finally moved to Flinton.

Well, she's in the process of moving. At nine this morning, Joie and I were hanging out in a hotel room while she went and closed on her new house. A couple hours later, she is officially a homeowner, and we're gearing up to spend the day unloading her U-Haul.

Okay, not the whole day. We have until five to get the truck back to the rental place. That gives us six hours to get it all done. The suitcases, boxes, and small furnishings were easy. Between the three adults and my niece and nephew, that went quickly. But now we have to do the big stuff, and I'm the only man here.

If it wasn't a Monday, I would have made the team help and called it "conditioning." But if I'd played that card and any one of them failed a final, it'd be my ass on the line. So instead, I'm thanking my lucky stars Joie skipped her classes for the first time ever because Hank and Matthews cancelled on me at the last minute, and there was no one else to help. Fuckers. I have no doubt they're both lying about being sick. I'm still trying to decide how to get them back for ditching me. I think a couple flat tires might do them some good next week.

So now I have to figure out how to get all the couches and dressers inside without completely throwing my back out. I'd use Oli. He's almost seventeen and big enough. But all this change has been hard on him, so I'm treading lightly.

At least until Joie stops arguing with me.

"Jack." My fiery woman stands inside the rental truck, hands on her hips. She's obviously irritated with me right now. "I can help you carry furniture. It's not that hard."

"No, but it's heavy," I argue. "I don't need you getting hurt."

"I don't think you're worried about me getting hurt. I think you're worried I'm going to drop something, and *you'll* get hurt."

Busted.

"Joie, it's a lot of furniture. Are you sure you have the stamina for this?"

From the way she's looking at me, I may as well stop arguing now. She's going to do what she wants no matter what I say.

"I'm a Texas woman. I can shoot a gun, cook a meal, and carry furniture all in the same day."

"First of all," I say, holding up my hand to stop her, "except for enchiladas, you can't cook worth a shit." She shrugs because she's knows I'm right. "And to my knowledge you've never even held a gun." Again with the shrug. "But since I have no other options at this point, fine. You can help me carry furniture."

She beams at me and claps her hands together. "Great! Where shall we start?"

Greer walks into the truck and leans over to pick up one of the few remaining boxes. It's labelled "towels." Of course she picked up the one light thing.

"Let's get these dressers out of the way. Greer, we might need your help."

"Sorry, I'm not a Texas woman," she says over her shoulder as she steps out of the truck. "I'm still from Kansas."

I shake my head in disappointment, but Joie laughs, taking it all in stride.

"I like her." She points in Greer's direction, wiggling her finger. "She's got sass."

"A little too much, if you ask me," I grumble, as we get in position to pick up the bedroom set.

It takes about an hour to finish unloading everything. Some of the furniture will still have to move around, but at least the heavy lifting part is over. My back is already aching.

Surprise of all surprises, Joie didn't complain once, and still, even while I'm in pain, she has a giant smile on her face and a spring in her step. Looks like I underestimated her. Or overestimated myself. Either way, I'm more than happy to take a break.

"How far is the U-Haul place from here?" I ask my sister, pulling a glass out of a box labeled "kitchenware" and grabbing some filtered water from the fridge. Thank goodness the previous owners had all new appliances and left this one here. I'd rather carry a couch than a fridge any day.

"It's just across town," Greer answers. She's busy wiping out drawers so she can organize all the silverware. Her main priority is getting this kitchen set up so they can stop eating out. Even Oli is getting sick of pizza, and it's his favorite food.

"Why don't I fold up all the moving blankets and take the truck back early so we can get that done? I can grab some food on the way back if you want."

She nods and looks off while she thinks for a second. "Is that sandwich shop still open? The mom and pop one over by the stadium?"

"Sullivan's Sandwiches?" I ask and she nods again. "Sure is. I ate there the other day."

"You think we could get that? I know it's still eating out, but it sounds way better than fast food." She makes a face at the thought of eating more grease. I get it. She started the moving process several weeks ago, so I'm sure they're ready for a home-cooked meal.

I grab the counter and lean my body back, stretching out my back. Joie comes up behind me and rubs the muscles next to my spine. If I wasn't in the presence of my sister, I might have let out an inappropriate groan. Instead, I answer her question. "I'll get them to cut the sandwiches in half and give me a family order of broccoli and cheese soup, too. It's not exactly homemade, but it might hit the spot."

She closes her eyes and makes a "mmmmmm" sound. I'll take that as confirmation that I'm getting the soup, too.

Standing up, I stretch my arms over my head, enjoying that the pain is beginning to go away. Joie's hands are practically magic. I have no idea how she has so much strength in her thumbs, but it comes in handy at times like this. Turning to face her, I pull her to me and kiss her on the top of the head.

"Thanks for the massage. Wanna come with me to get food? You can follow me in my truck and we can pick it all up after we drop off the U-Haul."

She gapes at me. "You mean I'll get to drive the precious Ford F-250?"

Greer snorts a laugh.

"It's a 350 and now I'm reconsidering since you don't even know what kind of vehicle you'd be driving. Ooof," I say, trying to catch my breath when she pokes me in the ribs.

"I don't care what kind of truck it is. I'm more interested in this soup."

"We're getting soup?" Oli ambles into the room, heading straight for the fridge. He looks disappointed when he finds it still empty.

"I figured soup and sandwiches might be a nice change. What do you think, Oli?"

He shrugs, but doesn't make eye contact with me. That's part of his disability.

Oliver was born by emergency C-section when his umbilical cord wrapped around his neck twice during Greer's labor. At first, the doctors thought he was okay, and it didn't cause any problems. But the older he got, the more apparent it was that something wasn't quite right.

It took until he was almost six, but it was finally determined that Oli had significant brain damage due to the oxygen deprivation. For the most part, he looks normal. But that's what makes it all so deceiving. It's the small things like not wanting to make eye contact and his inability to not stomp when he walks, not to mention completely missing most social cues and a severe lack of impulse control, particularly when he gets angry.

"Hey Mom?" he asks as he shuts the fridge. "Since I've been good all day, can I have my Kindle?"

If I didn't know her so well, I wouldn't catch it, but for a split second, Greer eyes close like she's preparing herself for what's coming. That immediately puts me on alert.

"Oli," she answers gently, "we talked about this. The cable guy can't get here until tomorrow, so we won't have any internet until then."

Oli's breathing gets heavier. "But, that's not fair, Mom. I've been good all day."

"You have been very good all day. But this isn't a punishment. We just don't have internet. None of us do."

Oli squeezes his eyes tightly and clenches his teeth. His closed fist comes up and he begins banging it against his forehead. "It isn't fair!" he yells. "You lied to me! You said I could have my Kindle if I was good!"

Joie stands frozen next to me as she watches the exchange. Greer, on the other hand, continues unpacking like Oli's reaction is a normal one, because to her, it is. When he doesn't get what he wants, no matter the reason, it's extremely hard for him to manage his frustration.

"I didn't lie to you, Oli. We talked about this, remember? We talked about how we wouldn't have any internet for a couple of days until it all get set up. But Oli"—Greer spins around, probably to assess how agitated he is—"we're getting it tomorrow. That's such good news! Sometimes it takes a week and it's only taking us a day!"

"No!" he yells and slams his hand on the counter. "You always do this to me because you hate me!" He begins pacing the room, breathing rapidly through his mouth, still banging on his forehead.

Out of the corner of my eye, I see Julie walk into the room. She stops, sees what's happening, and turns right back around. Julie is a good kid. At fourteen years old, she has a good head on her shoulders and is really smart. But she also got the short end of the stick. Her older brother is disabled. That means his needs almost always overshadow hers. In some ways, I'm glad she'll be going to college in a few years. I'm looking forward to seeing her blossom away from household action plans and constantly have to assess her brother's mood.

Greer continues to try to talk Oli off the ledge, but he's not having it. Within minutes, he's riled himself up so much, he tosses a bar stool and yells when he walks by it. I hear Joie gasp, but I calmly walk behind him and pick it up.

He whips around and bucks up to me. "Why are you following me?" he yells.

"I'm not following you, buddy," I say calmly.

This isn't my first showdown with Oli. Yes, I've lived in Flinton for a decade, but before that, I lived just a few blocks over from Greer. I saw the kids every few days. I was there when Oli was born, when he took his first step, and when Greer got her first phone call from the school about an outburst.

When it became clear that normal discipline didn't work, and he subsequently was diagnosed with a myriad of issues, I began following Greer's lead on how to handle delicate situations. She modeled patience and redirection, without overreaction, so I do the same. Over the years, even with short visits at holidays, it's become old hat for those of us who know Oli best.

That doesn't mean his outbursts aren't getting worse. It's not that he's doing anything new. He's just bigger. It won't be too long before he's strong enough to do some serious damage. "I just put the stool back where it belongs."

"Well, don't do that!" He leans over and topples another one. Knowing he's trying to engage me in a fight to get his own frustration out, I leave it.

Greer continues to try to redirect him by asking for his help unpacking, asking what color he wants to paint his room, talking about the new program at school, all kinds of different topics. It takes a solid ten or fifteen minutes of Greer and I discussing Pokémon (his favorite) and the new pet store in the area (also his favorite), but he's finally calm and stable enough to help Greer organize silverware.

Watching the entire exchange, I'm reminded again of how hard my sister's life really is. Having a disabled child isn't a cakewalk. There is no cure. He won't grow out of it. It's her life. Permanently. And I'm in awe of how well she handles it with such patience.

Peering over at Joie, I see a million unanswered questions in her eyes. Being the other permanent figure in my life, I can tell we need to have a very long talk about my nephew and why he is the way he is.

"Ready to get food?" I ask her, knowing this could be the only time we have to finish these errands before Oli remembers his inability to use his Kindle again. She nods blankly in response.

Once I make sure we have the correct sandwich orders, Joie and I caravan to the rental dealership, turning in the keys long before it's due. We thank the man for making the process so easy, and then I climb into the cab of my truck, which I appreciate so much more after driving in that rickety box of a vehicle we just returned. I crank the engine and twist my body toward Joie.

"I know you have questions."

Gotta love her. She doesn't pussyfoot around, and the first question out of her mouth is a doozy.

"Is he always like that?"

I sigh and put the truck in reverse, knowing this conversation may take longer than it does to get back to Greer's. Including the stop to order food.

"You know Oliver has brain damage."

"Yeah," Joie says with a shrug. "You told me that before."

"The brain damage has caused several issues for him. Besides being right on the borderline of the autism spectrum, which surprisingly, doesn't have anything to do with the oxygen deprivation, the part of his brain that was affected is the part that normally gives you your impulse control. His is severely damaged so when he gets fixated on something, he has a very hard time refocusing himself. What you saw back there …that's the result."

"So he just flips out and destroys things?" I know she's not meaning to sound insensitive, but it's clear that Joie doesn't get it. Most people don't when they're first introduced to my nephew. It's hard to understand that a kid who looks totally normal on the outside can be so damaged on the inside.

"Sometimes. Yes. But what you saw back there was mild. He toppled a couple stools and we redirected him within a few minutes. That's major improvement."

"It is?" she asks incredulously, which actually kind of pisses me off.

"It is," I say back with a hint of snark in my voice. "Three years ago, he was tossing tables and punching holes in the wall. His fits could easily last over an hour. He's matured a bit over the years, but what you see when he's banging his own head with his fist…that's Oli trying to calm himself down."

Joie leans her head back on the seat and blows out a breath. "It's so hard to watch. I can't imagine being Greer and doing it day in and day out. And I know it's not a disciplinary issue, but it's so hard to not just assume that if she would just ground him, he'd stop, ya know?"

Her comment irritates me. It's not said with malice, more as a statement, but it still goes back to one of the huge reasons Greer needed to be closer to me…no one understands the situation like I do. The massive amount of judgement she gets about her parenting skills is wearing on her. I hope explaining it will help Joie understand because if not, we're going to have some big problems.

"Joie, his short-term memory doesn't work right. You can ground him all day long, but the only thing that will do is cause him more frustration. He has to be dealt with moment by moment. He has to be rewarded for the fact that he didn't break anything. You're seeing this as the mom of a normal child. Isaac would respond to normal discipline. Oli wouldn't understand it within a few minutes and would think people are just being mean to him. Just because he doesn't look disabled on the outside doesn't mean he's not disabled on the inside. You can't just say 'Well if she'd discipline him differently,' because you don't get it. You don't know what it's like to live with it day in and day out. To try every form of therapy you can find and none of them work. This isn't a discipline issue. It's a brain function issue."

"I'm sorry," she says quietly, and I notice she's wringing her hands. "I didn't mean to sound insensitive. I've just never seen anything like that."

I sigh, disappointed in myself for my overreaction. Grabbing her hand, I intertwine our fingers and bring her knuckles to my lips, kissing them. "I'm sorry, too. I shouldn't have taken that tone with you. It's confusing right now because you haven't been around anyone with brain damage before. It'll become more normal the more you get to know him."

She nods and stares out the window. I let her absorb the information I've given her and wait for her to initiate more conversation. I don't want her to think Oli is a bad kid. He's not. He's loving and empathetic. He's inquisitive and tries really hard to be funny. He's so many things people don't see. All they see is a seventeen-year-old. They don't know he has the brain of an eight-year-old.

"Maybe..." she finally says, "maybe if I knew what his diagnoses are I could look up more information, so I could understand better, ya know?"

"Maybe." Hopefully. But just knowing she wants to understand and not make assumptions reassures me. "He's diagnosed with a major depressive disorder..."

She gasps. "He's got depression?"

I nod and look over at her quizzically. "Well yeah. He has brain damage, but he's smart enough to know he's not like everyone else and he wants to be. That alone probably takes a toll on his psyche."

"Oh, I didn't think about that. What else?"

"Something called Mood Dysregulation Disorder. Basically it means he has a hard time pulling himself back together when he gets upset, like you just saw. Then you add on the brain damage and the autism piece, and Oli is a cocktail of so many issues, it's unreal."

"I knew you said he had issues, Jack, but…wow." She shakes her head back and forth as she processes all the information. "I can't imagine what Greer must deal with every day."

I shrug. "Some days are better than others."

She goes quiet again as I drive to the sandwich shop. I squeeze her hand in reassurance. I love this woman. She owns me. I only hope she can learn to love Oli like I do.

"I'm going to do my best, Jack," she says, as I pull into the parking lot. "It might take me a little time, but this is your family. That makes them a part of my life now. No matter what the issue."

I squeeze her hand again as I park then pull her to me and kiss her hard.

"I love you," I say when I finally pull away. "Thank you."

She responds by cupping my cheek and kissing me again.

CHAPTER NINE

Joie

It has been long discouraging week.

It started when Isaac finally called me about his dad. He had initially been leery about Charlie's calls, but the more they talked, the more he was encouraged that maybe his dad was finally wanting a real relationship. Of course that made me concerned. Even though I know Isaac has a right to know his father, it's not easy for a mother to forgive years of hurt and disappointment.

As it turns out, there's no reason to forgive Charlie, anyway. Today, he called and asked Isaac for season passes for next year. So I got to listen to Isaac rant about the whole situation, while trying to remain calm, even though inside I was boiling over with fury. Mama Bear mode was in full force. But I couldn't let Isaac know that.

Then I had an honest conversation with myself about my reactions to Oli. It was hard for me to admit it, but I'm afraid of him. It's not the disability as much as it's his physical size with this kind of disability. So I did some research about brain damage. Unfortunately, there are so many kinds that basically no one's is the same. The only thing most everyone has in common is that once the brain is damaged, there's very little that can be done to fix it. So Oli will always be the way he is.

But this is Jack's family, so somehow I have to get my fear under control. I know I'll feel better when I get up to speed and understand Oli's condition better. It feels like such a daunting task, and I've only had a few days to wrap my brain around it.

To top it all off, it became clear that my Bio II professor is intent on killing my GPA. He sprung a pop quiz on us *just because*. With finals coming up, the last thing I needed was a *just because* quiz that wasn't on the syllabus. I understand that's why it's called a pop quiz, but this is college. We're adults. We don't need a professor springing additional grades on us to make a point about us needing to study more. We need to be taught the information so we can pass the tests that are listed on the syllabus.

After a full day of school, I'm really glad to be home. All I want to do is throw my hair up, take a nice, hot bubble bath, and drink a glass of wine. After everything that has happened, I really need some downtime.

Walking up my stoop and opening the door, I hear the tub calling my name, but I'm stopped in my tracks. I'm not even three steps in the house and already twitchy.

"Or not."

My already sour mood plummets. There is a pile of unfolded laundry on the couch. Jack's shoes are in the middle of the floor. A mostly empty pizza box, except for a few crusts, sits on the dining room table among papers strewn everywhere.

I can feel myself tensing as I walk around finding dirty dishes in the kitchen sink and two empty beer bottles on the counter. It's not even late. How can one man cause so much destruction in a couple hours?

Jack saunters into the kitchen, his face lighting up when he sees me. "Hey, I didn't hear you come in." He wraps his arms around me and pulls me into an embrace. I want to melt into him, but even being enveloped in him isn't helping my stress level this time.

"I just got home. What's going on in the dining room?"

"What's...? Oh, the paperwork." He kisses my head and walks over to the table. "These are last-minute scholarship requests. Hank and I have to go through them to finalize everything."

I don't pretend to understand the ins and outs of everything Jack does when it comes to the business side of football. Actually, I don't understand a lot of what they do, even the physical part. But it's the beginning of May. I thought this was already over.

"Wasn't this all done months ago? Isn't it really late to award scholarships?"

He sits down in his chair and stretches his legs out. "We always have some last-minute changes. Remember that kid, Tommy? The one who went to rehab?"

"Oh no. He's losing his scholarship?"

"Hell yeah," Jack says forcefully. "The investigation came back. Not only was he doping, he was dealing on the side."

I gasp. "Are you serious?"

"Yep. He was always really quiet, kept to himself. I thought he was an introvert or something. Nope. He was just keeping a low profile, keeping his side business away from the team. He'd have been caught a long time ago otherwise."

"And he would have gotten away with it if someone hadn't tipped you guys off."

"Yep." Jack absentmindedly rubs his knee, grimacing every once in a while. It must be bothering him. It's an old injury and still acts up when he's been sitting for too long. I don't think he realizes he rubs it sometimes, but it's one of those small things I've learned about him since he moved in. "And we lost a freshman tight end, too."

"What? How?"

"The dumb ass blew his knee skiing over spring break of all things. His first ortho told him he couldn't play football again, but he waited for a few weeks to get a second opinion before reneging his spot. Pissed me off he didn't give us a heads-up back in March."

"I take it the second doctor confirmed it?"

"Career-ending knee injury. The dumb ass knew better. It's almost better this way. We don't need stupid on this team."

I walk over to the sink and begin doing dishes. I might as well multitask because it'll irritate me until it's done anyway. So much for my relaxing evening. "That's not nice. You know he didn't do it on purpose."

"Every football player knows skiing is practically begging for a career-ending injury."

I cock an eyebrow at him. "Every single one?"

He watches me scrub but doesn't offer to help. "Every one that's gunning for a scholarship. He's probably been working for this since he was eight years old. It was a dumb move."

"I think you're being too hard on him."

Jack's lips quirk into a small smile before he stands up and walks out of the room. That's strange. When he returns, he has my phone in his hand.

"What are you doing?" I ask.

He angles my phone toward me to show me a text he just sent Isaac.

What do you think about going skiing in Tahoe for Thanksgiving this year?

I snicker. "You think he's going to turn that down?"

"He will if he's as smart as I think he is." Jack puts my phone down on the counter and leans against it while I begin drying the now clean plates that I really don't want to be doing. But what am I going to do? Let them mold? "Anyway, we have to decide who's going to get the money now. Someone we already have, or do we give a partial recipient a full ride? Hank's coming over in a bit so we can sort it out and get it all approved quickly."

I freeze. "Hank's coming here?"

"Yeah. His in-laws are in town, so he's looking for an excuse to get out of the house anyway."

"How long until he gets here?" Looking around the open concept room, I notice so much that has to be done before this house will be guest ready.

Jack shrugs like his friend seeing a messy house is no big deal. "Maybe an hour or so?"

"That doesn't give me enough time to clean up!" Panic overtakes me, and I feel my breathing start to get heavy. Keeping a clean home and always presenting a good front is important to me. I get squeamish if I know anyone besides Isaac, Jack, and myself will be coming into the house when it's anything less than spotless.

I don't have a lot of time to get things done. All I can do is race around the kitchen, wiping down counters and throwing bottles away. Jack looks at me with confusion.

"Joie, he doesn't care how messy our place is. He's coming to work."

"Do you not see how filthy this place is? Jack, I need your help. You made all this mess. You need to get it cleaned up."

"Joie, this isn't a big deal…"

"It's a big deal to me!" His eyes widen as I yell the words. I close my eyes and take a deep breath before speaking again. "It's a big deal to me, Jack. I know this is part of learning to live together, but I thought you knew this about me. I like having a clean home where everything is picked up and put in its place. I like having an empty, shiny sink. I like pulling my clothes out of a nice, neat dresser, not sorting through a clean pile for what I need. I like structure and organization. I need…just please help me pick up before Hank gets here. It will make me feel so much better."

He nods. "Okay," he says quietly. "I can respect that."

My phone buzzes and we both look at it. Picking it up, I read Isaac's response.

And risk blowing out my knee? No way. You can ski.
I'll hit on the snow bunnies by the fire.

If I hadn't just blown up at him, I'd show Jack the text and make a funny quip about it. Instead, all I can do is show him Isaac's response. Jack's lips begin to quirk up until I say quietly, "You win," and put the phone down on the counter.

His face immediately falls. I feel bad that a conversation about our day became a very tense situation. But I don't think he gets it. I've been trying so hard to let the little things go, like his shoes in the hall and the dishes in the sink, even though it makes me anxious. I'm trying to not be such a stick-in-the-mud, but I need Jack to meet me halfway, and right now I don't feel like he is.

Once the kitchen seems sufficiently cleaned, I tackle the next task…moving the giant pile of laundry to the bedroom. It needs to be done, but I don't think Hank will be going in our bedroom anyway, so at least I can do it last.

A quick run through of the house, and I feel confident that Jack has picked up enough of his crap to make it not look like "Jack's Bachelor pad" lives here, so I go back to the bedroom and begin folding.

"You don't want to do that in the living room in front of the TV?" Jack asks when he pokes his head into the room.

I can't even make eye contact with him, so instead I snap the wrinkles out of a towel before folding it in precise thirds. "I don't think Hank would appreciate hanging out on the couch with some of my panties."

"Joie, I really don't think he cares."

"I know that." I snap another towel. "But I care, Jack. And that's what should matter to you."

He nods and shifts to walk out of the room. "I'm just gonna go, uh, clean up the kitchen."

He leaves me to a pile of wrinkly clothes that I may have to iron. The realization makes me angry all over again.

Throwing a pair of shorts back into the pile, I toss myself back on the bed. I need to get out. I need to go have fun before I lose it completely. Fortunately, I know where I need to go and I know who with.

CHAPTER TEN

Jack

"**S**o we're in agreement about Franklin McCaw?" Hank drops the empty soy sauce packet on the counter and licks his finger. I didn't want any chicken fried rice from the shitty chain restaurant down the street anyway. But seeing how much MSG he's added makes my stomach roll. I swear he's addicted to the stuff.

"I think so." I flip through the papers, looking at the kid's stats again. He came out of nowhere recently, and we knew we'd run across someone special. He's good. Real good. Nine interceptions over seven games for a 1.3 average. He could easily be first string by his sophomore year. "We need to start grooming a couple more cornerbacks. I think he's got what it takes."

Hank plops down in the chair across from me, still eating straight from the takeout box. "I still can't believe we got him. How did no one find this kid before?"

"He's from a Triple-A school in the middle of nowhere Illinois. If Lennox hadn't tipped me off, I never would have opened up his highlight reel."

"That Lennox guy looking for a job? I'm sure we could make room on the coaching staff for him."

I smile and shake my head, grabbing a shitty eggroll out of the brown paper sack. "Pretty sure he's not going anywhere now that he's in a new relationship."

"Fucking young love. I hate recruiting, I was hoping to pass it off to him."

I chuckle under my breath as I put Franklin's paperwork aside. "But who will we have keeping an ear to the ground for us if we move him here?"

He signs in resignation. "Okay, fine. We'll keep doing all this bullshit ourselves. So where does that leave us?"

I flip through a few more papers, making sure I've got accurate information. "Uh...so we're recommending McCaw for the full ride." I make the note on my legal pad and cross out a couple other ideas we've had. "We only have a partial, but what if we give it to Anderson?"

Hank looks up and thinks while he chews and swallows. "Brian Anderson? I thought we already give him money."

"I think we do." A few more flips of the papers and I find what I'm looking for. "Okay, yeah. We give him tuition and expenses, but room and board come out-of-pocket." Leaning back, we begin tossing around our thoughts. "He's a good player. Solid on the field. Gets along with his teammates. Keeps his grades up and doesn't cause trouble."

He tosses the now empty container on the table and leans back. "You sure we don't want to use it to incentivize a quarterback recruit?"

317

"We could. But we've already got first and second string covered. Honestly, after talking to Anderson over the holidays, I'm worried we're gonna lose him if his parents can't afford to keep him here. We need a solid linebacker more than we need a third string QB right now. Anderson's good. His stats are solid, and he helps us win."

"Plus, it'd make your girlfriend happy if her little friend ended up with a full ride."

"Oh, please. She doesn't care one way or another who we throw scholarships at."

"Don't fool yourself, Pride. I know she's got a soft spot for that kid after they took that class together." I know he's just poking at me, but I see the challenge in his eyes. He knows the personal connection isn't why I'm recommending Anderson, but he needs to make *really* sure.

I look him dead in the eye and say, "I wouldn't have known his financial situation if Joie hadn't put together the holiday meals, but that's as far as the personal relationship goes. And I don't use my job to stay in my girlfriend's good graces. I don't need to."

"You sure about that?"

Looking down, I make a few notes on my legal pad again —mostly easy access statistics to justify our decisions. "What are you talking about?"

"I saw her walk out of here. There was mighty thick tension following behind her."

Stopping with my notes, I look up at Hank. He may be an asshole and a pain to work with sometimes, but he's still my best friend and right now, I could use his advice. I sigh and toss my pen on the table. "It was that obvious, huh?"

He looks at me like I'm crazy for not recognizing it myself. "Are you kidding? She ran out of here so fast I thought her panties were on fire. And that woman likes me. So if she's not stopping to chit chat, then yeah, it's obvious. What'd you do wrong?"

Scrubbing my face with my hand, I realize he's right. I've tried to pretend it has nothing to do with me, but considering she barely gave me a peck on the lips on her way out the door, it's clear I'm missing something.

"I honestly don't know," I admit. "Her biology class is giving her trouble, so she's really stressed about finals. And Isaac's dad showing up is really making her crazy."

Hank grimaces. "I hate when the daddies show up. It always fucks with these kids' heads."

"Tell me about it. He's handling it pretty good, so far, but Joie isn't doing as well." Shaking my head at the situation, all I feel is exasperated. "I don't know how to make it a less shitty situation."

"Pfft. I do," Hank retorts, causing me to raise an eyebrow at the shift in conversation. "Stop being so hard to live with."

I roll my eyes and pick up my pen to make more notes. I need advice, not jokes so I might as well get back to work. "We're doing fine living together, Hank."

"Really? Because you're a pig."

"What does that mean?"

He cocks his head and looks at me for a few seconds. It's unnerving because I know he's choosing his words carefully. Hank never does that, so when he does, it puts me on edge.

"Remember when you stayed with me for a couple weeks after your house sold and before the apartment was ready?"

"What does that have to do with anything?"

"A lot. You drove Renee crazy, never picking up after yourself and always leaving shit everywhere. She almost kicked your ass out a couple times, it made her so mad."

"Why didn't she?"

"I'm too good at using oral to make her relax." I smack my hand on my face, but he doesn't slow down. "Renee's pretty chill. We've raised a lot of kids, so not much bothers her. And if you drove *her* crazy, I can just imagine how Joie feels. I saw the color-coded Thanksgiving binders and the big rolly bag. That woman likes her shit neat and tidy, and you came in like a tornado and fucked it all up.

"Look around," he says, holding his arms out wide. "There are empty food containers everywhere. Soy sauce spilled all over the counter in the kitchen. I saw a couple socks on the living room floor, so don't even tell me there wasn't a pile of clean laundry out there when Joie got home. And if I went and looked right now, I bet there's toothpaste in the sink. Am I right?"

I scoff. "First of all, all those Chinese food containers are yours. I don't eat shitty take out. Second, you're the one that spilled the soy sauce. And third, you're wrong about the bathroom."

He scoots away from the table and leaves the room. When he comes back in a few seconds later, he shoves his finger in my face. "I found this toothpaste in the sink."

"Get your hand out of my face, asshole," I shove him away. "So you found toothpaste in the sink. Big deal. That doesn't make me a pig."

"No. But it helps prove my point. How do you explain the socks?"

Narrowing my eyes at him, I know he's got me again. "I must have missed them when we put away all the laundry before you got here."

"Was this before or after she freaked out about company coming over while the house was a mess?"

"The house isn't a mess, Hank. Besides, none of this has anything to do with why Joie is stressed and how I can help her."

He laughs at me. Not with me. At me, and it makes me want to punch him in the nuts. If he wasn't technically my boss, I probably would.

I open my mouth to spout off his direction, but then I begin looking around the room. No, those aren't my Chinese food containers, but that is my pizza box. Those were my beer bottles Joie threw out in a panic. That is my toothpaste in the sink, and I bet it was next to a dirty towel I forgot to throw in the hamper. It hits me, and as much as I hate to admit it, he's probably right.

I'm a slob. And while it doesn't bother me, it probably makes Joie completely crazy.

"Oh shit," I say under my breath as the realization hits me.

"You see it now, don't you?" I nod as I keep looking around the room at my clean socks, my shoes, the spare change and receipts sitting on the counter from where I dumped them when I walked in hours ago.

"Oh shit," I say more forcefully. "I knew I wasn't helping her feel better, but I didn't realize I was making her feel worse."

"Well, you are," he says all matter-of-factly. "So now you can fix it."

"How? How am I going to fix this? I've never been good at keeping a clean house. Sheila used to do all of that, so I don't even know where to start."

"I'm glad you asked, my friend." Hank reaches into his bag and pulls out a colorful package. When he drops the brick on the table it makes a loud bang, which I'm sure he planned for dramatic effect.

"What is that?"

He smirks and waggles his eyebrows. "Sticky notes. In the variety color pack."

I stare at him blankly until he gives up and rolls his eyes.

"The best way to remember things is to have sticky notes as reminders. It's even better if they're color-coded. She'll appreciate the extra effort."

I pick up the square papers and my pen, ready to jot down more notes. Only this time, it's not to build a case about a scholarship, it's to build a case for Joie not kicking my unorganized ass to the curb.

CHAPTER
ELEVEN

Joie

The base of the music is the only thing I can hear. Actually I can hear everything, but I have to concentrate reeeeeeeally hard for it to make sense.

That's what happens when I've had four pineapple chipotle martinis. Four? Five? Four? I lost count after the free Dirty Red shot the bartender gave us. I have no idea what was in it, but it was goooooood.

But I don't care because I feel so relaxed and happy. I don't care about the mess at home or my finals or Isaac's stupid dad. Because the music I can't hear and the white noise of people talking around me make me happy.

Amanda makes me happy. She's my bestest friend ever.

Will, the bartender, makes me happy. He's so cute. He's way too young for me, and he's not my Jack, but he's a little flirt and gave me a free shot. Plus, he makes sure my drinks are full so I love him. So, so much.

I bring the glass to my lips to down the rest of my martini and...wait. The glass is empty.

"Well how did that happen?" I try to get my eyes to focus across the bar. There he is! "Will! Woohoo! Wiiiiiill!"

He looks up from the tap he's pulling and smiles at me, mouthing *one second*. See? He's such a cutie and takes such good care of me. Even though I'm old enough to be his mother. And I know because I'm old enough to be Isaac's mother. Which I am. Isaac's mother.

Suddenly Amanda is right here next to me. I put my arm around her shoulder and pull her close.

"I love you, Amanda. So, so much."

"Okay." She laughs. "I think it might be time for you to stop drinking. Affectionate Joie is here."

Pulling back quickly, I almost fall off the stool. Who makes the seats so much smaller than my butt? "What's wrong with affectionate Joie?"

"Nothing's wrong with affectionate Joie. She's just the beginning of the end is all."

I drop my jaw and look her up and down. How dare she imply I'm going to pass out soon...Oh, Will's here!

"What can I get you?" he asks me.

I sigh and shake my head at him. "Will, you are such a good bartender."

"Thanks." He smiles at me and puts a fresh napkin in front of me. Just like a true gentleman. Because Will is a true gentleman.

"I think I need another one of"—my fingers won't work right so I use my whoooole hand to point at my glass—"that one. I need another of that one."

"The pineapple chipotle martini?" he asks with a flirty little smirk. Because Will is a flirty little bartender. And I *like him*.

"Yes, please. Oh and Will."

"Yeah?"

"If only you were about twenty years older."

He chuckles. "You've said that a few times already. You sure you want another one?"

I gasp. "I have not said that before! Maybe. I don't know. Just make me another martini!"

He raps his knuckles on the bar once and smiles at me. "On it."

"Are you sure you need another one?" Amanda asks as I try to drain the last drops of my martini. If only my tongue was just a little…bit…longer…

The glass is suddenly pulled away from me.

"Hey, I was drinking that!"

"You were not," Amanda says as she puts it down on the counter closer to Will. Sweet, sweet Will who needs a cute girlfriend. I wonder if Isaac knows anyone. "You were practically giving the glass head."

I drop my jaw again. "That was not a very ladylike thing to say. You should have more class."

"Oh good!" She raises her fists in victory, but jokes on her. She didn't do anything victorious. "Mean Drunk Joie is here!"

If I could feel my face, I would have felt it fall. "Am I really a mean drunk?"

Her shoulders move up and down. I think it was a shrug. "You're not terrible, but you can get kind of ugly."

Oh no. I don't want to be a mean drunk. No one likes a mean drunk.

"Oh no," Amanda says as Will puts my drink down in front of me. "Don't you get those weepy, puppy dog eyes. I'll take Mean Drunk Joie over Crying Joie any day."

"But I hurt your feelings, and I don't like hurting your feelings."

"You didn't hurt my feelings. See? I'm smiling." Her smile is so wide, she looks like a clown. But I don't think she'd like if I told her that, so I don't. I'm very, very good at practicing not being Mean Drunk Joie. "No feelings are hurt here."

"Oh good." I take a big sigh of relief and almost fall down again. Seriously. Who shrunk my seat? Or did my butt magically get bigger? It could go either way.

All the people on the dance floor are whirling around and it kind of makes me dizzy. So dizzy I really am falling off my chair. Wait...no I'm not. Some guy just pulled me off the stool and dragged me to the dance floor. Yay! Dancing!

I move to the music, not caring that I can't hear it very well or that I'm the oldest one out here. I've got mooooooooves these kids haven't ever seen. Including the guy I'm dancing with. Who is he?

Looking up I try really hard to focus on him. He's tall, over six feet. He's got blond hair and a tie wrapped around his head. Why does he have a tie wrapped around his head? Does he think he's the Karate Kid? That was the best movie. Ralph Macchio was a total babe.

But this guy isn't Ralph, which is good because Ralph is like eighty, so looking at him probably would make me ralph these days. Get it? Ralph would make me ralph?

I burst out laughing because I am way funny when I'm drinking.

"Why are you laughing?" Tie Guy yells over the crowd at me.

"Because Ralph will make me ralph. Get it?"

He smiles and nods and says, "No. I don't get it."

I shake my head and his unfortunate lack of all things ralph related. "It's because you're too young for me." I pat his arm. "You just don't know."

Something glitters on his hand and I pull on his wrist so I can see better. I gasp because I know what it is. "Where is your wife, Tie Guy? And why are you dancing without her?"

"Because I love dancing!"

I try very hard to throw his hand down, but I think it just slipped out of my grasp. Whatever. "So do other women! Women who love to break up marriages. Don't you know what kind of danger you're in? Where is your wife?"

"She's in the room asleep." He twirls around like he has no cares in the world when clearly he's in danger of cheating on her.

"Why is she sleeping when she could be dancing with the Karate Kid?"

He gestures a big bump over his stomach. "Because she's pregnant."

I stop dancing. That is the most wonderful news ever! "Oh my gosh! Is it your first baby?"

He nods and smiles and twirls. How is he not falling over?

"Tie Guy! Focus!" I yell and grab him, stopping him from dancing. "I'm so happy for you! Do you just love her so much now?"

He stops moving completely, looks me dead in the eye and says, "She's my everything."

If I wasn't in serious danger of passing out, I would have swooned so hard I would have needed smelling salts, because that was the nicest thing anyone could ever say. I have to tell Amanda.

I race back to the bar and plop down next to her. Dammit, the seat got smaller again! "Will, stop changing my seat!"

He looks at me like he has no idea what he's talking about. He's not tricking me, I'm not that drunk.

"Amanda, Ralph is having a baby."

She finishes her sip of something that looks awfully close to my martini. I'll have to investigate that later. "Who's Ralph?"

I roll my eyes. "The Karate Kid?"

"Joie, I am so confused right now. You need to think more carefully about your words."

I huff. "Amanda. Ralph is the Karate Kid who is Tie Guy whose wife is having their first baby and she's his everything. Now who do you think has had too much to drink, *Amanda*?" I take a giant gulp of the spicy, fruity goodness, now that I've made my point.

"Oh well, clearly it's me who needs to slow down on the booze." I love it when Amanda agrees with me. "And yes, that's a very sweet story."

"It is, right?" I love it when people have babies. And when they're happy. And when men are so excited to be dads and love their wives and...wait. "Wait." I smack Amanda's arm. "We have to warn him about what happens when you have a baby."

"Uh…what part of it are we warning him about?"

"Seriously? Keep up! We have to warn him. Hey Ralph!" I yell across the dance floor because I can't hear hardly anything anyway so maybe he'll hear me. "Ralph! Tie guy!" He looks up and waves at me, so I wave back. "Come here!"

It takes him a few seconds, or maybe a year, I just don't know what time is right now, and he comes over to us.

"Ooh! Is that a martini?" he asks and grabs it off the bar and drinks it.

"Yep. It's Amanda's but you can have it."

"Hey!" she says. We ignore her because it's not nice to not share.

"Hey, listen, Ralph." I smack his arm a couple times so he'll look at me. "You need to listen to me. This is very important. It's about your wife."

His eyes get big. "I love her so much. I'm listening."

"Okay, good. So listen. After she has the baby, things aren't always going to work the same down there." I gesture toward my lady bits in case he doesn't know what I'm talking about. I think he does since he got a baby in there, but you can never be too sure.

"Oh God, here we go," Amanda grumbles.

I shush her because this is very important information. "You need to know, Ralph, that someday soon, after the baby is here, when she sneezes, she's going to pee a little. And you're just going to have to love her anyway."

He looks at me, really understanding what I'm saying and says, "I like to eat butt, so…"

I blink a few times, trying to decide if he said that out loud or if I just heard it in my foggy, mushy brain. But Amanda is laughing hard enough that I think he said it out loud. And if he likes that level of kink...

"Okay. So I guess you're good then," I say to him because, what else can I say that won't be rude?

He smiles and nods at me and dances away.

My brain still is trying to figure out if that just happened. Kids these days are just so odd. Is that a real thing?

"I wonder if Jack likes to eat butt," I muse out loud.

This time Amanda laughs so hard, she falls right off the stool.

CHAPTER
TWELVE

Jack

Pulling into the Holiday Inn parking lot, I look around. Of all the places Amanda could have brought Joie to-night, why in the world did they come here? It's on the outskirts of town, practically in the middle of nowhere, and it's a hotel. Not a restaurant downtown or even a random dive. I asked when she called and told me it was my turn for drunk babysitting duties. She tried to convince me it's a nice little bar, but I still think it's weird.

I can hear the music from the back of the packed parking lot. That's not a juke box. That's a live band. It's my first ink-ling that maybe I had the wrong idea about this place. The neighborhood isn't bad. The building itself isn't run-down or anything. There are a lot of people walking in and out, and they're mostly dressed up. I feel kind of out of place wearing jeans. Maybe Amanda's right. I guess I'm about to find out.

Pulling open the door, I'm immediately stopped by a security guard.

"Ho, wait a minute." He puts his hand up to stop me. He's not much older than I am, but he's definitely worse for wear. Not only is he completely grey and his face is weathered and wrinkly, but he has a pot belly for days. He doesn't bother to stand up to make sure I follow instructions. The words "security guard" might actually be a stretch for what he's doing. "This is a closed event. Do you have a wedding invitation?"

"A wedding invitation? People are getting hitched here?"

He chuckles. "Nah. The wedding is long over. Groom already got in a big fight with his new father-in-law. Something about holding up his end of the bargain and never agreeing to a honeymoon in the Caribbean. Who knows? This is the after party. They rented out the bar."

The dresses and suits everyone is wearing makes sense now. "Sounds like they need all the booze they can get if he doesn't even want to go on vacation with his new bride."

"That's what I thought." He crosses his legs at the ankles and relaxes into the stool. I guess I passed his test and am not perceived as a threat. "For a minute I thought I was going to have to kick them both out. Wouldn't that have been a fun way to end a wedding."

"Just another reason not to get hitched any time soon. But I'm not here to crash the party. I got a call to come pick up my girlfriend. I'm not sure how she got past you, but from what I hear, she's pretty smashed."

He sizes me up, probably to make sure I'm not telling a story to prey on an innocent victim. I appreciate it, but I'm starting to get antsy that I can't get to Joie.

"You Joie's guy?" he finally asks, narrowing his eyes as he waits for my answer.

Why does his question not surprise me? Oh yeah. Because she's a social butterfly. "I see she's made friends since she got here. How bad off is she?"

Another chuckle, but he still doesn't make a move to get up. "She's gonna be hurting in the morning. She's a nice lady, though. Funny. Real funny. Got here before the party started so she's been living it up."

"I've never seen her drunk before, so this is gonna be an experience for me."

He shakes his head in amusement. "Brace yourself. She's something else."

A little more small talk, and he lets me pass, despite it being a closed event. I wander around the room, trying to find her. I see Amanda first. She's sitting at the bar, playing on her phone, with Joie nowhere around her. Pushing through the wedding guests, I finally see her hands waving in the air in time to the music. Okay, not really in time to the music. She's very off-beat. But at least she's sweating out some of the alcohol dancing with some young guy who...does he have a tie on his head?

It's not hard to get through the crowd of drunks. With as much as they've had to drink, I can pretty much knock them out of my way. Soon I'm standing right behind her. She whirls around and stops as soon as she sees me. More like she stumbles, but eventually she stops.

"Jack!" Launching herself into my arms, she begins kissing all over my face and neck. "I missed you! Did you miss me?"

Chuckling to myself, I'm already starting to understand what the security guard meant when he said I should brace myself. She normally has an excess of energy, but it seems magnified right now. "It's been four hours. Who are you dancing with anyway?"

She pulls away and looks around for the drunkard who got his head tangled up in his tie when getting undressed. "Oh there he is! Ralph! Ralph come here!"

"Ralph?" I ask under my breath. That's an unusual name for a kid his age.

"Like Ralph from Karate Kid?" Joie looks at me like I'm an idiot. "Seriously? Why does no one get this? He looks like he knows karate because of the tie."

Honestly, I'm surprised she has enough brain power left to put all that together coherently. I'm even more surprised that "Ralph" comes bounding over.

"Jack this is Tie Guy. We call him Ralph. And his wife is having a baby, so I'm dancing with him to make sure no one else does because he doesn't need a floozy to take advantage of him when he's drunk because his wife is super pregnant, and she's his everything." I have my arm around her waist, holding her up so she doesn't tumble to the floor. She spins and gets so close to me I can smell the booze. Gin. Yeah, she's headed for a nasty hangover. "Am I your everything, Jack?"

"You're my everything, babe."

"No really. Am I? Because you're mine, and I want to be yours, but I never ever want to have another baby, okay? We'll let Ralph do that."

I snicker. "Okay. We can let Ralph have the babies." Whoever this Ralph guy is, he's already dancing with someone else. So much for my girlfriend protecting his virtue.

"Okay. Are you taking me home?" She begins to snuggle into me, but pops back up when she has a thought. "Oh! Where's Amanda?"

"She's right here." I guide my very drunk girlfriend back over to the bar and sit her on the stool next to her friend. "Exactly how much has she had to drink?" I ask Amanda.

She drops her phone on the bar, an exasperated look on her face. "Good. You're here. She's had four martinis and a shot."

"Five," Joie mumbles into my chest.

"Four, honey. That last one was a virgin."

Joie pushes away from me, looking like a pissed off kitten …all snarky and wild, but without the coordination to back it up. "You gave me a virgin? You bitch! And Will," she yells over the bar, pointing at some bartender, "you're dead to me!"

He gives her a questioning look, but quickly turns away to take care of a customer.

"As you can see," Amanda says, "we've had a lot of fun, but this one has about hit her limit."

Joie collapses her body into my chest and begins to fall asleep. "I can see that. I hope she didn't ruin your night."

Amanda has a sudden change in demeanor. "Oh my gosh, no! We had a great time!" She holds up her phone. "My idiot son is just pulling a bunch of bullshit right now, and my husband won't stop texting me about it. It's been a total buzzkill. Joie has actually been the most entertaining part of the evening. Well, and Tie Guy," she says with a laugh.

"I feel like I'm missing his appeal."

"Oh, I'm sure you'll hear all about it in the car." She snickers again. "Let's just say, neither one of them have a filter when they're drinking. The conversations have been quite entertaining."

Joie gets a sudden burst of energy and sits straight up. "Do you like to eat butt?"

Amanda barks a laugh. "Told ya."

I blink and shake my head, trying to wrap my brain around what's happening. "What?"

"Do you like to eat butt?" Joie stares off into space as she spews her thoughts. "I've never done that before, and I don't get it. I mean, maybe I do. But I think you'd get sick from the poop and probably pink eye. I don't know. So, would you eat my butt?"

Amanda continues laughing as I stand here, completely baffled as to what the hell is going on. So I shrug and answer honestly, whispering in her ear. "I have no desire to eat your butt. But my tongue is ready to lick your pussy, so if we can hurry this up, I'd like to take you home and get on that."

"Oh my," she breathes and then leans toward Amanda. "He won't eat my butt, but he's gonna eat my other things."

My head drops as I try not to laugh. Amanda isn't trying as hard as I am. In fact, I'm pretty sure she might fall on the floor, she's laughing so hard.

"I think that's my cue to get you outta here," I finally say. Joie seems to have other plans as she melts into me again. I wouldn't be surprised if she actually falls asleep in the middle of all this noise. "Amanda, do you need a ride, too?"

She shakes her head and waves over the bar tender. "Nah. I cut myself off when I realized she needed to kill brain cells way more than I did."

I grimace. "She's still that stressed, isn't she?"

She shrugs. "Do you blame her? The woman is a control freak, and she's had a tremendous amount of stress thrown at her in a very short amount of time. She'll get there. It's just going to take her a minute to get back into her comfort zone."

"Yeah, I hope I can help with some of that."

The bartender drops a black check folder in front of Amanda and looks at me rubbing my hand up and down Joie's back before turning back to her. "Does Joie know that guy?"

She nods. "That's the boyfriend she's been talking about all night."

He holds his hand out to me. "I'm Will. She's gonna need some aspirin, a lot of water, and maybe even a mimosa in the morning to get rid of the headache."

"She made friends fast, didn't she?" I ask no one in particular as I shake his hand.

"That's our Joie. She's not shy." Amanda tosses a few twenties in the folder and hands it back to Will. "Keep the change. And thanks so much for everything."

He winks at her. "My pleasure. You guys come back any time. I had more fun tonight than usual."

"Will!" Joie yells and pops up again. Her ability to regain random comprehension is impressive.

"Yo!" Will responds. "What's up? You still feeling good?"

"Yeah." She nods so hard her hair flies in her face. She doesn't seem to notice. "Will, do you eat butt? Is this like a generational thing?"

Gotta love the bartender who has fielded so many random conversations at his job that he doesn't even skip a beat. "I've done it. It's not my fav, but she seemed to like it okay. And yes, in my observations as an almost thirty something, it's gaining popularity. Particularly on the college campuses."

Amanda grimaces and Joie puts her hands over her ears. "Ack! I don't need to know that! My son goes to a college campus! I can't look at anyone in my study group again!"

Will shrugs. "She asked."

"That she did," I agree, trying to really hard not to remember how many mouth pieces I've picked up in a college locker room over the years. "Are you ladies ready to go?"

"Yep," Amanda says as she pops off the stool. "I need to get home and deal with my ridiculous child."

"That bad, huh?" I help Joie stand and situate her under my arm so I can help guide her to the car.

"Who knows? My husband seems to freak out over every little thing and wants to jump right in and fix it. My theory is, spend the night in jail one time and you're less likely to get arrested for peeing on the side of a church and public intoxication again." We walk past the security guard who nods in agreement with her statement as he holds the door open for us. "How we choose to discipline him has been a fundamental disagreement in our marriage since the day he was born. Obviously the inconsistency has done wonders for his ability to make good decisions as an adult."

We walk Amanda to her car and make sure she gets settled. She thanks me for coming to pick Joie up so she can go straight home and calm her husband down. I like Amanda. As we head to my truck, I make a mental note to tell Joie I'd be happy to get her and her husband seats to a home game. Maybe we can do dinner afterward. I'm curious if they're polar opposites on more than just discipline issues.

"I love you, Jack," Joie mumbles as I help her into the truck. And by help, I mean lift her up and set her down. Good thing she's tiny.

"I love you, too, babydoll." Wiping a stray hair off her forehead, I kiss her quickly and seat belt her in. "You can go to sleep. I'll make sure we get home safe."

"Okay." She never opens her eyes, just leans back and begins to snore gently. She'd better enjoy the rest now. Tomorrow is going to be brutal.

CHAPTER THIRTEEN

Joie

I would open my eyes, but if the pounding in my head is any indication of what's to come, I don't think I'll be able to handle the light.

Hangovers in my twenties were pretty bad. But this... wow. I don't know what happened when I hit forty, but this is something else. Something worse. The pain itself might not actually be worse, but I definitely crossed the line from buzzed to hurting-in-the-morning a lot faster than I used to. Did Amanda say they gave me a virgin martini at one point? I'll have to thank her later.

Trying to roll over so my back is facing the window, I groan. It's going to be a rough day. Thank goodness there's nothing pressing on the agenda. As much as I'd like to get up and clean, I'm almost positive it will make me hurl, and mopping up morning-after vomit is not on my to-do list.

A warm hand brushes some hair off my face, and lips press gently to my forehead. "Good morning, sunshine. Are you awake?"

"I think I'm dead." The words come out like a groan, and he laughs. How rude for him to be laughing at my pain.

I hear him rooting around on the bedside table. "You'd be feeling worse if it weren't for the aspirin and bottle of water you drank before bed."

"I don't think it worked."

"With as drunk as you were, maybe not. Can you sit up? I have more medicine for you."

I take a deep breath and use all my strength to get into a sitting position. Jack has to help me because my muscles are apparently all still asleep. Finally peeling my eyes open, I have to squint to see anything. The blinds are closed and the light is off, but it's still very much daytime. Ugh. This is going to be a long day.

Jack hands me two pills and a glass with orange juice in it. "Here. This will help."

It takes longer than normal to get the pills down because I have to move so slowly, but I finally complete the task and lean back against the headboard, sighing. "Remind me never to drink that much again."

Jack laughs and sprawls out on the bed next to me, his head resting on his hand. "Sad thing is, you didn't even have that much. You're just a lightweight."

"You're lucky I'm a cheap date."

I feel the rumble of the vibrations from his chest when he laughs quietly. He rubs my thigh, which feels really, really good compared to the rest of me. I'm throbbing all over—my head, my shoulders, even my feet. It's like I can feel my heartbeat over my entire body. I also notice a slight shake in my hand when I bring the glass to my lips. The small sip tastes funny, but I'm not sure if it's the juice or my cotton mouth.

"Is this straight orange juice?"

"Mimosa," Jack says. "Hair of the dog will thin your blood a bit and help you feel better."

I nod my head in appreciation and take another sip. He continues rubbing my leg. This is what Jack does. He takes care of me. He's not perfect. But he loves me more than anyone in the entire world. I know I've been taking his imperfections personally instead of focusing on the perfect way he loves me. And I need to own up to it.

"I'm sorry, Jack." I open my eyes as wide as my headache will let me, which isn't much. "I've been a real pain to be around lately."

He shakes his head in protest. "You haven't been a pain to be around. Last night was a little rough, but even then, you weren't a pain."

I try to think back to last night, but there's not much there. "I don't mean about last night. I mean for a few weeks now. I guess I'm so used to having my own space and having things exactly the way I like that I haven't exactly been welcoming in my home. In *our* home."

Jack sits up and leans next to me against the headboard, grabbing my free hand to hold it. "Joie, honey, you are a control freak."

"I am not." I try hard to protest, but it comes out much weaker than I intend.

"You are," he argues. "You like things to be done in a particular order. You don't like change very much. And you certainly like being right smack in the middle of certain things when they do change." I start to protest, but he cuts me off before I can say anything. "There's nothing wrong with those things. They're part of who you are, and I love who you are. But I think Charlie coming back, and there's nothing you can do about it, has thrown you for a loop."

He's got me there. I hate that Isaac went to Jack before me. I hate that I have no say in whether or not Charlie gets to see my son. I hate that I don't even have a right to know what Isaac's decision is. Letting go and trusting Isaac to make his own decisions about his father is one of the hardest things I've ever had to do as a mother. I wasn't expecting that.

"Add onto that, your biology class has been more fly-by-the-seat-of-your-pants than you like," Jack continues. "So when you come home, you want things neat and organized, and I'm not that guy."

I lean my head on his shoulder. "You're right. About all of it. And you're right...you're not that guy. But I love the guy you are."

He leans over and kisses the top of my head. "I'm trying really hard to be better about the mess. It's weird because I don't see it. Not like I ignore it. I just don't see it."

"How can you not see it? When I walk in, the first thing I see is how messy the room is."

He shrugs, causing my head to move, and I groan in response. "Oh sorry," he apologizes. "When I first walk in, I don't see the overall room. I see the path to the kitchen. I guess it's like tunnel vision."

I giggle just a little. The mimosa and aspirin must be working. "You tunnel-vision to the fridge, don't you?"

The movement of his cheeks when he smiles can be felt against my hair. "I do. I don't understand why, but it's like my brain can only focus on one task at a time, and that task is nourishment. But I'm going to make an effort to look around the room and really see it from now on."

"I appreciate that. And I'm going to work on letting it go. Yes, I like my organized, clean space. But if it comes between clean and organized or a happy relationship, I choose you."

He pats my leg and kisses the top of my head again. "If you feel up to it, why don't you go brush your teeth, because your breath smells terrible." My eyes widen, and I immediately clap my hand over my mouth. Jack just laughs. "Stop. It's fine. I just figured you might want to get rid of the gross taste and freshen up a bit. I'm making eggs and bacon to help sober you up."

"You're so good to me."

He shrugs like it's not a big deal, even though to me, it really is. Kissing me one more time, he saunters out of the room and leaves me to slowly peel myself out from under the sheets. It takes a few minutes to finally get myself into the bathroom. Yeah. My binge drinking days are definitely over.

Twisting the water faucet on, I glance in the mirror. What catches my attention isn't the black eye makeup smeared all over my face, although I make a mental note to fix that quickly, it's what is stuck to the mirror. A bright pink sticky note with: *Clean the toothpaste out of the sink* written on it hangs before me. He made himself a note to remember?

I turn to open the drawer and grab my toothbrush when another one catches my eye. This one is over the towel holder and says: *throw dirty hand towel in hamper.* Did he leave little reminders for himself all over?

Looking around the room, I find two more. One is over the toilet and says: *Put the seat down*, which makes me smile. The other is next to the shower and says: *Close the curtain*.

I'm stunned. When Jack said he was trying to be better because he knows I need my space to be organized and clean, he wasn't just tossing words out there. He really meant it.

Anxious to let Jack know I found his notes, I wash my face and brush my teeth as quickly as my hangover will let me. I forgo the hair for now and throw it up in a ponytail. A very long, very hot shower is in order for the near future anyway. There's no reason to put in that much effort. I'm still a little wobbly, so I slowly pad down the hallway, coming across another note.

Put your shoes away. It's right where Jack normally leaves his shoes when he kicks them off. And there are no shoes in sight.

Rounding the corner to the kitchen, Jack looks over and smiles. I realize, he's put his money where his mouth is. It's time to return the favor.

"I want you to put your chair in the living room," I blurt out before I can change my mind.

He looks at me quizzically as he stirs the eggs and flips some bacon. "What? Why?"

"Because that's not a man cave. It's an office. And this is your house, too."

He smiles again, and I know in his mind, this is his version of finding sticky notes. It's a way of recognizing living together is hard. We're individuals with different priorities and comfort levels. But ultimately, our goal is to make the other one happy. And that's what's going to make this work.

"I appreciate that, babe. Are you sure you're okay with it?"

I nod. "I'm sure. As long as I get to recover it with new material first."

He laughs a hearty, belly laugh. "You have a deal."

I smile as I watch him cook, ideas for a color palate binder racing through my brain. All of the sudden, I have a random memory of the night before.

"Did I...?" I ask as the memory takes on my clarity. "Did I ask you to eat my butt?"

Jack laughs so hard at my sudden realization that he has to drop his hands to his knees. I narrow my eyes as he keeps laughing at my humiliation. I may have to reconsider moving his chair, after all.

CHAPTER FOURTEEN

Jack

Football doesn't end just because the season is over. Practices aren't as intense, sure, but every player still has a grade point average to maintain and a physique to continue to work on. As a staff, we meet with the academic advisors daily to get updates on grades and what kind of tutoring needs to be in place. This close to finals, it's intense. A different kind of intense than the rest of the year, but intense nonetheless.

I can hear rustling in the locker room, a sure indicator that morning workouts are over. I'm not paying much attention, though. I'm up to my ears in grade point averages and tutoring schedules. Not to mention double checking to make sure everyone has a place to live over the summer. Yes, we have people who do all this, but I don't like things slipping through the cracks, so I prefer to monitor it all myself.

My phone rings, and I'm both relieved and pissed off for the distraction.

"Pride," I growl into the receiver, only halfway paying attention, more focused on the housing forms sitting in front of me.

"Hey, Jack Pride!" the male voice practically yells through the phone. "I didn't expect to actually be transferred straight to the top! How cool is this?"

Immediately I know something's up, and my focus is solely on this conversation. "They don't normally. Must be an important situation. What can I do for you?"

"Sure is important. You're coaching my son, and I can't reach him."

My hackles rise, knowing something is wrong. If a parent can't get ahold of his kid, it's usually because the kid is avoiding him. And I have a sick feeling he's talking about the only kid I know who might be avoiding his so-called parent right now.

"Well, I'll see what I can do. Who am I speaking to?"

"Charlie Stevens."

Bingo. The exact person I don't want to talk to is, of course, the one person who our receptionist put through. That tells me he's been hounding her for a while, and she finally had enough of his shit.

"I've been trying to reach my son, Isaac, but he's not calling me back."

"Sure, sure." I'm sounding calmer than I feel, but I know this is about to get ugly before it ends once and for all. "I know everyone is really busy right now with finals just around the corner. Are you just checking up on him? I can have him call you if need be."

"Nah," he says, and I have a bad feeling I know what's coming. "We had talked about getting me season passes for next year, but I haven't been able to reach him. I know those seats go fast, so I need to make sure we're all good to go. But now that I have you on the line, this is even better. Parents get the good tickets, right?"

I'm practically shaking with fury. Situations like this always piss me off, but this one is so much more personal. Everything Joie was worried about is coming to fruition right here, right now. Everything I warned Isaac about was dead-on. I hoped we were all wrong because no one wants to be right about stuff like this.

"I'll have to see what I can do. But hey, Charlie, can I put you on hold for a second? I'm right in the middle of something, and I want to make sure I do this the right way."

"Yeah, absolutely!" he says with excitement. "This is great!"

I press the hold button and do my best not to slam the receiver down on the cradle. Taking a few deep breaths, I ready myself for what has to be done. Pushing back my chair and standing up, I take a few more deep breaths. This is it. This is the moment we've been waiting for. This is where Isaac's decision will be made and the ramifications of it will begin.

"Stevens," I yell when my office door is open.

He looks up, a quizzical expression on his face. He hears it in my tone. From the look on everyone else's face, they all do. "Coach?"

"In my office. Now."

"Okay, Coach." He fist-bumps Anderson and makes his way around the benches to my door. I know he's confused, but

I'm not doing this emotional shit in front of everyone else. He'll thank me for that later.

"Is something wrong?" he asks as soon as the door latches behind us.

"Isaac."

His face pales when I call him by his first name. He knows this is personal. "Is it my mom? Did something happen?"

"No! No. She's fine. Everyone's fine." Except now I feel like a dick for making him panic.

He takes a deep breath. "Oh good. Sorry. You just called me by my name and..." He breathes again.

"I know. I'm sorry. You just need to know which hat I'm wearing right now."

He nods and sinks down into the chair in front of my desk. "Gotcha. What's going on?"

"Your dad is on the phone."

This time his face doesn't get pale. No, this time it's bright red from anger. His jaw clenches and his hands curl into fists. "What the fuck does he want?"

From his reaction, I think it's clear he already knows. "Season passes."

"Son of a bitch." He jumps out of the chair and begins pacing, which is hard to do considering what a small room it is.

"I take it he already hit you up for them?"

"I figured he'd get the hint that the answer was no when I didn't call him back. I guess not."

I lean against the wall, crossing my arms and legs, and glance at the phone to make sure the hold button is still blinking. This isn't the first time I've seen one of these kids realize the depth of a deadbeat parent's betrayal. Somehow, though, I feel it much more deeply myself. It's different watching your girlfriend's son go through it. No, we're not married, but Isaac is family. That makes it so much worse.

He finally quits pacing and turns to me, putting his hands on his hips. "So what do I do?"

"That depends. The big question here is, do you want me to give him the passes?"

"Fuck, no," Isaac spits out. "I'd rather give them to the devil himself."

I nod in agreement. "Understood. Second question, do you want a relationship with your dad?"

His eyes soften. This is the question they all have to decide. They know that not caving to their parents' demands means the opportunity will likely never come around again. Regardless of how bad a parent has been, never seeing or talking to them again is still the toughest pill anyone could swallow.

"He doesn't want me," he says quietly and licks his lips. "He never did."

His eyes glisten as he admits the truth to himself, probably for the very first time. I grab him by the back of the neck and bring our foreheads together.

"You listen to me." He nods. "I will never be your daddy. That ship has sailed. But you are family now. And that may not mean anything to you, but it means something to me. You aren't alone in any of this. Not in this situation. Not prepping for the draft. Not figuring out what to get your mother for Christmas. So don't you think for one second you're losing out on anything special by cutting him out. Okay? I've got your back from here on out, Isaac. I'm not leaving your mother, and that means I'm not leaving you. Got it?"

He nods again, and I pull away. We may never discuss our relationship like this again, but now that it's out there, we're on the same page.

"So," I continue, "here's what we're gonna do. I'm gonna put him on speaker, and we're going to tell him together, in a very professional way, to go fuck himself. Sound good?"

Isaac straightens his back and takes another breath. "I'm sure you've done this before, so I'll follow your lead."

"Right. Let's do this."

Isaac makes himself comfortable in the chair, or at least as comfortable as he can be, considering. I don't bother sitting. I have too much pent-up energy. Pressing the speaker button, the showdown begins.

"Mr. Stevens, sorry to keep you on hold," I start. "Before we authorize any tickets, we have to verify with the player in question. I'm sure you understand."

"Oh totally," he responds, sounding as cocky and arrogant as they always do. It always makes me wonder why so many men think being a sperm donor gives them rights to all the benefits of a kid, but doesn't make a dent in their understanding of taking on the responsibility. "I guess you tracked him down and got his blessing?"

Isaac glances up at me. The fury in his eyes gives me encouragement. He'll be all right. He'll say his piece. He'll have a good cry when he's alone. And he'll move on.

"Well, we seem to have a little misunderstanding here."

"Misunderstanding?" Charlie doesn't seem so confident now. It almost makes me want to laugh. Almost. "What kind of misunderstanding?"

"Mr. Stevens, I have Isaac sitting in my office right now, and he says he never talked to you about any season passes."

"What the fuck?" Just like I anticipated, the nice-guy mask comes off quickly. "We talked about it last week."

"No, Dad," Isaac jumps in, surprising me. But this is his show, and I'm not going to stop him. "*You* brought it up. I never answered you."

"That's because I haven't been able to reach you. I've been calling every day."

"And leaving messages asking about the fucking tickets." Isaac's voice rises as he gets it all out. "You haven't asked about my grades or if I have a girlfriend or how my mom is. The only thing you ask me about is football and getting tickets. How do you think that feels, huh? I haven't seen you since *middle school*. And the minute I get a full ride, *now* I'm good enough for you?"

"That's not how it is, boy," Charlie argues. "You know your mama wouldn't let me see you."

I feel myself stiffen, but bite my tongue from defending Joie. It'll only make it worse if he knows we're living together. Plus, I don't need to take away from Isaac's moment.

"No, she wouldn't let you *use* me," Isaac spouts. "You could have come to any one of my games in high school, but you chose not to. You're welcome to come to all of my games next year. I'd actually love that. But you'll have to pay your own way like everyone else."

"Why you ungrateful little...I'm your father—" Charlie starts, but I cut him off.

"Mr. Stevens, I'm sure you understand that I can't author-ize those tickets now. But we're grateful for your support, so

I'm gonna send you a coupon for a discount on your next ticket purchase. Consider it a personal thank you from me to you."

I smirk at Isaac who is stifling a laugh. He knows I'm not really feeling generous and am getting a kick out of digging the knife in a little more, but you can't have a position like mine without playing a little politics sometimes.

"Yeah," Charlie responds, sounding like someone just kicked his dog. "Yeah, thanks."

"No problem. I'll have that over to you today. Have a great afternoon." And I click the speaker button and cut off the phone call. Isaac's head is hanging down, elbows on his knees. "You okay?"

It takes him a minute to figure out how to respond. It's clear when he looks up that he's not, but that he knows he will be. It's a look I've seen before, and it never gets any easier to witness.

"I think..." He stands up and thinks again. "I think I need to go for a run."

"Don't you have class?"

He shakes his head. "Not until one."

As he moves toward the door, I realize how tense I am as well. I've been waiting for this situation to come to a head, but I didn't realize how badly I would feel. How hurt I would feel for Isaac and how upset I would feel for Joie. I've felt hatred in situations like these, but this one is on a whole different level. As much as I need to stay and double check these housing reports, Isaac has the right idea.

"Hey wait up. If you don't mind, I'll come with you."

"Yeah. Yeah, that'd be cool." I'm grabbing my gym bag from under my desk when he drops another bomb on me. "You know you get to tell Mom about all this, right?"

"Yeah, I know." Because I do. I knew it the minute I answered that phone.

"I'd make sure to get the purple flowers on the way home," he jokes as we walk through the locker room.

"I was thinking more like vacuuming and offering a foot rub."

Isaac laughs. "You've learned quickly."

He claps me on the back and goes to put his running shoes on before we head out into the Flinton heat and humidity.

CHAPTER FIFTEEN

Joie

Two years later

The house is packed with people and laughter, but for me, the tension has never been higher. Isaac was supposed to be snatched up in the fourth round. It's the now the sixth round and so far, nothing.

He's gotten several phone calls saying he's up next, but none of it has panned out. Jack and Hank both say that's pretty normal. Deals are being made behind the scenes the whole time, and any of those deals can change things in an instant. That doesn't make it any easier though. And for all their calming words, the tension radiating off the two coaches, Jack in particular, is obvious.

This is what we've all been working for. What we've all sacrificed for. All that gear my former co-workers gave us because I couldn't afford it when he was in high school, the hours upon hours of travel Amanda and I did in support, the scholarship Jack gave him long before we'd met—it all led up to this moment.

The NFL Draft.

We expected a long two days. We just didn't expect for it to be this long. And the more names that are knocked off the board, the more Jack's shoulders rise. He's nervous. Really nervous. And there's nothing any of us can do to eliminate those nerves.

Jack and Isaac have become relatively close over the last two years. It's not like a father/son relationship. More like a mentoring friendship. They've moved past only talking football. They talk relationships and future options. They talk about when Jack played in college, and the lessons he learned there. Nothing is off limits.

And Jack has been vital in helping us through this draft thing. He already knew of a good agent, highly recommended by some former players of his who had gone pro, as well as a financial planner to help Isaac through contract issues. I never would have known where to go with all that, so I'm beyond grateful. I know he would have done it for any of his players, but knowing Jack, he went above and beyond for our family.

As anticipated, the minute Isaac's name and "the draft" started being spoken in the same sentence, Charlie showed up again. This time it was short-lived. Isaac answered his call one time and told Charlie he looked forward to seeing him in the stands if he ever went to a game. It shut Charlie down quickly. But I'm proud of Isaac. He didn't shut the door on a relationship with his father. He merely put the ball back in his dad's court. I know he still has hope that his dad will be an upstanding guy someday. I don't have the same hope, but maybe that's the mom in me.

For the last two days, our friends and family have kept us relatively calm and entertained during the down times. Renee, Amanda, and my mom have been keeping the food stocked and the house clean while I kind of wander around in a daze, not really sure what to do.

Greg and Elena's four girls have been doing talent and fashion shows for us. I'm pretty sure only Greg, Elena, and I actually find it cute. Everyone else just tolerates it. But my house, my rules, so later on we'll all be getting our hair and nails done during beauty parlor time. I've already picked out the color for Hank's fingers. He's less than thrilled by how happy it makes me that Renee is forcing him to participate.

Greer and her family are also here. Oli has done a really good job of staying calm and focused, despite the stress level surrounding him. He started working on a ranch a couple years ago and we all agree it's helped calm him tremendously. Like having a connection with the animals cures a part of him that was broken. It's weird how finding that one thing that makes you happy can sometimes be the key to so many of your problems.

The downside is, since he still has some resistance to doing the basic daily chores required to maintain good hygiene, he smells like a cow pretty much all the time. But I'm not complaining. One battle at a time.

Oli's new baby sister may have helped him a bit, too. Yes, I said baby sister. That's a story in and of itself. She came as a huge surprise to everyone, especially Greer, but she's been a joy to all of us. And today, she's also been a good distraction. Well, for a while. There's only so long you can make faces at an infant before your mind starts wandering again.

I'm feeling so much pressure, and I can't imagine how hard it must be on my son. I know he's discouraged and second guessing his entire career. Did he do enough? Did he train hard enough? Did he push as hard as he could at the draft combine? I'm sure his mind is running in circles and somewhere around the 160th draft pick, he disappeared. That was hours ago. I'd look for him, but I know he needs this time alone. And probably he needs time away from the roomful of people that keep shooting him pitying glances whenever he doesn't get called. They're all rooting for him, but they know how let down he feels every time the pick goes to someone else.

"Joie!" I hear Jack call from the living room. "It's on!"

I walk back into the room and sit down next to him, clasping our hands together. His thumb pushes the full-carat rock back and forth on my finger. He loves that ring. About six months ago he asked me to marry him, and of course I said yes. Will we actually go through with it? Who knows? But being engaged seemed to solidify to any doubters that we're in this for the long haul. Not that the doubters matter. We just wanted something more officially than just "living together" so it works for us.

I squeeze Jack's hand and bite my lip. He bounces his knee up and down. We've done this 185 times already. 185 times someone official has stood on that podium and announced another draft pick. 185 times of us having a sliver of hope that my son is about to reach his goal. 185 times we've all felt his defeat. 185 times of reminding ourselves that there are still more spots open.

We watch as a representative of the Detroit Lions stands on the stage. There are several people with him, but I have no idea who they are. Nor do I care. I squeeze Jack's hand harder as my nerves get the best of me.

"Here we go," I vaguely hear Hank say from the chair next to us.

"In the 186th pick by the Detroit Lions, they've chosen offensive lineman from Flinton State University, Isaac Stevens."

I stare at the television in disbelief. The only sound I hear is the blood rushing in my ears, despite knowing there are cheers all around me. Suddenly, Isaac's name crosses the screen and it hits me that it's happening. This is real. He did it. My son is going to the NFL.

As quickly as it hits me, I'm lifted off the feet I didn't realize I was standing on and hoisted into Isaac's arms.

"We did it, Mama," he whispers in my ear, his voice clogged with emotion. "We did it. I'm going to the pros!"

"I'm so proud of you, baby," I say, my own voice full of happy tears. "You worked so far for this."

"Dammit. Now I have to stock up on Lions memorabilia." I barely register Hank's latest gripe as I embrace my son. After a long moment, he sets me down and wipes his eyes, not caring that people are seeing him cry while he accepts their congratulations. For the first time, he doesn't look like my little boy to me. He looks like a grown-up. A grown man who is ready to be out on his own. Who I feel confident will make good choices and decisions. A grown man I'm proud to say I raised to be a *good* man.

Jack pulls me to him as the tears continue to roll down my face. "You okay?"

I nod up at him. "Yeah. I'm damn near perfect."

He smirks at my choice of language and holds me tighter.

Sure, it's been a long road getting to where we are now, and an even longer day, but I wouldn't change a thing. I've never been more full of pride and joy.

Curious about Jack's sister, Greer?
Look for her story coming Summer 2018!

Acknowledgements

It takes a village to write a book and in this case, it's more true than most. For whatever reason, my brain didn't want to cooperate with this story so there are multiple people I have to thank for getting me through the hardest write of my life.

Andrea Johnston and Kate Spitzer for the daily check ins and encouragement. For reminding me to rest and let myself take breaks.

Melinda Knight, Marisol Scott and Katie Pettigrew for getting me organized (I can finally use the online calendar!) and never making me feel bad for being a disorganized mess.

Andrea Johnston, Andee Michelle, Melinda Knight, Marisol Scott, Kate Spitzer and Amber Higbie for having eagle eyes and good judgement when it comes to making this story come together the way it did. I think Jack Pride and Joie Stevens are better because of it.

Erin Noelle and Karen Lawson for constantly rearranging their schedules and squeezing me in for edits and proofs as I would get things done. You have such different styles of editing, yet they complement each other so well. It was a great experience in that aspect.

Murphy Rae for these covers. These beautiful, beautiful co-vers. I'm kind of glad the first version didn't work out. These are so much better!

Julie Titus for going above and beyond the call of duty every. Time. Stop trying to give me free stuff.

And to my muse, the woman "Joie" was inspired by. You know who you are. Thank you for always having a smile on your face and for never being a push over. You are a daily inspiration.

Give Me Books for being so easy to work with and doing a spectacular job getting the word out.

Carter's Cheerleaders and Nerdy Little Book Herd for my daily fun and motivation. You guys truly feed my soul and make me feel accomplished. I don't think you can ever understand the depths of my appreciation.

The Walk. You ladies came into my life unexpectedly and I don't think you can ever understand the gravity of the impact you make. Just knowing you're there and you "get it" makes all the difference as I sort through my own crap.

My parents and kids for trying to understand and give me grace as I try to build and run a business while being a single mom. I think we're finally getting into a groove. Hopefully soon we'll be in a good routine and won't feel so discombobu-lated.

Thank you, Lord, for getting me through this book!!! It was a hard experience, but I've been stretched in ways I didn't know I could be. I suppose that's the silver lining.

ABOUT THE AUTHOR

Mother, reader, storyteller—ME Carter never set out to write books. But when a friend practically forced a copy of Twilight into her hands, the love of the written word she had lost as a child was rekindled. With a story always rolling around in her head, it should come as no surprise that she finally started putting them on paper. She lives in Texas with her four children, Mary, Elizabeth, Carter and Bug, who sadly was born long after her pen name was created, and will probably need extensive therapy because of it.

You can follow her on Facebook at
https://www.facebook.com/authorMECarter,
on Twitter at https://twitter.com/AuthorMECarter,
Instagram at
https://www.instagram.com/authormecarter/?hl=en
or email her at AuthorMECarter@gmail.com

Other Titles by M.E. Carter

Hart Series

Change of Hart
Hart to Heart

Texas Mutiny Series

Juked
Groupie
Goalie
Megged

#MyNewLife Series

Getting a Grip
Balance Check
Pride & Joie.